The Ugly Parts of Me

E.K. Clark

For permissions requests or inquiries, contact:
ekclarkauthor@gmail.com

Paperback ISBN: 979-8-218-64291-4
Ebook ISBN:
Cover Design by Nerd Sisters Design Group
Edited by Sara Oestreich and Jen S.

Printed in the United States of America
First Edition: 2025

FOREWORD

This book contains heavy topics that are not suitable for everyone. Please refer to the back of the book for a full list of content warnings. Due to the sensitive subject matter, reader discretion is advised.

One day you will
tell your story of how
you overcame what you
went through and it will
be someone else's survival guide.
-Brene Brown

PROLOGUE

16 Months Ago

HINDSIGHT IS A REAL bitch.

That's the only coherent thought breaking through the ringing in my ears as I sit here with five sets of narrowed eyes trained on me. My forehead burns with the heat from that little invisible red bulls-eye that feels painted on my skull.

Based on my limited research, not being a lawyer and all, I don't think they have grounds to arrest me. But what do I know?

"Maddie, how are you, dear?" My caseworker, Jackie, swings the door closed as she steps out from her hiding place in this tiny office.

Oh yeah, that's not good. Jackie's nice and all, but she only checks in when she's required to, and that's typically a quick text or phone call. I haven't seen her in person in over a year.

"Um, honestly, pretty confused," I admit. My lungs fight for a pocket of fresh air in the stale, overcrowded room.

She folds her hands in front of her and nods. "We need to ask you some questions, dear. Please understand that this is a safe space, okay? You can be honest with us—in fact, I insist on it. We're all here because we care about you and your well-being." Her gentle brown eyes droop with the weight that can only come from years of trying to stay above water in a shattered system.

Reality crashes down. Her words, the grim expressions plastered across the faces currently staring at me, the urgent summons down here.

This is happening.

My heart thumps so loud inside my chest I would bet the entire building can hear it. The air is thick and hard to breathe—like inhaling smoke. I want to cough, to force it from my lungs.

But it won't help.

They all stare at me as I hyperventilate.

I think I just confirmed everything they feared without ever saying a word.

As if reading from a list of stage directions, a light knock rings out behind me before a tall, clean-shaven gentleman in a telling blue uniform eases the door open and crams his way into this congested shoebox of an office.

Buzzing, like a thousand cicadas all screaming my name, surrounds me as it drowns out the surreal conversation taking place on my behalf. If I join them in their incessant chirping, would my screams be enough for them to haul me off? I don't hate the idea of being drugged to escape this nightmare.

An hour ago, I was sitting in front of a blank piece of paper meant to be my Algebra II quiz, panicked over what would happen to my grade when I failed it. The black ink against the stark white page taunted me, screaming my incompetence.

"We're in the middle of a quiz; can it wait?"

Some pimple-faced freshman stands at the front of the stuffy classroom, whispering with Mrs. Cutz, clutching a blue slip of paper used to pull students out of class. My teacher purses her lips and narrows her eyes as she hisses at the poor girl.

For her part, the lanky kid is trying to inch her way backward to avoid any more of the spit shower flying from my math teacher's mouth as she snarls back at her.

"They, uh, said it was urgent, ma'am."

Mrs. Cutz snatches the paper from the girl's hand, scans it over for herself and then looks up, locking dark, narrowed eyes with me.

Crap, busted.

I drop my gaze back to the nonsense on the page, hoping if I stare at it long enough, the numbers will morph into something that makes sense. After studying my ass off, it's still like trying to read Latin.

"Madalynn!" The sharp snap of my name pulls my eyes back up to the witch. She gets off on punishing me, all because I hate the subject she so cherishes. Can't she let me sit here and fail all on my own? I don't need her rubbing my nose in it.

She stares at me like I'm an ant crawling across her kitchen counter.

Am I supposed to know what she wants?

"For the love of God, Miss Klein. Come here!"

It finally occurs to me that the little blue slip of paper is meant for me. My friend Allison shoots me a "what the hell?" look as I gather my things. I respond with my own silent "not a clue."

As I reach my teacher, I slip the empty quiz on her desk upside down, snag the pass she hands me, and rush from the room before she can flip it over and see my failure. As soon as I'm in the safety of the hallway, I start to question who wants me and why. Shit, has something happened to Kelly? Andrew would have said something, right?

I pull my phone from the pocket of my bag to check for any missed calls. There are none. Only a simple text is waiting.

Andrew: Hope you're having a great day, baby.

My stomach rolls.

Maddie: Same shit, different day. Miss you!

I shoot the text off as I walk, trying to ignore the anxiety building inside me with every step. Between Andrew, worrying about college, the fat zero I imagine Mrs. Cutz just slapped on my paper with a smirk, and now whatever hot water I seem to have landed myself in, I think I'm getting an ulcer.

Some days, I just want to scream at the sky and beg, why me?

The thought leaves a sour taste in my mouth. Things used to be so much worse. Sort of. Now, I'm in an actual home with a literal white picket fence and two grown adults who go to work, buy groceries, cook meals, and pay the bills. I don't have to worry about any of it for once.

I need to remember to be grateful for that; it could all be taken away so easily.

The walk to the main office takes forever in this massive building, but I'm not in a position to complain. I'd rather delay this as long as possible, knowing whatever I'm walking into won't be good.

In the office, I hand the slip over to the secretary, a typically cheery middle-aged lady who likes to tell anybody who will listen about her pet ferret. It never fails to make my skin crawl.

I'm so thankful when she avoids looking at me that it doesn't cross my mind to question her somber mood. All I care about is avoiding her stories about the furry little beast.

She nods toward the chairs against the wall and resumes her work as if I didn't notice her playing solitaire. I sit and wait, tapping my foot for several long, quiet minutes.

"*Vice Principal Gill is ready for you, Madalynn.*" *Her shaky voice is barely loud enough to hear.*

What's her deal? And why in the hell does Gill want to see me? I hate that guy. *I wish the slip would have said who was requesting my presence. I would have blown it off and hid in the library instead.*

I make my way toward the back of a hallway lined with doors, each one belonging to a different administrator, until I reach the gold plaque which reads V.P. Albert Gill.

Inside, I'm confused by the odd party of individuals waiting for me. Not only is my douchebag of a principal wiping sweat from his furrowed brow, but Mrs. Simms, my guidance counselor, is here as well, perched on a chair like a bird, refusing to look me in the eye. Miss VanHue throws me off the most. What could my history teacher be doing here?

She gives me a tight smile as a single tear leaks from the corner of her eye.

Andrew is my final thought before the buzzing consumes my mind. After this all plays out, I don't know where I'm going to end up, but I have a pretty good idea of where he's headed. Orange never looked good on him.

My stomach rolls again at the idea, right before I lose my lunch all over Miss VanHue's shoes.

Chapter One

Present Day

SENIOR YEAR IS SUPPOSED to be significant—a milestone to be remembered. I used to picture it: standing outside the building, staring at the fading red brick, overcome with all of these happy memories. Maybe I would cry a bit, bittersweet about the beginning of an end. I was so eager to go from that confused, dorky kid who couldn't figure out their damn locker combination to this confident, mature senior.

Instead, I stand here with a heaping pile of bitterness and not an ounce of anything sweet.

I'm no longer the same girl that first entered these halls. She was young and naïve. Life has enjoyed kicking my ass these past four years and boy, am I ready to be done with it all.

I have the sudden urge to find a brick and throw it through one of the windows. But what good would that do?

Instead, like the mature eighteen-year-old I am, I kick the bottom step leading up to the giant metal doors and pretend my toe isn't throbbing like hell from the impact as I march my way into the building to face the day—and year—before me.

I heave open the large doors and take an immediate right, entering the main office where sounds of ringing phones, an extremely outdated fax machine, and the buzz of staff chatting all around greet me.

I see, or rather smell, the secretary, Ms. I-don't-remember-her-name and her dead rose perfume, before she sees me. Stepping up to the desk, her beaming smile falls, and her chocolate-brown eyes dart back down toward her desk. I never knew being a walking, talking buzzkill could feel so...depressing. I should be used to it by now, but that sting never fully fades.

On the bright side, no ferret stories for the last year. Yay for me.

My feet drag as I approach her desk, wishing there was a way to skip this and avoid the need to talk to her, but I kind of need my schedule. Looks like I'll have to suck it up.

"Miss Klein," she speaks without looking up. "Do you have an excuse for being late today?"

I raise an eyebrow, not that she sees it. "Like a doctor's note? No. I overslept." I try to keep the snark from my tone, but it's not working as well as I would like. I don't mean to be a bitch, it just naturally oozes from me, especially at times like this.

"In that case, we need a note from your—" Her words come to an abrupt halt, her eyes widen, and her lips snap shut. The entire office seems to fall silent right along with her.

Is she serious?

"A note from...my parents?" I finish, no longer trying to hide my disdain. "Nope, haven't got those either."

Her cheeks flame red. When I notice her hands shaking, I almost feel bad. It's not her fault nobody knows how to treat me. I am a reminder of the world's ugliness, which apparently dampens the mood. At least, I assume that's why most people go out of their way to avoid me.

"Look, I just need my schedule, and I'll be on my way."

Her fingers fly across her keyboard. In less than a minute, I have the paper printed and in my hand. I guess somebody wants to be done with this interaction as well. Fair enough, lady.

Without bothering to look it over, I toss my bag over my shoulder, eager to leave. Before I can walk away, a swinging door to my left grabs my attention. I don't need to see the guy's face to recognize his massive frame. My counselor, Wyatt, emerges, engrossed in his phone, tapping away like he's sending a text. As he finishes, he glances up, right at me, and smiles.

Since I like the guy, I do him a favor and tip my head, silently pointing out Ferret Lady. Eyebrows pinched together, he looks ready to question my sanity until he realizes what I'm trying to tell him. One look to my side has him turning on his heel and darting back into his office before she sees him. Looks like I'm not the only one bothered by her creepy stories. He owes me for that.

With my business here finished, I gladly take my leave and head back out to the main building. My lungs deflate as the door swings closed behind me. I can breathe again.

The vibration of my phone has me shoving my schedule into the side pocket of my bag and pulling the device from the same pocket. A text notification from my best friend flashes across the screen.

Kenna: Where are you?

Maddie: Office. Just got my schedule.

Kenna: Stay there.

Maddie: Yes, boss.

She sends me back an eye-roll emoji that has me smiling as I wait.

It takes less than two minutes before I hear that bright sunshine voice I've missed so much over the past three months. "Oh, Madalynn!" She looks like a damn Barbie prancing toward me, and I wonder, not for the first time, how we are friends.

She's got on a plain gray crewneck sweatshirt, a pair of high-waisted jean shorts that look like they came from a bin at Goodwill but probably cost more than my car, tall white socks, and a white pair of sneakers. She doesn't try, and everything about her is perfect. I sort of hate her for it.

Kenna glides toward me, steam rising from a to-go cup of coffee in her perfectly manicured hand. Her platinum-blonde hair is neatly curled around her face, highlighting her golden tan.

Kenna nears me, blinking rapidly beneath furrowed brows. I might as well have grown a third head over the summer. Let's be honest; that would have been more likely.

"Um, Maddie. What in the heck are you wearing?" she asks as she reaches up and presses her hand to my forehead, which I promptly swat away. My gaze drops once again to the foam cup in her hand.

Throwing my head back, I groan at the reminder of my morning from hell, then fill her in, starting with oversleeping. I recall my infuriating search for clean clothes, which she kindly reminds me wouldn't happen if I just sucked it up and did some laundry now and again. She's right, but I flip her off anyway.

"I got so desperate; I even searched the dirty clothes pile. I really thought I had caught a break when I found my favorite pair of jeans—"

"The ones that make your butt look *ahhmazing*?" she interjects.

"Not the point. But yes, that pair. So anyway, I found them, and they weren't visibly dirty *and* didn't smell like a wet gym bag, so don't judge me, but it was my only option." I shrug. "Until I pull them on, and my fat ass rips the seam right down the center." I'm still eyeing that coffee in her hands. It's calling my name—screaming, in fact. It's taking every ounce of restraint I have not to yank it away and guzzle down the rich, nutty goodness before she can protest.

"You have got to be kidding."

"My thoughts exactly. With the jeans no longer an option, I was back at square one. You've seen my closet, Kenna. It's pathetic." She doesn't even bother pretending and just nods in agreement. "So, there I am, standing in front of my pitiful closet, praying to the gods for something to appear magically, and lo-and-behold, I find this ridiculous dress buried behind sweatshirts and a winter coat." I'm riled up just enough to be dramatic and not care.

"Here." Kenna pushes that glorious brown paper cup into my hands. I could kiss her.

"Sweet Jesus, thank you! I didn't even have time to make myself some this morning, and I quite literally might slip into a coma without it." The liquid hits my tongue, and I can't hold back my moan of delight. Medium roast, black, and still steaming hot, just like I like it.

"I figured as much. Consider it a favor for the entire student body."

She knows me too well.

We slowly make our way through the halls of Ridge Valley High. Memories flood back and remind me of why this place feels like its own circle of hell.

The smell is exactly as I remember: sweat, musty books, and water damage.

"You do realize that's my dress, right? I've been looking for it all summer."

I tug at the hem for the hundredth time today. Kenna might be four inches taller than me, but where the fabric would drape delicately down her thin frame, it sucks to every inch of my much fuller figure, making it end far higher up on my thighs than would hers.

"That explains why my boobs are moments away from ripping this thing to shreds. I feel like a fucking highlighter. No offense."

She shrugs one shoulder and gives me a little smirk. "None taken. Besides, I would rather look like a highlighter than a model for Hot Topic." Kenna's elbow jabs into my side as she pokes fun at my typically monochromatic wardrobe.

The small gesture sparks a flicker of hope over the year ahead. With my diner job and her family responsibilities, I rarely see my friend outside these halls. May's uncertainty urges me to make the most of our time together. I guess that's reason enough to endure the day, even if she's gleefully skipping beside me, excited about all the "fun" of being a senior.

Dork.

With the little money I have, I'd bet she has her schedule printed, laminated, and delicately placed in her backpack, along with color-coordinated notebooks and folders for each class. I'm sure she has at least two brand new packs of multicolored pens—blue for definitions, red for key concepts—nerdy things like that.

"So," she stops skipping and shoots a somber look back in my direction. "It's not like you to oversleep." The layers upon layers of meaning packed into such an innocent question would make an archeologist drool.

"Dinner ran late and pushed the whole night back so it was nearly two by the time I made it back to my apartment."

"Maddie—" She starts but stops herself, reconsidering her words. "Look, I love you and I worry, okay? Please don't be mad at me for that." Powerless against the bright blue eyes blinking back at me, I turn and start walking again without commenting.

First period has a few minutes left, but I still don't know what class I have next, so I need to get my butt moving if I want to avoid another red mark on today's shitty day.

"You know I'm incapable of being mad at you." I roll my eyes with a smile, then reach into my pocket to pull out my schedule, smoothing the crumpled paper against my bare leg. Kenna glances over my shoulder as we scan through the courses and respective teachers.

"Maddie, you sure you can manage all of that?" she asks. "I'm not implying you can't handle the honors classes, but to do it *and* work a full-time job? Do you have enough time for everything?"

"Says the girl with as many honors classes and what, four extracurriculars? Besides, it's not any different from last year. It's not that bad, really. I can usually get two ten-hour days in on the weekends, and then it's just a matter of spreading out another twenty during the week, which isn't as hard as it sounds." I take another long drink of coffee and attempt to keep my tone light as I ease her concerns.

"Besides, what choice do I have? I can't risk dropping any of the honors courses. Not only will it hurt my chances of getting into my top schools, but also the scholarships I need in order to attend if I'm accepted."

I can feel Kenna's skeptical frown lines burning into the side of my cheek. "Regarding work, my options are nonexistent. My budget has zero wiggle room, so as long as I feel like having a roof over my head, this is what I have to keep doing."

My attempt to ease her worries fails. Apparently, I didn't hide my exhaustion from the same grueling schedule last year as well as I thought I did. I understand where she's coming from, but I wish she could see it from my point of view. She understands my need to escape this town. It's not only that, though; I need to make something of myself to prove to, I don't know who exactly—the world, maybe—that I'm more than the crappy circumstances that have been thrown my way.

"Can we drop this, please?"

She gives me a tight nod, reluctantly agreeing not to say anything more.

Annoyed, I turn my attention back to my schedule. I recognize all but one teacher. The relief about sends me to my knees when Miss VanHue's name doesn't appear anywhere on the page. As uncalled for as it might be, the idea of seeing her again fills me with more dread than I care to admit. I still haven't decided if I love or hate her for what she did.

I suppose it's irrelevant.

"Any idea who this James chick is?" I ask. Kenna would be the one to know.

The pep in her voice is back at the chance to share what she knows of the latest gossip. "Well, first off, not chick. He is the new English guy. I've been told there is even a group chat dedicated to pictures of his rear end circling the school. Talk about completely invasive. Anyway, I have him fifth period for A.P. Lit. You?"

"Me too, thank God." Another superficial victory.

I want to fist pump, *Breakfast Club* style, but it's far too early for that. There is still plenty of time for the day to go back to complete shit. In fact, I'm counting on it. I always am.

Before I can say anymore, the warning bell rings out, causing me to jump. I sure as hell did not miss that sound. "I gotta go. My next class is on the fourth floor." I wave a hand behind me, already rushing toward the stairs. As I climb, I focus on keeping my breathing slow while I run through my schedule again.

I'm faced with four advanced placement courses and two regular ones because, well, fuck math. The end of my day has a surprising, yet welcome free period. It would give me extra time to study, but I need to talk to Wyatt before I get too excited. The last I knew, I needed a full course load this year to stay on track.

I'm entering Mr. Olsen's room when a text from my boss comes through. I pull out my phone, happy to have an excuse to avoid entering said shitty math class, even if only for ten more seconds.

Bea: Any chance you can come in an hr early?

The low fuel light flashing on my dashboard this morning makes it an easy choice.

Me: Yup, see you at 4

After four hours of classes I couldn't care less about, my shoulders drop with relief as I head down the stairs for English.

I find Kenna sitting, much to my annoyance, in the very front row. Whispers and giggles greet me as I enter. I flip the group responsible the bird as I approach

Kenna, barely settling into my seat before she's flinging questions at me, asking about my day. The questions are typical and innocent to any outsider, but I know her well enough to see through them. She's worried about me and while I appreciate the concern, it also bugs me.

Not that I can ever tell her that.

It's not her fault I'm a jaded bitch who wants to hide from the world.

There isn't much to be said, but I fill her in on my classes anyway. I've kept to myself, ignoring the pointed stares and whispers. You would think they would have moved on from that shit by now, but no such luck.

Now that I'm thinking about it, I realize Kenna is the first person I've spoken to all day, apart from Ferret Lady, and she doesn't count. I'd be lying if I said that didn't sort of suck.

After sharing the few details I have, Kenna updates me on her day. We commiserate over a few teachers, and I play the part of best friend, nodding at all the right times and listening intently. The ins and outs of high school might feel trivial to me, but they matter to Kenna.

Where this place might as well be Hades in my book, I get that it's her sanctuary. Our situations might be different, but I know her home life sucks in its own way.

Until now, I have paid little to no attention to the man sitting at the teacher's desk a few feet away. I've been too wrapped up in the tornado living in my head to remember the fuss over the new guy. A smooth, deep "Hello" a few minutes after the bell rings interrupts my conversation with Kenna and draws my attention to the owner of that surprisingly sexy voice.

Kenna watches me, watching him, with raised eyebrows and a shit-eating grin on her face. I'm waiting for her to extend her long, delicate finger and use it to reconnect my jaw to the rest of my face.

I take in the not-quite-shaggy sand-colored hair, longer on top and cropped short on the sides, rustled to perfection, though it doesn't look like he tried to make it that way. His jaw is sharp under a beard that's slightly more than a five o'clock shadow, high cheekbones, and full, plump lips.

He's tall, over six feet, if I had to guess. He's not overly bulky, but I'd be shocked if he didn't work out. And that ass...I can't go there. No wonder there is an entire thread dedicated to it. I wonder if I can sneak my way in on that?

Dammit, this is the last thing I need. How am I supposed to pay attention when the man teaching my favorite subject of all time is my walking wet dream?

When my eyes finally reach his, I want to disappear into my chair as I find him staring at me; eyes locked on mine like he's looking into my soul.

Well shit.

Chapter Two

M Y PHONE VIBRATES FROM my desk as the last of my fourth-period students beeline out of my classroom. "Hey Lee, I only have a minute. What's up?" I answer, seeing my sister's face fill the screen.

"I just wanted to check in to see how your first day was going!"

I scrub my hand down my face. "As expected—painful. Just a bunch of mind-numbing red tape to go through. My first four classes are nothing but freshman who either think they're something special now that they're in high school or who haven't figured out how to wipe the doe-eyed, in-over-my-head looks from their faces." I sigh.

"Wow, tell me how you really feel."

"It's been a long morning."

"Sounds painful. But the real question is, is it better or worse than teaching middle school?" She asks.

"Better. Without a doubt. You couldn't pay me enough to go back to those little dementors."

My sister's laugh gives me my first genuine smile of the day. I truly do enjoy teaching, but I wish I could skip the first week, even two, until things fall into a normal routine.

"That being said, being the low man on the totem pole again, sucks. There is one tiny little wing of the school that doesn't have air, and since I'm the new guy, guess who got stuck there? I've had a steady stream of sweat dripping down my back since nine this morning."

"That's disgusting," my sister snorts. I can hear the laughter in her tone, mocking me, as she says, "So, my friend Jenny just moved back to town." Harleigh attempts to sound casual, but I can see right through her.

"Not interested."

"Oh, come on. At least give it a chance. One date. That's it."

"Harleigh, I said no. I get enough of this from Mom, I don't need it from you too," I snap.

"Okay, okay. I'm sorry. You're a good guy Harrison. You deserve to be happy. That's all I'm saying." Harleigh sighs and it makes guilt course through me for getting so irritated. She means well, even if it's misplaced.

"I know you do but trust me, that's not in the cards for me. My only concern right now is my career. I just want to focus on finding my footing here and making the most of the school year."

"Alright, alright. Consider it dropped. For now."

I roll my eyes, knowing that "for now" will only last a short time. "Thank you."

"So anyway, what I really called for—"

I'm only half-listening to my sister chattering about the new plant that is putting my house one step closer to being zoned as a damn jungle as I glance toward the schedule printed on the corner of my desk, curious about my next class.

Honors Literature. Finally, a much-needed break from the underclassman.

Loud voices interrupt my thoughts as the first few students file in. I'm just hanging up with my sister and shoving my phone back into my pocket when a student skips—literally skips—across the room toward me. She comes to an abrupt halt at my feet and extends her hand.

"Mr. James, it is a pleasure to meet you. I'm McKenna Kamp, but please call me Kenna." Everything about this strange interaction screams "kiss ass" to me, except for the way her smile lights up her entire face. It's genuine and kind, paired with her gentle voice and a strong air of confidence.

"Babe, I'm telling you, that is not the same guy!" Two more students walk into the room side by side in the middle of a heated conversation. The bright red-headed girl has a smirk on her face, while the guy's hands fly to his head, pulling at his moppy brown hair.

"I don't believe you. It's freaking Dumbledore. They can't replace him and have nobody notice."

The word Dumbledore instantly grabs my attention and summons my inner geek. I should stay out of it, but I can't help but listen in.

"How many times have we watched those movies, Grace? You can't seriously tell me you have never realized it is an entirely different actor?"

Now, I can't help but laugh. This kid is still pulling on his hair, eyes bugging out while his girlfriend just laughs.

I feel bad enough for him that I have to interject. "At the risk of starting off on the wrong foot, he's right. In the first two movies, Richard Harris played him, but he got cancer and was too sick to keep filming, so they replaced him with Michael Gambon, the guy who plays Gandalf in *Lord of the Rings*."

I can picture my sister rolling her eyes, calling me a nerd as the words leave my mouth.

The boy leaps in the air and darts over to give me a high-five, then turns back to his companion. "Thank you! See, I told you!"

I smile, hopeful I have won over at least one student today. They move toward their seats, but not before the girl peeks over her shoulder and throws me a wink and a smile. She squeezes her boyfriend's hand, confirming my suspicion that she was messing with him the whole time.

I smile back as they find their seats, only remembering the girl standing beside me when she leans in close and whispers, "That's Grace Wallace and Woods Stafford. Been together since like sixth grade. They got engaged over the summer, and everybody thinks they're crazy, but trust me, they'll make it. It's stupidly adorable. Oh, and they are total dorks, but they own it and don't give a monkey's butt what anybody else's opinion is, so instead of being made fun of, everybody sort of loves them for it."

The pang in my chest strikes with enough force that I have to physically rub it away.

I turn my attention back to my human newspaper. "Nice to meet you, Kenna. Mr. James." I return her hand-shake.

After giving me one more grin, Kenna nods slightly as if our business is momentarily finished, and then she turns to find herself a seat in the front row to my left.

As students continue to filter in, they all acknowledge or greet Kenna in some capacity. Some smile and wave; others stop to say hi or ask how her summer went. Even the kids who slink right toward the back offer something to her. She treats each one with the same effortless smile and warm acceptance that she showed me.

The minutes tick by, and right before the last bell rings, my final student barrels through the door and immediately knocks me on my ass. I stumble back, the sharp metal of the desk digging into the backs of my thighs with a strong bite. One glance is all it takes to have me fighting for air while my lungs turn to stone.

Fallon.

Except, it can't be.

This girl has the same rich, chocolate-brown hair spilling out from a bun haphazardly piled on the top of her head, with random loose curls bouncing around her face. The same heart-shaped face with a narrow jaw and subtly pointed chin and high cheekbones. She's around the same height from what I remember, but then again, it's been over ten years since I last saw Fallon, so my memory can't be fully trusted.

The eyes set her apart. She doesn't even have to look in my direction for them to pierce through me. Those eyes are the palest shade of green I have ever seen, framed by dark brown eyelashes and brows that match her hair. The contrast is so striking it feels like trying to look into the sun.

I want to stare, but the effort is blinding.

As she walks, she tugs at the hem of a bright green dress like she's trying to make it grow a few inches longer while also trying to pull the top up at the same time. The girl squirms around, scrunching up her face as she does.

She's coming in at the last possible second, so I expect her to head toward one of the open seats at the very back of the room. I'm thrown off as she beelines straight for Kenna, who appears to be holding in a laugh.

As she finds her desk, a few girls giggle. I wouldn't have assumed much of it, but she flips them off without bothering to turn her head. The slight pinch of her eyes and extra breath are the only indication she's affected by it.

Is that a regular thing?

She continues chatting with her friend as if nothing happened. Something about the interaction leaves me feeling a bit of pride for this green-eyed girl. I don't know her, but I know that high school girls can be brutal, so I'm glad to see her standing up for herself. I should probably reprimand her for the rude gesture, but I won't.

It takes every ounce of effort in me to tear my eyes from the girl and back toward the twenty-five other faces staring expectantly up at me. Even while my eyes are on them, my attention stays glued to the girl in the green dress.

"Hello, everyone. My name is Mr. James, and as you have likely already guessed, I'm new to Ridge Valley High this year." My gaze travels around the room as I speak, noting how many people are paying attention, and to my surprise, it's the majority.

"I'll start by telling you about me, and then we can go around the room so you all can do the same and yes, I know it's probably been the same song and dance most of the day, and you're all sick of it by now, but it is the best way for me to match names and faces, so just bear with me and know it's as painful for me as it is for you" I'm only half joking.

I catch a few groans; one kid drops his head to his desk and checks out. I can't say I blame him.

The green-eyed girl is sitting upright, shoulders back in a way that makes me believe I have her full attention, even as she picks nonchalantly at the skin around her fingernails. No matter how much I try, I can't keep my attention away from her for more than a few seconds. Every time I look away, all I see in my peripheral is Fallon.

It's fucking with my head.

"So, I was born and raised right here in Ridge Valley, but went to school across town. I love to run, so you might find me in the workout room occasionally, though I prefer running outdoors." I catch a look of pure disgust from the green-eyed girl out of the corner of my eye. It's one I have seen many, many times. I have found that there are generally two kinds of people. The type that loves to run and the type that thinks running is the worst form of torture imaginable. Green-eyes must be the latter.

"Let's see. What else can I tell you? I graduated from Belton State with my undergrad and master's in English.

Obviously, I love to read. I'm also a huge Belton Buckeyes fan, so please feel free to attempt bribery in the form of shirts, hats, mugs, or whatever you wish. It won't work, but I'll take whatever you offer with a smile and a high five for your efforts." I attempt a joke but feel about as lame as I sound.

A few kids smile and exchange glances, but otherwise, crickets. I wish I had been more creative and could have devised some fun activity or game to get them engaged, but it's a little late for that.

"Before we turn the ball over to you all, does anybody have questions for me?"

Hands dart up all around the room. Can't say I expected that, but at least they're paying attention.

I point to a random kid first, giving her the floor.

"How old are you?" I want to roll my eyes but refrain.

"Not relevant."

Next.

"Are you married?"

"Also not relevant, but no."

Next.

"Kids?"

"Nope." I'm regretting opening the floor up for this right about now.

"Favorite movie?"

Okay, that one is a little better. "*Twister*." The guy who asked gives a nod of appreciation while most of his classmates look confused.

"Favorite band?"

"Red Hot Chili Peppers." If this pointless questioning helps them get to know me better, I suppose I can humor them for today.

"How long would you survive in a zombie apocalypse?"

I laugh out loud—*good one, kid*. "Well, I said I'm a runner, so longer than some, but I'm also no Daryl Dixon."

The kid grins. Maybe I'm not starting off too bad after all. I have at least won over a few of these kids today, so I'll take what I can get. I have to say, so far, they are a much easier crowd than the middle schoolers used to be.

Kenna raises her hand, so I call on her, noting the way her green-eyed friend is chewing on her fingernails, looking anywhere but at me.

"If you were to write a book, what would it be about?" Kenna asks. A couple of her peers raise their eyebrows and nod, liking her question. I'm with them on that. The girl is smart.

"Great question, but I will tell you, as much as I love to read, I'm a terrible writer. Love the idea, suck at the practice. If I could, I think I would want to write crime novels. I like the intrigue and the puzzle to solve, figuring out who did it, so I think it would be neat to be the man behind the curtain, so to speak."

I want to end on a positive note before the questions get out of hand, so I leave that as my final answer and redirect the attention back toward the students.

Perched on the edge of my desk, I listen as they go around the room and tell me about themselves, fighting to keep my attention on each speaker and far away from green-eyes.

While they speak, I try to pick out some feature or something unique about each one that will help me remember their names. The first girl to share is Casey, who has the highest pitched voice I have ever heard in my life.

Then comes Darrien, who shares that his father is a senator. I try not to stereotype, but that kid screams brown-noser. Zombie boy in the back is Finch, who prefers to go by his last name and wears a dark hoodie pulled up to cover his eyes.

I listen to every one of them speak until it's *her* turn. I'm anxious as hell to hear from her. I need to know her name. I need something more than just those eyes to tell me she isn't the one person that still haunts my dreams.

The girl seems lost in her thoughts and completely unaware that it's her turn. Kenna attempts to help her out subtly by faking a cough.

It doesn't work.

So, she clears her throat. Nothing. Once more, but significantly louder.

Finally, the girl looks up and glares at her friend. They share a few silent words until she slowly turns to me. Her gaze travels up my legs and torso, and then those green eyes lock with mine.

Chapter Three

M R. JAMES FINISHES HIS spiel about himself before handing it over to Casey Welter on the opposite side of the room. I take it as my opportunity to go over the syllabus that was waiting on each desk when class started. I have zero interest in learning anything more about my peers.

I scan the page, searching for the list of books for the semester so that I can copy the titles down on a page in my notebook. I then stuff it into the front pocket of my bag for later. The school gives us all copies of the books to use, but those copies suck. They are always all tattered up with penis drawings on the inside covers or underlines in all the wrong places.

I have nothing against a good used book; in fact, I love them, but schoolbooks are a different story. For those, I would much rather buy my own copies, fresh and new, waiting for my own notes, highlights, and dog-eared pages. Buying the novels myself will require a bit of extra penny-pinching for the month, but it's worth it to have a fresh start with a new book. The satisfaction of cracking the spine for the first time, feeling the weight of the paper, and sniffing the pages.

Yup, worth it.

After making and safely stashing away my list, I work on copying assignment due dates into the calendar app on my phone. Like the books, the school provides a planner for each student, but I'm constantly losing the damn thing. Besides, since my phone is always with me, I can look up due dates and assignments no matter where I am.

It's one way I have learned to keep myself painstakingly organized with my time. That way, on days I'm running around unable to tell my head from my ass, which is more days than not, at least I know I have one aspect of my life in order. I'm so focused on my task I forget where I am.

Kenna clears her throat, making me look up with a glare. Out of the corner of my eye, I see a pair of long legs with medium-wash jeans clinging to muscular thighs I want to sink my teeth into.

Jesus, where did that come from? That is so far out of the question, Maddie!

My eyes travel up the body I refuse to acknowledge and accidentally land directly on his. For a moment, we both stare. His eyes are steel-gray and yet have this warmth to them. There is a kindness there that reminds me of Kenna. Right below his left eye is a small but deep scar.

I can almost picture him as a little boy, climbing the tree in his backyard when a branch snaps, swinging back to gash open his adorable little face.

The longer we stay locked like this, the more I squirm. A difficult task given the way the backs of my thighs are sticking to the chair beneath me.

I hate being the center of attention. Can't he skip me?

"Madalynn Klein," I mutter, barely loud enough for him to hear. I leave it at that and hope he can understand how much I don't want to take part in this game. No such luck.

"Care to tell me anything more about yourself, Madalynn?" His tone carries a hint of amusement, but my attention is drawn to the loud whispers filling the room. I might not have much to share about myself, but my classmates could probably write a book. It might be fictional, but try convincing them of that.

"Not much to tell." I'm not trying to be funny so much as trying to end this awful interaction. I should feed him a line or two of bullshit to get him off my back, but I can't think straight with everyone staring at me.

Besides, I want him to get the hint that I'm not a "participation" kind of student. I work hard and get good grades, but I'm not one for engaging in class chitchat.

"There has to be something," he urges.

I make a face, raising my eyebrows, with my lips drawn together in a tight line, and shrug my shoulders at him in a "what can you do" way. He sighs and moves on.

Kenna more than makes up for my poor attitude with her bubbly, spirited introduction. She's the last student to go through his monkey dance. When she is done, Mr. James resumes his position at the front of the class and instructs everyone to turn their attention to the syllabus. The one I have already read through twice now.

The repetition allows me to tune out his words. I study him instead, noting how annoyingly attractive he is. In a way that is both confident and commanding, he pulls back his wide shoulders. The way he chooses to perch on the edge of his desk, crossing his feet at his ankles, makes him seem completely at ease in the front of the room.

I want to ask about his scar, but I won't.

He's got a golden-brown tan, like Kenna. Probably from all that running. But I do not need the image of him running shirtless with sweat dripping down what I imagine being some nicely tanned abs stuck in my head.

He is likely in his late twenties, no older than thirty. I try my damnedest to ignore how the black Ridge Valley Ravens t-shirt clings to his biceps, straining the fabric, his muscles threatening to rip through the flimsy material at any given moment. The entire staff was wearing the same shirt today, and not one pulled it off as well as he does.

I seriously need to stop thinking about him like that or it's going to be a painfully long semester.

"Maddie, you coming?" Kenna's voice kills my internal monologue and pulls my attention toward her. She is standing at my desk with a strange look as she studies me.

Class has ended, and my ass is still firmly planted in this seat. "Shit, yeah, sorry. I spaced." I start to stand, wincing when the skin on my legs wants to stay behind, molded to the seat beneath me.

I bend to gather my things, trying to save my dignity by holding the back of the stupid dress. The obscene length and the way my boobs are trying to make a defiant escape make me feel like a tramp.

"Wait, no. I have my next class here too." I stop and quickly plop back down at the desk before somebody gets an unintentional view of my ass. "Creative Writing," I explain.

"You okay?" Kenna questions my weird behavior.

"I'm fine, mother." Her eyes roll at my comment.

"Fine. I'll see you later."

She's still staring at me like I've lost it, which, to be fair, I think I might have. I'll blame lack of sleep, as usual.

She finally tosses me one more worried gaze but turns and heads toward her next class, allowing me to settle back in my seat and pull my book from my bag.

I'm in the middle of an extra spicy scene when a hand lands on my arm.

Every individual hair on my body stands at attention; a cold sweat breaks out across my forehead, and my heartbeat triples. I jerk my arm away with far more force than I need to. It takes every ounce of my energy to keep myself firmly planted in my chair. The owner of the offending hand finally registers in my brain and allows me to inhale deeply to try to calm my nerves.

"Whoa, Maddie, relax. It's just me."

I don't know which I hate worse—being touched or being told to relax.

Fucking idiot.

Before I can say anything, Mr. James is flying across the room, thrusting his arm between me and Clark Something, a douche-bag jock from the football team. Mr. James uses his leverage to jerk his arm and make Clark stumble backward into the desk behind him, putting a few feet of distance between us.

"If I ever see you put your hands on somebody again without their permission, it will be the last time you set foot in this school," Mr. James hisses and takes a step toward Clark, his gray eyes turning a deep, stormy black. Holy fuck.

I wouldn't be surprised to look down and find a wet stream painting the front of Clark's pants. His eyes go wide and he takes another step back, forgetting about the desk directly behind him and sending it screeching back another several inches.

"I wasn't hurting her. I just wanted to ask if she wanted to hang Friday." The moron has the audacity to peer around Mr. James and raise an eyebrow at me, like he still thinks it's okay to ask.

The way my knuckles twitch with the urge to punch the asshole in the stomach overshadows my shock over our teacher's reaction. I know what he means when he says "hang," and no, it's not so much Netflix as it is "chill."

I should have known.

One more thing to blame Andrew for.

I could only do so much to hide the countless hickeys he left lining my neck and collarbones over the last few years, and because teenagers are, well, teenagers and like to gossip, it didn't take long for the rumor mill to get started and somehow I became the school slut.

"Fuck off, Clark." I attempt to appear unbothered as I give him my answer, so he walks away, muttering something about me being a bitch.

I want to holler after him to tell his friends, so maybe they get the memo and leave me the hell alone, but I don't.

"You okay?" Mr. James' voice remains low, shielded from the ears of my classmates.

I give a small nod, ready to be done with whatever the hell just happened. He nods in return and, thankfully, straightens the desk and moves back toward his perch.

I shake the thoughts away and turn back to my book. I don't even get through another page when the bell rings, and Mr. James tells everyone to settle.

"I have seen many of your faces throughout the day already today, but I also see some new ones, so for those I have not met yet, my name is Mr. James. I know you are all sick of—" He trails off as his eyes land on me again, and then he perks up with this cocky smirk.

"On second thought, I'm going to bet you are about as tired of the introduce yourself with a fun fact crap as I am. Let's try something different before we all lose our minds, okay?"

Well, color me surprised.

"I do still want to hear you say your names—I'm an auditory learner, so that part helps me remember them all, but given that one goal of this class is to be creative, let's try to channel that into something a bit more... interesting. Plus, this way, I can better understand your writing style and skill levels. So, how about you all write a brief excerpt for me, pretending to be an object?" He pauses, as if considering the idea he just blurted out, and smirks. "Pick anything you feel fits your personality and describe that object from another person's perspective. Clear as mud?"

Damn, I just had to be an asshole with my introduction earlier. I really don't want to be an object, and I sure as shit don't want anyone reading about how I view myself. Maybe I can get away with using a locked box or a brick wall?

I better not, if only because I don't know if this assignment is going to be graded or not, and I would rather not risk flunking it for the sake of being a smartass. Every single assignment and grade counts right now. I need to take this seriously.

With that in mind, I pull out a notebook and pen and get to work. Surprisingly, the words flow out faster than my hand can keep up with. I scribble away, and within no more than twenty minutes, I finish. I proofread line by line, leaving it at that. I'm aware that if I thoroughly reread what I've written, I would discard the entire thing, so I only pay attention to grammar and details, not the piece as a whole.

Once that part is complete, I flip the paper over and glance around the room. I must be the first person finished, as every other head in the room is still down, scratching away. My scan ends on the standard issue, brown vinyl-topped teacher desk only ten feet in front of me.

The way Mr. James is watching me makes me question if it's because I'm done or if it's due to something else, like my attitude or reputation. His gaze on me is unnerving.

I don't like anybody looking at me, let alone the hot, super-off-limits teacher.

The less people pay attention to me, the better. For both me and them.

CHAPTER FOUR

M Y BLOOD IS STILL just below a simmer from watching the fear in Maddie when that kid touched her. It brought back every painful memory I have fought so hard to overcome and instead of thinking rationally, I just acted. It was stupid and impulsive and I'm just thankful that the kid didn't make a scene over the way I shoved him.

Losing my job on day one probably wouldn't bode well.

I shove aside the hurricane building inside me made of a thousand thoughts and memories all swirling together into a storm that will knock me on my ass as soon as I have a moment to myself. But for right now, I need to be a teacher. I can't lose my shit in front of a class full of students.

With that in mind, I hand out their assignment and take a seat behind my desk and put all my energy into keeping my cool.

The easiest way to achieve that is to stay present in the moment, which brings my thoughts back to the assignment I just made up on the fly. I'd be lying if I said my last-minute change in plans didn't involve a particularly defiant student. I'm quite pleased with myself for coming up with the change so quickly.

I meant it when I told them it would help me gauge their skills to know what areas we wanted or needed to focus on the most. I have a loose plan for how I want the semester to go, but I'm more than open to adjusting it as I see fit.

Besides, it gives me a chance to try to get a little more out of Madalynn Klein since she refused to share anything about herself in the last class. Everything about her is a contradiction. I'm inclined to believe that even without the haunting resemblance to Fallon, the misaligned pieces that make up this girl would still be holding me captive.

That bright green dress, which was a little too short and far too tight to be appropriate for school, doesn't match the messy bun, dirty canvas sneakers and ratty backpack. Most kids show up at school the first day with brand new things, but not her.

Her voice, from the little I got to hear, is low and raspy and it reminds me of an actress in my favorite crime show.

Shit, what is her name? S-something. Sandy? Sammy? Sophie!

That's it, Sophia Bush.

Madalynn sounds exactly like her.

Then there is the friendship she appears to have with Kenna—a girl who is bright, outgoing, and bubbly. I could bet money she is a cheerleader, top of her class, student council, or something, if not all the above.

The class has fallen silent except for the occasional crinkle of paper, a pen click, or an eraser squeak. I'm eager to see what they come up with for this assignment and how it might help me get to know them better.

I allow myself a quick glance back at Madalynn and find I'm both surprised and pleased to see her pinched brows. Her hand flies across a piece of paper already almost fully covered in black ink. I half expected her to turn in a blank page with nothing but her name to spite me.

Although it could be nonsense, the white knuckle grip on her pen, and the scrunch of her nose tells me otherwise.

My mind drifts back to her earlier interaction with that tall, black-haired kid. Clark, I think. When he first approached her, I assumed they were friends or maybe dating. He seemed to have no problem reaching for her like they were, but then I saw the panic wash over her entire body in seconds, and I knew that I was very wrong. He could have been an ex, but the look in her eyes didn't read that way.

I still can't shake that fear I had seen in her the moment his hand landed on her arm.

As she works, I'm tempted to pull her file up to get an idea of what I'm dealing with here, but something keeps stopping me. There's this mental block telling me that the information I'm looking for isn't whatever might be housed in that little electronic folder. I'm half convinced I would find detention notices, in-school suspensions, behavior reports, and that sort of thing. With a mouth and attitude like that, she screams trouble.

And yet, everything in me tells me that label doesn't fit. I can't imagine she would have made it this far with nothing more than a snarky attitude, but more than that, I can tell Madalynn has a story. There's a haunted look that seems to slip through her hard exterior that reminds me of the same expression greeting me in the mirror each morning.

A shrill ring blasts through the room and gives rise to the screeching sound of chairs scraping across the floor and the shuffle of students weaving their way out the door. They smack their papers down on the corner of my desk as they exit while I impatiently wait for the room to empty so I can snatch them up and begin reading.

Pouring over their papers makes me wish I had come up with this little exercise earlier in the day. For something I bullshitted my way into, it's telling me a lot about these kids, especially how they see themselves and the world around them.

Many are exactly what I would expect from a bunch of teenagers—full of that theme of "who am I?" and "where is my place in the world?". It's just as clear who has an excessively large ego as it is those who have none. I can't begin to guess the meaning behind the kid who compared himself to a plate. Perhaps I need to pull Wyatt in for an analysis on that one. Regardless, it makes me laugh, so who knows, maybe that was the whole point.

I finally flip over one of the last papers to find Madalynn's name in small, almost block-like letters pressed firmly into the paper in deep, bold lines. I take a breath and dive in.

I'm a book.

Not a picture book that kids flip through and smile at. Not the book at the top of the best-seller list. I'm not a classic novel studied by students across the country—the kind that people write essays about and meet for book clubs.

No.

I'm the book that sits atop the list marked BANNED. I don't fit into their neat little boxes. My words are not written to please their audience or inflate egos. I don't make them swoon over a sappy love story they long to find one day.

I scare them.

Not the good kind of way, either, like in a horror or thriller novel.

I'm different, so they toss me aside and tell me I'm not good enough. My cover is worn and tattered, though it's not a result of being well-loved. It's the wear and tear of being cast aside, shuffled out of the way for something better.

Easier. Cleaner. Neater.

Inside, you'll find my pages untouched; nobody bothers to look past that worn, dirty cover to see what lies beneath. They judge based on the stains and cracks along my spine, deeming me unworthy of their time. I'm messy and hard to read. I challenge what they think they know. Some days, I hate the binding that holds me together. I want to rip some out, rewrite others, and burn the whole thing in a dumpster at the back of an abandoned alley.

But I can't.

I don't get to choose my words. My story. That's a task left for others.

And yet, I get the blame for what they choose to write, with little say in how the story goes. I'm a book gathering dust on an old, forgotten shelf. Shove me aside; find something new, shiny, and bright.

Forget I exist.

I reread it again and again and again. Then I read it one more time.

I feel as if that last sentence is meant as a warning, but maybe I'm making something out of nothing. I'm shocked at the raw emotion, practically stabbed into the page, especially after having to pry something as simple as her name from her just over an hour ago.

The longer I stare, the heavier the weight of her words grows, and once again, I can't help but compare her to Fallon. Is that how she felt, too? Is this the same cry for help that I never heard all those years ago? If it isn't and I say something, I risk breaking this girl's trust and doing more harm than good, but maybe that's a risk I have to take.

Sitting here staring at a piece of paper that holds enough power to hurtle me back down the darkest moments of my life doesn't seem to be doing me any good. Instead, I take advantage of the empty classroom and snatch my gym bag from where I crammed it into the bottom drawer of my desk this morning.

I throw the red duffle over my shoulder, lock up my classroom, and head downstairs to the locker room to get changed. Then, I find a small pocket of peace out on the track as the rubber soles of my shoes beat out a familiar tune.

CHAPTER FIVE

"I NEED YOU TO tell me you're joking. Please, for the love of God, say you are joking, Wyatt. I can't deal with this." One fucking elective. That's what I need. One tiny little class to graduate on time. It should be simple, only I walked into my counselor's office today to find out that it was not simple at all; in fact, I was about to be royally fucked because every single goddamn elective is full.

How does that even happen?

So, it has to be a joke. That is the only thing I can tell myself because if it isn't, I'm going to lose my shit, and I do not have the time or energy to lose my shit right now. Besides, that wouldn't be fair to Wyatt, since it isn't his fault. He's a cog in a fucking awful machine of suck that is the public school system.

The longer I wait for the smile or laugh I know isn't coming, the hotter my skin feels. It's like tiny little electric bugs dancing below the surface of my flesh. A lump forms in my throat, telling me that my voice will tremble and shake if I try to speak. I need to calm down, but how in the hell am I supposed to do that right about now?

"I'm so sorry, Maddie, but my hands are tied. The school administration switched the scheduling to a new AI-powered software and there have been a few kinks." He swipes a hand down his face then cracks his knuckles. "Somebody was supposed to be in charge of making sure this kind of thing didn't happen. If there was anything I could do, I hope you know I would, but I can't see any solution here. Every class is full."

My guidance counselor, turned almost friend, sounds distressed, and maybe it's wrong of me, but I find a small amount of comfort in that.

I breathe, swallow down that lump and keep my voice as steady as I can manage. "So, you're saying I don't get to graduate on time? Is that right? I have been killing myself this entire time for what?" My voice has grown louder with every word until I find myself shouting across the desk. I close my eyes, suck in another lungful of air, and try again to remain calm.

"I need this, Wyatt. You know how badly I need this. I can't go to college without a scholarship. Don't get me wrong, you know I love the diner, but it's not exactly a long-term career. I can't stay here."

The walls are closing in. My future feels like it is circling the drain, dragging my entire life down with it.

"Please, is there anything, anything at all? I will take auto shop or shit, throw me in with the freshman art class! Sewing? Knitting? There has to be something! I'll mop the damn floors every night if I can get credit for it." I sound pathetic, but this is important, and I will be damned if I let my pride stand in the way of begging if it means making something work.

Silence hangs heavy in the room, except for the frantic tapping of my fingers against the inflexible, smooth, plastic armrest on the chair and the matching tap, tap, tap, of my anxiously bouncing foot.

I'm trying to channel all of my frustration and anger into not crying.

I hate being one of those people who cries when I get mad. It makes me feel weak and emotional, and that downright pisses me off.

So, I try not to focus on it.

Instead, I study Wyatt's face as he scrolls through what I assume to be the course calendar for the semester. His forehead is creased with deep, angry lines while his eyes bore holes into the screen.

For all I know, he's mad because he's sick of dealing with my ass, and I truly can't say I blame him for that. Though I suppose I can easily argue that he brought the whole dumpster fire that is Maddie Klein on himself.

The longer he stays quiet, that familiar brooding look on his scruffy face, the lighter my head starts to feel. My vision gets hazy. A familiar, high-pitched ringing rattles my eardrums, and the room starts to feel like a carousel.

It won't be the first time I have sat in this tiny, stuffy office, parked in the same faded blue, off-balance chair, and lost it. I need to get myself under control before I'm too far gone. I don't want to send Wyatt into shrink mode on me right now when we have bigger problems to deal with than my fucked-up head.

A tickle in the back of my mind tugs a fact out of the chaos. Wyatt once told me that when a person goes into fight-or-flight mode like I am right now, the prefrontal cortex shuts down, and some other part of the brain takes over. Science and anatomy are not my strongest areas, so I had no idea what nonsense he was spewing at the time.

In layman's terms, he explained, you lose the ability to think logically, so thinking your way out of an anxiety attack is pretty impossible. It's a lot like trying to logic a toddler out of a tantrum. I've babysat enough to understand the analogy.

So, after that, we spent the next few days learning "tools," as he called them, to override rational thought but still be able to calm me down. After practicing and being coached through it a few times, I picked up the trick pretty fast.

It still irks me that he was right about the whole thing. I was so sure that he was full of shit, telling me I could breathe my way through episodes that paralyzed my body and sucked me into that terrifying state of helplessness.

But alas, it does work, so now, when this feeling starts to settle into my chest, I can revert straight to those ridiculous techniques that help ground me in the moment and calm my pathetic brain.

Wyatt is still grumbling at his computer, unaware of my pending meltdown. I inhale deeply through my nose and out through my mouth and notice how the chair's smooth, almost oily plastic presses into the bare skin of my thighs. My ears zero in on the soft *tick*, *tick*, *tick* of the clock hanging far above my head.

I track Wyatt's chest, gently rising and falling with each breath he takes, and I focus on matching my breathing to his. With each inhale, I feel my heart rate start to decline. The room comes back into focus. My head feels back to an appropriate weight, firmly attached to my shoulders.

It wasn't long ago when allowing anybody close enough to have such a calming effect on me would be an automatic trigger. I would have either run like hell in the opposite direction or flung myself at him like a desperate spider monkey, which I'm still embarrassed to admit that I did try when we first met.

Letting myself get so vulnerable with anybody still unnerves me. I have to give him credit; he has earned as much of my trust as I have to give. To most people, that morsel I give him is far below what might be considered normal, but for me, it speaks to how far I've come.

He's taken everything I've shared, even when I've purposely dug up the worst of what I could speak out loud to test him, push him, and make him walk away; it's never worked. He takes it all in stride, never bats an eye and jumps right into helping me work through my shit. I've never once felt judged or shamed in this office, and for that, I will never be able to thank the guy enough.

The silly little mental exercises have helped ground me and brought me to a much calmer state of mind. I'm getting ready to apologize when I see the little light bulb moment flash in Wyatt's eyes. I know that look, and it's exactly what I need right now. *Work your magic, buddy, please!*

"Wait here a minute, will ya?"

I nod eagerly and pull out my phone, checking an email alert I heard go off a few minutes ago. It's from my lawyer, undoubtedly about the upcoming trial I want to pretend isn't going to happen. Despite the subject line marked URGENT, I mark it as unread without bothering to open it, and close the app. I can't deal with that right now.

Instead, I put the phone away and pull my book out while I wait. I haven't even cracked it open when the sound of Wyatt shouting bleeds through the heavy wood door. I can't make out what he is saying, but I don't need to. The sound is shocking all on its own. In all the time I have known him, I've never once heard him so much as raise his voice, let alone yell and boy have I tried. I've succeeded in truly pissing him off a few times, but never once did he lose control or yell like that. I can't imagine what would have him so worked up. Guilt crashes down on me at the realization that it's most likely on my behalf.

Amidst that guilt is a slight twinge of happiness.

The first time I was summoned down here after things blew up sophomore year, it never would have crossed my mind that anybody, let alone a virtual stranger, would ever care enough about me enough to get emotionally involved. I wasn't the kind of person that people flocked to or rallied behind. That would be Kenna, and I was the exact opposite.

Something about the line of thinking brings back memories of the first time I sat in this chair. I remember every detail in painfully vivid HD, like it or not. And I really, really do not.

"Maddie, it's nice to meet you. My name is Mr. Bailey; I'm the school counselor. Forgive me if we've met before. It's a big school, and I have a lot of students coming through my door every day." The man barely bothers looking up at me when he speaks.

"I'm gonna need a first name." I manage to stop from slapping my hand over my mouth as the words fly out without my permission.

In my head, I can hear the little animated sound they play in cartoons when a character blinks their enormous eyes as his head jerks up and he stares back at me. The little gears in his head churn, trying to figure me out.

Good luck with that. Even I haven't figured out where my head is lately. It changes from moment to moment. One minute, I want to burn the world to the ground, and the next, curl up in a ball and cry from pain.

These last weeks have been the absolute worst of my life and have left me a mess. Everything I thought I knew vanished in a matter of hours. I'm scared and confused and angry and sad and a lot of other shit I can't name.

Most days, I can't think about eating. Every bite of food feels like lead in my stomach.

Mr. Bailey finally replies, "I'm not sure that's appropriate."

I almost laugh. "Interesting. Does it seem fair that you get to call me by my first name, but I don't get to do the same? Your job and age somehow make you better than me? I've never had a job, so I can't be sure, but I've never heard of anybody calling their boss by their last name, so why would I do that for you? I assume you brought me here to spill my guts and tell you all my problems and maybe to make sure

I won't go off myself anytime soon. So, given that you want all my dirty little secrets, don't you think I should at least get to use your first name?"

I can't tell if he's more shocked or I am at the words flying out of my mouth. I hate confrontation; I do what I'm told: work, study, and mind my business. I'm not good at saying no to people. Maybe this is part of who I am now. Hell, if I know. I don't care much about anything right now, though, so maybe that lack of caring has burned my brain-to-mouth filter up in the fiery explosion that is my life.

My life that has been flipped upside down, backward, set on fire and then stomped on a few times for good measure, so what have I got to lose?

I wouldn't have stepped through those doors to this building again if I wasn't required to be here as a stipulation of my emancipation. I have to prove to the court that I'm mature enough to make it on my own, and a high school dropout doesn't exactly scream "competent adult who makes good choices." Since there is no way in hell that I'm going back into the system, here I am, like it or not.

"You make a fair point, Maddie. My name is Wyatt. Is that better?"

Well, shit, I wasn't expecting him to concede.

My surprise must show on my face if that slight uptick in the corner of Wyatt's mouth says anything. He thinks he won some of my trust or respect, but the jokes on him. It won't take long for him to learn that I'm not easily won over. At least, not anymore.

I can respect that he considered my point, understood where I was coming from, and changed his stance, but that only makes me suspicious. The entire world has an agenda, even if they don't all like to share it.

Wyatt relaxes back in his chair across the cheap metal desk between us. I take in his appearance for the first time since stepping in here. He doesn't look at all like a school counselor. Mrs. Simms is usually the counselor I work with for my scheduling and all that nonsense. The two of them could not be any more different.

Mrs. Simms looks like the kind of person who lives alone with forty-two cats and knits in her free time. She's tiny and frail-looking, with beady, dark-brown eyes and these horrible thin-framed glasses perched on the end of her strange pointy nose. All that is missing is a giant wart on her chin. But I suppose she's nice enough, so I shouldn't judge her like that.

Now Wyatt, on the other hand. He's hot.

Not my type, but attractive, nonetheless. If I had to guess, I would put him in his early thirties, with chestnut-brown hair that's on the longer side, a thick, full beard and this lumberjack kind of vibe. Plus, the man is big. Huge. He towers over me at well over six feet with shoulders so wide that I don't know how he fits through the door frame.

The squeak of the door hinges pulls me from my trip down memory lane. When Wyatt returns with a broad smile, the only emotion I can feel is this massive sense of relief. I knew I could count on him.

The relief is short-lived once he fills me in on the actual plan. Technically, there is no reason it should be an issue, and I truly am glad to have an option. Yet, I would have rather gone with the mopping the floor's choice than this.

Fluttering fills my stomach, along with the profound sense that this might be a horrible idea.

Chapter Six

I T TAKES EVERYTHING I have to drag myself out of bed this morning following a restless night where ghosts lingered in every corner of my mind. I hoped a shower might wash away the memories, but after forty-five minutes, I'm resigned that it's just going to be a long day.

In fact, the entire year is going to be long and painful if I don't address the walking, talking reminder of my past. It isn't Madalynn's fault, but I'm not strong enough to face her day in and day out looking so much like Fallon. I can't believe Wyatt didn't warn me.

My drive across town isn't any easier; every storefront or restaurant I pass just seems to flip the switch on a different memory. It's not until I look down that I realize I'm going fifteen over the speed limit trying to outrun them all. Clearly that isn't going to work either.

As I ease my car into the staff parking lot of the school, I let out a soft exhale of relief and hope that my day will keep me busy enough that my mind will be occupied with anything but Fallon. And Madalynn.

With my mind made up about the situation, I know I need to talk to Wyatt right away this morning and get her removed from my classes.

I have about forty minutes before my first class starts, which leaves me time to pop into my classroom and drop off my bag and then I can go chat with my old friend about things. If anybody can understand, I would think it has to be him.

I approach my classroom only to find the unlocked door and a grinning 250-pound hulk of a man kicked back in my chair, dirty cowboy boots marring the top of my previously clean desktop. Guess I won't need to track him down after all.

"Wyatt."

"Hey man, how'd the first day go?" he asks, getting up and dragging a chair from one of the student desks to mine.

It screeches across the floor and makes me wince. As he sits, I half-expect and half-hope that the tiny chair will collapse under his size and send his monstrous ass to the floor. He seems oblivious to the situation, and I have to wonder if he doesn't know Madalynn or just doesn't know that I've met her. Maybe it's all in my head and that uncanny resemblance isn't as gut wrenching as it felt yesterday.

"I'm not gonna lie, it was rough." I admit as I flop into my chair and scrub my hand over my face.

I met Wyatt when I was four and my family moved into the house next door to him. Wyatt would have been eight, his older brother Gabe was thirteen, and his little sister was just a year younger than me. Our moms became instant friends, and we spent most of our days running around outside, playing in his backyard or tearing apart the basement at my house. Most of our childhood, I was his little sister's pesky friend that was constantly trying to tag along with him and his friends.

I worshiped Wyatt, and it bugged the shit out of him.

As Wyatt got older, he embraced that big brother role, to the point that he was the one coaching me through my first date, standing on the sidelines with both our parents at every sporting event or spelling bee. Whatever it was, no matter how boring he thought it might be, Wyatt was there.

He also stood up to bullies for me and knocked a few teeth in when I got stuffed in a locker for being the tiny, dorky kid with his nose in a book. I'm grateful to have a friend like him, though, no matter how big of a pain he might be. And speaking of the pain in the ass, I know well enough to ask, "What do you need?"

"Who says I need anything?"

"Your face," I deadpan.

Wyatt grins, "Fair enough. This will be one of those, ask for forgiveness, not permission moments, okay? Well, shit, no. That makes it sound bad, but it isn't. More like a favor to you, if you look at it the right way, and so on that note, I suppose I should say, you're welcome."

"Holy shit, man, spit it out already."

He rolls his eyes as if I'm the one being annoying here. "I need your help with this student. She's super smart, but not in the nerdy and obvious way like you are. She's talented but has had a rough go of it, and you know that means a lot coming from me."

I intentionally ignore how he calls me nerdy, but I still wonder what this has to do with me.

"I signed her up to be your TA."

"TA? I thought that was a college thing. What would I need a TA for in a high school class?"

"She can help grade papers for other classes as long as you don't give her anything from her own classes, obviously. You can have her run to the printer, input grades, type shit up. Hell, ask her to organize your classroom or get your coffee. Think of it like a secretary or something. You get the extra help, and she gets to graduate on time. Trust me, man, you will be doing both of us a big favor. She might hang me up by my toes if I can't make this work."

He chuckles with a clear fondness for this person. "Look, you don't need to talk to her much. She'd probably prefer you didn't. It's a win-win. Not only that but it's during your planning period, which makes it even easier. Give her a task, and then go about your business. Pretend she's not there."

"Okay, so what's the catch then? If this is as perfect as you make it out to be, why are you being so weird about it?"

"No catch, I swear!" He throws his hands up by his shoulders in one of those "I surrender" moves.

"So, then, who's the student?" I ask, still suspicious.

"Madalynn Klein," he answers, but quickly jumps into an explanation. "Look, I know Maddie enough to guess she may not have made the best first impression." He lifts a single shoulder with a pinched expression. "She can be prickly, but hell, if you knew half the things I did, you would understand. Trust me on this one and give her a chance, okay? She's a great person and strong as hell. Can be pretty damn funny too. It just takes a while to get below the layers to see any of that. Kinda like Shrek...she's an onion. Fuck, don't tell her I said that!" Wyatt's eyes widen and his gaze darts around the room as if he's checking to make sure she didn't hear him.

I almost laugh, but my mind's too caught up on hearing her name again.

I shake my head and jump to my feet, no longer capable of sitting still as that anxious energy drags me back down.

So, I pace.

Back and forth across the front of the room while Wyatt tracks my movement, eyeing me like the tiger that just escaped his cage at the zoo.

"I don't know that I can do that," I manage to get out through gritted teeth. My fists clench and unclench at my sides. I'm trying like hell not to get angry, but Jesus. "How could you not tell me? Didn't I at least deserve a heads up?" I finally come to a stop and turn to Wyatt, whose face has gone whiter than the stack of papers on my desk at my mention of Fallon, his little sister.

"You see it too? Fuck, all this time I thought it was in my head." Wyatt leans forward in his chair, rests his elbows on his knees and buries his face in his hands.

Seeing his pain makes me feel like a jackass because, as hard as it is for me, I can only imagine what it would be like to work face to face with somebody who might as well be a clone of your dead little sister. He seems to need a minute to collect his thoughts, so I remain quiet and figure out where my own head is at.

Based on yesterday alone, I don't know that I can remain professional around this girl. Part of me wants to go up and just hold her in an enormous hug, and the other part wants to shove her out the door and never see her again. None of that should fall on her to deal with, especially given the little information I have about her that makes me believe she's not an average student. I know I should question Wyatt more about that. I should also take a look at her student records to find out what I am dealing with and yet, I haven't. And I don't intend to.

I remember my senior year of high school and how it felt to have everybody staring at me, whispering behind my back, talking shit about things they knew nothing about. Above all that, I distinctly remember how angry it made me that not one of my teachers bothered to let me tell my own story. They saw that little red flag in my file and read a few sentences about a singular moment over the summer and assumed they knew everything they needed to know about me. I refuse to do that to Maddie.

Whatever her story is, it's hers to tell if and when she feels comfortable doing so and I'll be damned if I take that away from her.

Wyatt finally pulls himself from memory lane and rises to his feet, towering over my desk and looks down with his red eyes, knocks his fists against the cheap laminate desktop and sighs. "Look, if it's too much, I get it. I won't force you into it. But at least think about it, for her sake?"

Against my better judgment and despite having a plan to come in here this morning and demand this girl be removed from my class roster, I find myself agreeing.

He breaks out with a huge smile and claps his hands as he unfolds himself from the chair. Before he leaves, he stops and turns around, filling up the doorframe, surly expression firmly back in place. "One last thing, don't touch her, okay? In fact, keep a few feet of distance at all times and don't sneak up on her." I wait, expecting him to laugh at his joke, but it doesn't come.

"Jesus, man, does she have rabies or something? You aren't exactly making me feel great about this idea."

Most of the time, despite knowing he is a giant teddy bear, he walks around looking like he's on his way to snap somebody in two. What's the male equivalent to resting bitch face?

Whatever it is, Wyatt has it.

But, despite his looks, he's an empath, and when he cares about somebody, he shoulders their pain like it's his own. He cares about this girl and helping her. Perhaps, like me, that need to help ties back to his sister, but knowing Wyatt, it's much more than that.

"Don't listen to the gossip. It circles this place like a virus in a petri dish, but it's pure bullshit. Don't let the mouth and snark fool you. She's strong, but most days, I'm pretty sure she's hanging on by a thread, so take what she says with a grain of salt and know it's all a defense mechanism to keep people away." I nod again, taking in all the information but unsure what to do about it.

"Last thing. She was emancipated last year. She's eighteen now so it doesn't mean much at this point but I'm telling you so you're aware that she works a full-time job, pays her own bills, buys her own groceries, and shit like that. She's doing everything completely solo and as a full-time honors student.

"Now, I'm not saying you should treat her any differently because of it, but it might be something to be aware of in case she shows up looking like she's strung out on drugs or something. It's only because she hardly sleeps. Take a look at her file and you'll understand what I mean."

With that, he finally pushes through the doorway and heads off down the hall toward his office, leaving me questioning my decision to continue working with this girl and what the cost is going to be on my sanity.

Chapter Seven

With the start of school comes earlier bedtimes for kids and their families, fewer summer activities and more family dinners at home, making work dreadfully slow tonight.

I have no homework to keep me occupied, and my mind is racing far too much to read or write. So, I clean.

I spend my time scrubbing down everything in sight, including places that are already spotless. Bea runs a tight ship.

I go so far as to use a toothpick and scratch away at the soap scum and hard water buildup around the bathroom faucets, all while texting Kenna.

I'm in the middle of round three of mopping when another alert pings my phone across the room.

Kenna: By the way, how'd the meeting about your schedule go?

I groan, not wanting to think about it, let alone rehash the details. It's too much to text, though, and I know she won't stop bugging me about it until I fill her in.

With a tomato-red face and sweat dripping down my spine and forehead, I press the little camera button that opens a video call. She's seen me at my worst, so I don't care how disgusting I look so long as she can't smell me.

"Whoa, what happened?" is the greeting I get.

"Gee, thanks. Way to make a girl feel good about herself."

"Crap, no! That's not what I mean. I meant you look, um, hot..." Her eyes go wide and then drop, feeling guilty.

"Chill, I'm messing with you. I know I'm a mess. Been cleaning."

"Uh oh. How bad is it?" Her understanding of my weird habits freaks me out.

I tend to go on these crazy cleaning sprees when my mind gets to this point where it feels too crowded and heavy, and I can't focus on any thought long enough to pin it down and work through it.

I run a hand down my overheated face, grimacing at the moisture coating my palm when I pull it away. Since I'm already filthy, I wipe it on the leg of my pants.

"It could be worse. But it could also be a whole lot better."

With her face covered in green goop and some weird noodle-looking things all over her head, Kenna levels me with an annoyed stare. "Can you spit it out already?"

"Sheesh, what got into you?"

Whatever her issue is, it makes her grumble, muttering under her breath, but not loud or coherent enough that I can hear it. "We're not talking about me right now."

I roll my eyes but let her have her moment. "Fine. I fucked up, as usual, and got off on the wrong foot, as you saw, with the one teacher I need to help save my ass this year. Turns out, I'm a credit short and have no other options but to TA for Mr. James."

Kenna's eyebrows raise as much as the dried mud on her face will allow. "You're joking? How did that happen?"

"I don't know, but it did." I snatch a condiment bottle and use it to prop up my phone while we talk. There's no reason I can't wipe down salt and pepper shakers and refill them while I sit here. Kenna hates it when I pick at my fingers, which is exactly what I'll do if my hands are left idle for too long.

"So, what's that mean?" She's painting her nails and I wonder how long this girl spends on her beauty regime every day. It sounds exhausting if you ask me. I barely remember to put on mascara or lip balm in the morning.

"That I am now stuck in Mr. Hottie Pants's class for three hours a day, knowing he probably thinks I'm a dick."

"You kind of are, though." She pulls her focus from her perfectly pink nails long enough to wink and stick her tongue out at me. "Oh, and don't think I missed that Hottie Pants comment either." She smirks at me again. It's a good thing my face is already as red as it can get. "I think you are blowing this out of proportion, though. Just apologize. I doubt he thought twice about it."

I sigh and throw my head back, annoyed with myself and this shitshow of a day. "I'm sure that I am. The idea of being lumped into this defiant, bratty teenager stereotype bothers the hell out of me though. I hate that it's the impression I left."

"I know, I know. Look, apologize. Simple as that. Throw in some nerdy book talk, and he will forget all about it. English teachers love nerds, and Maddie, you might hide it well, but you're a nerd, at least when it comes to English-type stuff. It practically solves itself!"

God, I hate her preppy, positive attitude sometimes. Mostly when she's right, and I don't want to admit it.

"So, where are the parents this time."

Even with her eyes down, I catch the exaggerated eye roll. "China, I think. At least, that's what Dad's LinkedIn says." Kenna tries to hide it with a mask of indifference, but I catch the pain in her voice.

"They didn't tell you?" I can't say I know much about parenting, but it seems weird to leave the country and not bother to tell your kid.

"Nope." There's a soft knock in the background. Kenna must mute the phone; she's talking to somebody out of view but I only hear silence.

"Maddie, I'm sorry. I've got to go. But try not to stress about this. And for the love of God, stop cleaning!" With that, she taps the screen and is gone.

Ignoring her threat, I finish up my salt and pepper shakers and squat to the floor to scrub the underside of each table. It's disgusting how much crap ends up under there. I don't want to think about what it all might be.

With Kenna's voice in my head, I pulled on my big girl pants, clean ones even without a tear in sight, shoved my pride into a tiny little box that it lives in more often than not, and walked as confidently as I could muster up to Mr. James's desk before class this morning.

"Look," I jump right in; no need to dance around with pleasantries. "I wanted to apologize for being an asshat yesterday. It was pretty uncalled for, and well, yeah, I'm sorry." There, that was mostly painless. So why am I drumming my fingers incessantly against his desktop?

Mr. James' deep voice sends chills down my arms and pulls my gaze upward. I get a small glimmer of satisfaction at the surprised look my words have cast over his handsome face.

"I appreciate the apology, unnecessary as it was. Please know that I want to be respectful to those students who aren't as outspoken or social, but I do need some level of participation from time to time. Sound fair?"

It is. Probably too fair, which throws up a red flag. What has he heard?

I spent all last year dealing with teachers tip-toeing around me, whispering behind my back when they thought I couldn't hear. I'm pretty sure a mass email was sent to the entire faculty with the subject line: ***Ticking Time Bomb Returns: Beware!***

A new teacher was supposed to mean a blank slate. I had the slightest glimmer of hope that perhaps, with him,

I wouldn't have to question if every A I got was earned or just given out of pity. I should've known better. It never seems to be that simple for me.

I know people talk. I've heard the whispers and seen the stares; truthfully, I don't exactly blame them. It's not every day that one of their peers gets escorted out of the building by the cops and then drops off the face of the Earth for months, only to pop back up with little to no explanation.

Everything I thought I knew was flipped upside down in the course of a few hours. The next months I spent dealing with the fallout of that day only upended things even further. So, by the time I came back, I no longer had the energy to pretend to care.

I was digging at the ground of rock bottom, barely managing to get myself out of bed in the morning. The last thing I cared about was pep rallies and group projects. My head was so fucked up at that point that I could barely function to get through the day, let alone get caught up in the drama and tedious nonsense of whatever was happening within the walls of Ridge Valley High.

The only positive was that it helped make my goals pretty clear: to get the hell out of Dodge and put this place as far behind me as possible. Making friends along the way is the last thing I want or need.

Besides, most of the gossip about me now is bullshit anyway. Sometimes, it makes me laugh to hear what new theory they have come up with. My favorite is that I got knocked up and went away to have the baby.

So yeah, I don't care too much about their gossip.

As much as I wish I didn't care about the teachers, though, their opinions worry me. As far as I know, they were all given a general heads up about my situation, but considering even the cops don't know the half of things, that little memo doesn't scratch the surface.

There isn't a single soul that understands what the last five years of my life have been like and as long as I have a say in it, they never will. That includes Wyatt.

He may know more than most, but I try my best to guard even him from the worst of it. I can't imagine how he would look at me if he knew some of the darkest pieces of that story. I might never admit it to his face, but I like the guy and care what he thinks, so I prefer he not hate me.

My brain latches onto that horrible thought like a leech, sucking blood and tripling in size. I have this horrendous picture of what he would say and do if he could read my mind. I can picture his face. Kenna's face. The way they would stare in horror and disgust.

I get caught up in the spiral so fast, I don't realize what is happening until it's too late. What started as a simple apology has gotten so derailed in my head, bringing forward this tingling sensation that breaks out all over my body.

My head is heavy.

Too heavy.

My ears feel like they have been stuffed with cotton but are simultaneously ringing. I feel like I'm breathing through a pillow, fighting to get enough air. It's what I imagine suffocating is like.

That familiar feeling pulls me under.

I drop to the floor, fighting for breath, my legs too weak to support the weight of my body. No matter how much air I suck in, my lungs turn to shriveled-up raisins while I tug and pull at the collar of my black t-shirt. I want to rip the fucking thing off, but I at least have enough sense to know I can't.

Even if the lightweight fabric feels more like a weighted blanket on my body that itches everywhere it connects with my bare skin. Fire rages in my belly. The sensations too much for me to handle.

The noise inside my mind drowns out the rest of the world until all I hear is this incessant swooshing and a high-pitched bell chiming in the distance.

"Maddie! Maddie, can you hear me?"

A large hand lands on my arm firmly, drawing all my awareness directly to it. All logic tumbles out of my ears.

The only thought I have is him.

He's here. He's touching me.

How is he here!?

He's supposed to be in jail.

I can't do this. Can't see him. Face him. Talk to him.

Fuck, don't touch me!

Then it all goes blissfully dark, and I fade into the deepest layers of the Earth, far away from their terrible world.

"Kenna, what do we do? Is she okay? Has this happened before? Call 911!"

So much for fading away for good.

My eyelids are still too heavy to open. Everything spins. The weight of my head is too much to lift. So, I stay immobilized on the floor, but aware enough to hear the muffled voices around me.

The fear in Kenna's voice makes me want to fight through the haze. To open my eyes and tell them I'm okay.

Dear God, please do not call 911.

I'm too caught up in my own fear of looking up to find twenty-five pairs of judgmental eyes peering down at me like the freak show that I am.

Although it is oddly quiet. I expect at least some whispering.

"I...she has. I mean, I've never seen it before! I don't... um... Call Mr. Bailey!" I want to reach my arms out and hug her. I can't though. Or maybe I could, but I won't.

God, I suck.

I'm embarrassed, struggling to catch my breath, and none of that begins to touch the anger I feel at my life. At him.

He's two hours away, behind bars, under lock and key, and I don't know how many guards and yet, he's still right here with me. He's in my head at every given moment. I hear his voice, his whisper.

Sometimes, when I open my mouth, it feels like his words come out instead of mine. He tainted me. Broke me. Poisoned my mind and my body and I don't know how to fix it. If I didn't already hate myself, that thought alone would be enough to push me over the edge.

I'm so damn tired.

I don't sleep because, surprise, surprise—he's there too. Each time I'm right on the edge of drifting off, this painful thought pops into my head to remind me that one day, those dreams will pull me so far into that dark space that I won't be able to get out.

I almost laugh because I hear Wyatt's voice in my head telling me that it isn't supposed to be this way.

He likes to mention that I have been living in survival mode for the past several years. That kind of thing wears a person down. He seems to think I'm not irreparably broken, but that's something we strongly disagree on. He doesn't understand how deep the damage runs.

"Maddie." I can't suppress the groan. Speak of the devil. Guess they called in the reinforcements after all. "Harrison, back up man. You need to give her some space. You too, Miss Kamp." There is a sharp bite to Wyatt's voice. He's like my own version of a guard dog. I'd pat his head if I could reach. The thought is almost enough to make me laugh. Almost.

Instead, I groan again and finally will myself to open my damn eyes. "Jesus, I don't bite." I attempt a joke that fails miserably. The faces looking down at me are filled with concern and a bit of fear. Not even a half-smile in sight. Losers.

I pull my body up slowly so I'm at least sitting. I don't want to think about the disgusting things my hair just mopped off the floor.

"Wyatt." I give him a pointed glare. "It's not them I'm scared of."

I don't register the slip-up. Not until I see the pronounced grimace on Mr. James' face and the not-so-subtle wince from Kenna.

Fuck, how many people heard me say that?

A glance around the room shows me it's blissfully, beautifully empty—Hallelujah for small miracles.

"I sent the class to the library, so it's only us here, okay? Would you like me to leave?" Mr. James's voice is calm and steady, his features have softened, if only slightly. I saw what he tried to hide—the horror at a few small words that barely touched the surface of my damage.

He gains a few points in for volunteering to leave. It's thoughtful but unnecessary, so I tell him as much. The worst is over, and leaving for a few minutes won't prevent me from having to face him again later, so what's the point? He might as well stay.

It takes me a minute to gather my bearings and feel steady enough to trust my feet, but I finally manage to pull myself up to a desk and settle into a chair.

My mind starts to slip away.

Tick, tick, tick.

The clock sounds the same as the one in Wyatt's office. And any other clock in pretty much any other place. Something about the consistency of that comforts me. It's familiar and reliable and never changing.

I inhale deeply, noticing the smell of pencil shavings and that same scent you would find in an old bookstore. It washes over me like warm water in the hot sun.

There is also this new scent mixed in that I can't place, but I want to burrow into it and stay there. It's warm and rich and reminds me of scenes in cheesy Hallmark movies where the couple is curled up on an old leather sofa, sipping hot chocolate in front of a crackling fireplace. God, I could get high from that smell. I need to find out where it's coming from.

For now, though, I turn my attention back to the room, hoping to slow my racing heart.

I continue my scan of the room, noticing each predictable element: long white tables, two chairs tucked neatly under each one, make-up row after row of desks.

Bookshelves line the back wall with thirty or more copies of the same book, one after the other. The standard-issue teacher's desk that has been in every single classroom since kindergarten sits bare at the front left of the room to avoid blocking the view of the board, smeared with the remains of dry-erase markers who refuse to disappear.

My eyes eventually land on Mr. James, who looks at me like he wants to see inside my head, to know what makes me tick and what secrets I'm hiding below the surface. It's unnerving to say the least.

I will be the first to admit that the idea of having even one person who could know everything there is to know about me, my thoughts, my past, all of it. To have no secrets or hidden meanings and to not have to filter everything that comes out of my mouth. I would kill for somebody who I can be one hundred percent myself around, no matter how ugly that gets.

Yeah, that sounds pretty damn amazing.

Too bad it can never happen.

I choose not to dwell on the idea. Too much of that, and it starts to get downright depressing.

"Maddie, are you okay? What do you need? I can grab you some water or something?" Kenna's voice interrupts my thoughts. She leans in like she's going to hug me and then stops herself.

Fuck, I hate that she stops.

I need that damn hug, even if I can't ask for it. And because I hate that my best friend, who used to leap into my arms and laugh when I pretended to protest her affection, now feels like she can't touch me. Is she scared of me? Worried I will go all looney tunes again?

I want to scream and tell the world that I'm not a time bomb. To tell them to stop tiptoeing around me all the time. It's making me crazy! But I can't because I don't fully believe my words. There are absolutely moments when I feel like I'm on the verge of self-destructing. A bottle, all shaken up and ready to pop the lid off at any second, spraying anybody in my path. I can't predict if and when that could happen, so maybe they are right to treat me like glass.

So, instead of reaching out for that hug, I keep my arms firmly planted on the table in front of me and bow my head in shame.

Kenna chooses to plop herself into the seat next to me. "You know you can talk to me about...things, right? I won't scare away easily, and nothing you say can or would change the way I see you. You've been my best friend my whole life and I know I won't ever be able to understand the things you've been through, but Maddie, you don't have to always face it alone."

Tears sting my eyes. I fight them off. I refuse to cry, no matter how much those words mean to me. I can't risk taking her up on that offer, as tempting as it might be.

"Wyatt, mind if I talk to you for a moment?" Mr. James strides across the room, motioning for Wyatt to follow. I don't care to know what they might be saying about me, so I turn back to Kenna.

"Thanks. I appreciate that more than I can tell you." I sigh. "Sorry about that whole..." I wave my hand around to avoid saying the words. Admitting to my panic attacks out loud feels weak. "Talk about embarrassing. How many people saw?"

She smiles tenderly at me. "Just Mr. James and me. As soon as you went down, he ran out and threw something on the door, telling students that class was canceled. I don't think he is allowed to do that, but it was impressive. We were both a little freaked, so he sent me to get Mr. Bailey." she explains. "So, uh, is he usually like that?" There is a slight flush to her cheeks as she stares across the room where the men are talking.

Holy shit, is she crushing on the new guy?

"I have no idea. I only met the guy yesterday, same as you."

"Huh?" She tilts her head, confused, which confuses me. "Oh! No, I meant Mr. Bailey." Her voice comes out in this weirdly distant tone, like she's lost in her thoughts. The uncertainty stands out for a girl I have always known to be as self-assured and as confident as they come. I've always joked that she was a Southern belle in a past life. She carries herself with such grace and kindness, but also knows exactly who she is and what she wants. Kenna isn't afraid to charge headfirst after whatever that might be.

"Always like what?" I question with a raised brow.

"I don't know. I guess I was surprised by him. Just now, I mean, he was so in control. I was so freaked, and he kept his cool and had this confident presence. He knew exactly what to do. I know I shouldn't be surprised. If you trust him, he has to be halfway competent, but I don't know why; I have always gotten this big, dumb, meathead impression from him. He always looks so angry."

I can't help but laugh out loud. "Kenna, he's a damn counselor. How would that equate to dumb meathead?"

"I never said it made sense! But come on, look at the guy. You know how you read about a person or hear about them, and you form this mental picture of what they look like and fill in all these blanks about them based on their name? Well, my brain decided that was what it would fill in for him. I mean, he is built like a darn NFL linebacker, so what can you expect from me?"

I can't help but laugh and send a silent thank you to whoever gave me a friend like Kenna. "Wyatt is a great guy. I know I hated him at first, but that was never his fault. He's been nothing but kind and makes me feel like he cares. I feel safe with him, so that should tell you a lot," I admit with a shrug.

"Sounds like somebody has a little crush!" she teases, elbowing me in the side.

I can't help but laugh out loud for the second time. Not a chance in hell. "Yeah, no. Not even a little. He's like a brother. And not in the *Game of Thrones* way." Kenna lives under a rock and doesn't get my joke, but I'm proud of it regardless.

We both turn our heads back toward the man in question, who is still standing near the far side of the room, talking with a fired-up Mr. James. I can only hope he isn't too pissed that I messed up his class. I also hope to hell that he won't get in trouble for canceling class. I don't know for sure, but I'm pretty sure high school teachers don't have the authority to do that.

For somebody who likes to slip into the shadows, I have been making a hell of a scene these past two days.

Nice job, Maddie.

Chapter Eight

Y EARS OF ANGER MANAGEMENT classes have taught me to be Zen as a fucking monk. In most situations, I've mastered the ability to keep a calm head and think clearly. That's not even taking into account the fact that I've taught middle school. And work in a female-dominated field. I ooze patience.

All of that flies out the window in a few short minutes. Seeing Maddie collapse to the floor like that brought me right back to that house and that excruciatingly helpless feeling of watching the trigger draw back just moments too late.

But this isn't that. I'm not seventeen, and Maddie isn't Fallon.

I'll keep repeating that over and over as long as it takes to make my brain understand.

"Alright, Wyatt, I know there's confidentiality and all that shit so you can't tell me much but you at least need to walk me through how to stop that from happening again. How do I help her?"

"Well for starters, you need to remain calm. Getting worked up is just going to escalate and add tension so keep yourself in check. She's getting better at knowing how to manage it and bring herself out of a panic attack like that."

He clasps a hand firmly on my shoulder. "She's fine. I'll talk to her about it later and see if we can determine what the deal was. If it happens again, though, you have to give her space but don't leave. Do a breathing exercise with her. She will know what that means. And talk to her. Distractions can help pull her mind from whatever hole it's spiraling down. But otherwise, I'm right down the hall, so call or text me if you need to. I don't think they happen that often unless she is lying to me, so don't worry too much about it. Alright?"

"How do you do it? Every time I look at her, all I see is Fal. I'm right back to that place. It's all I can think about. All I see. It haunted my dreams last night. I haven't had a nightmare in years!" I'm back to pacing the back of the room, trying to put the lid back on my own heaping pile of shit.

I want to help this girl. I want to make a difference in a way nobody could for my friend all those years ago. In a way that I couldn't back then. But at what cost? Is losing my peace, my sanity, myself, in the process, worth it?

Yes. Of course it is. It's not even a question.

My words catch Wyatt by surprise. Once again, I'm left feeling like a jerk for pulling him back into something he had clearly already worked through or made his own peace with.

I take my cue to give him a minute and return my attention to the girls. I find Kenna watching Wyatt curiously. She might not know what happened, but she knows she saw something. She's too polite to question it, though, no matter how badly I can tell she wants to.

Then there is Maddie.

Apart from the people in this room, she seems pretty alone. From what Wyatt told me about her emancipation yesterday, I can only assume she doesn't have much for family and judging by her limited interactions with her peers yesterday, it seems she doesn't fit in here either. I know how lonely that can be. To an extent.

Her slip-up about not being scared of us springs back to mind. If I take that, combined with how she was with that boy yesterday, Wyatt insisting not to get too close to her. It all starts to come together into a pretty ugly picture. Maybe I don't want to know more about her past. The different scenarios that swirl around in my head are enough to make me sick to my stomach.

Logic tells me I need to let this go, that digging my heels in is a bad idea, but I know I can't. Maybe Maddie is my second chance? My redemption. Can I save her in a way I couldn't save Fallon?

CHAPTER NINE

MOST OF MY PEERS started getting part-time jobs about the time we all turned sixteen. With their new cars and freedom, they craved the independence that a little gas and spending money granted them.

No matter how much I wanted that freedom, I wasn't allowed. I knew without asking that the answer would be something along the lines of them buying me anything I needed, and it would cut into our time together, which was a big fat no.

When I found out I had to acquire and maintain steady employment for the court to approve my emancipation, I was pretty excited about the idea. I remember feeling a little overwhelmed and scared since I had no skills and zero experience, but what seventeen-year-old did?

My problem, though, was I had more bills and responsibilities than most people my age, which meant I needed more than minimum wage from a fast-food place if I wanted to cover rent, insurance, gas, utilities, and be able to eat. Unlike my peers, I had to be able to support myself while also working around my school schedule. A process that started with hope and excitement quickly turned miserable and frustrating. It hadn't taken long to figure out my options were minimal.

I don't even need a full hand to count the number of times that luck seemed to be on my side, but stumbling upon Bea's just happened to be one of them. Getting her to hire me with my winning personality was another.

Tonight is no different from normal. I get here on time, bust my ass through dinner, and then spend another hour or so running around getting cleaned up from that mess. Then, I work through the weekly and monthly cleaning tasks. If I can knock those out early in the week, it frees up my time for the remaining days.

Once all is said and done, I settle into the cozy little nook in the corner of the diner, my signature place when I'm not actively working, and switch gears into school mode. I drown out the quiet with my headphones, giving me the perfect backdrop to study.

Pauly, the night cook, spends his evenings sitting out back on the patio, chain-smoking, and listening to this little portable radio he carries in his pocket. It can be pouring down rain or snowing; a damn tornado could pass right by us, and he would still be sitting in that same spot. It's totally old-school and weird, and I love it.

If a customer does wander in, he saunters his way back to the kitchen, whips up an amazing, juicy burger and then goes right back to his place on the patio without ever saying a word. It's rare that I need him, so we typically spend our nights in our respective locations, content to do our own thing until close.

Two weeks into school now and so far, I'm not struggling as much as I was expecting. I'm halfway through our current English novel when the little bell above the front door chimes. My spine straightens, and a cold sweat breaks out on my brow.

Nobody comes in this late, and in the rare instances that they do, my reaction is always the same. It doesn't seem to matter how often I remind myself that he's in jail; I'm safe now.

He doesn't know where I live or work. But the fear never goes away, even when it is entirely irrational. Running into him is a scenario that plays in my head often, though every time it does, I imagine a different reaction.

There are days I run in fear, days I stand my ground and scream at the top of my lungs, days I pound my fists into him over and over, demanding answers. Then there are the days that haunt me the most, that tear me up inside with guilt, disgust. They make me feel dirty and broken. Those are the days I feel so lonely and lost, when I imagine myself lunging into his arms, wrapping them around his body, burying my face in his familiar chest, afraid to let go.

Fuck those days.

I hate him. More than that, I hate myself for missing him.

Knowing there is going to come a day soon that I will have to face him again in court makes a shiver crawl down my spine and my heart gallop inside my chest.

Looking up, I see a harmless-looking girl glancing around the empty building. The sight of her washes away those fears, if only for the moment.

She appears to be slightly older than me, I'd guess early twenties. Everything about her fits right into this place, too, and I can totally picture her hitting it off with Bea.

The girl has honey-blonde hair pulled into a side braid, trailing over her shoulder. She's carrying a tattered, vintage messenger bag with little buttons pinned over every surface. They say cheesy shit like *It's a great day to smile* and *Be the good*.

She's tall, lean, and appears to float through the room. Everything about her screams hipster, but not the kind that wants to power their car with cow shit. More like the kind that does puzzles, watches Bob Ross and probably has like thirty plants in her house. My interest is piqued.

That doesn't happen often. I don't give a flying fuck about most people, but I want to know more about this chick. I offer a small wave, letting her know I will be right over, then flop my book down on the chair beneath me. I pat the pockets of my apron and glance around the coffee table, the chair, and the floor, but I can't find my damn order pad anywhere. Eh, fuck it. I can remember a simple drink.

"Hi, I'm Maddie. What can I get for you?"

I cringe at the bright, over-the-top smile that greets me. "Maddie, hi! I *loooove* your shirt!" Her voice is as sugary sweet as her smile. Why the hell am I always surrounded by all these peppy, bubbly people? Jesus.

I glance down at my shirt because I can't remember what I threw on this morning and almost laugh at the vintage band tee. I own about twenty of them. This one happens to be Johnny Cash, because, of course, it is. I might know one or two songs, whereas she looks like the type that might actually listen to his music.

I seriously hope she doesn't want to chat about it, or I'll look like the ass-wad that I am.

I only own this, and all others like it because the material is soft and comfortable, and the neckline isn't so high that it chokes me. That and it's black, which is always a bonus.

It's completely obnoxious when people wear bands they don't know, but whatever. Sue me.

"Oh, thanks," I mutter. "Need a minute with the menu?"

"What were you reading?" I can't decide if I'm annoyed, intrigued, or smitten with this stranger. She's everything I wish I was. Confident, kind, open, straightforward. I'm leaning toward liking her, but I suck at peopling, so at the same time, having her talk to me is making beads of sweat drip down my back.

"Um, Ellison. Invisible Man. It's for school." I shift my weight to my other foot, wishing I had found my notepad, so I had something to do with my hands.

"You're joking! My brother is reading the same thing right now!"

That's probably my cue to ask who her brother is. Chances are he goes to the same school, likely the same class. Even if we are across town. As far as I know, only the honors class reads this particular novel. But I don't ask because, frankly, I don't give a shit, and I would prefer, if her brother is in my class, that she not go home and tell him she ran into me here. The less people know about me, the better.

"Sweet." I don't know how much more uninterested I can sound before she gets the hint that I do not want to talk.

"You don't talk much, do you?" Ah, there it is. She just doesn't give up.

"Nope."

"How come?"

"Not much to say, I guess."

Apparently, that's the wrong answer. Instead of accepting that I'm a bitch and letting it go, Hippie Girl looks at me. Like really looks.

She stares into my eyes until I squirm and look away. Then she moves down, taking in my shirt, ripped jeans, and worn tennis shoes. The hairband squeezing my wrist. She catalogs each of the unruly strands of hair popping up around my head, refusing to stay in the bun with the rest of my hair no matter how many times I redo the damn thing.

Her eyes appraise my pale, flat nose, my sunken eyes shadowed in purple bags, and my lack of makeup. And then back to my eyes. She is trying to figure me out; it scares the shit out of me to think what she might see.

It might scare me more that she cares to look at all.

"I have a feeling that is far from true."

Chapter Ten

"How are those papers coming along, Maddie?"

It's taken a month, but I'm finally starting to feel like we're getting in the groove. Maddie and I had gotten off to a rocky start; the uncomfortable silence paired with a lack of anything to give her to do was enough to drive me insane, and I'm sure she was ready to throw in the towel. But we both stuck it out, and I think she would agree that we have fallen into a good rhythm these last few days.

Outside of a few difficult years, I've never struggled to talk to people before. I might be a geek, but I think because of that, my parents both made sure to socialize the hell out of me as a kid, so I would never feel awkward and out of place. It was an adapt-to-survive situation, with my parents and sister being major extroverts. I got good at watching them and learning how to converse with almost anybody. I could work the room at a party without breaking a sweat, so why is this one eighteen-year-old girl sending me scrambling?

We're both busy with our respective tasks when I feel eyes on me. I glance up, and Maddie raises her eyebrows at me without moving her head. The unspoken words are clear—some of these kids are idiots. As a professional, I can't agree with her out loud. But I also can't say she's wrong.

"Now, now, Miss. Klein. It's not nice to judge your fellow students. Not everybody can be book nerds like us," I joke.

To my surprise, she smiles. It doesn't touch her eyes, but I'm guessing it's as sincere as she can manage. I catch a twinkle of mischief shining back in those astonishing green eyes. "Who says I'm judging? I suck major ass at math, and I know it. I don't care if people aren't good at something. We can't all excel at the same things, or this world would be pretty one-dimensional."

She gives a huge eye roll and flaps the paper in her hand between us. "But," she continues, "it bugs the shit out of me that some of these people don't even try. This kid filled in A, B, C, D, E. They couldn't even do that part right!" She throws her hands up in the air again. "*E* wasn't an option on this quiz! Everyone knows that if you don't know the damn answers, you need to stick with the same letter for everything. That way, you at least get a quarter of them right. The way he did it, it's possible to get literally every single answer wrong. I mean, come on!" She rubs her forehead, exasperated, and it makes me chuckle.

"Tell me how you really feel." That comment earns me a scowl that only makes me laugh more. "Hold on a second. Did Madalynn Klein just reveal something personal about herself?"

My words surprise her as she looks up, trying to remember what she said. Being bad at math might not be the most groundbreaking revelation, but it goes to show how little she lets people in.

Sometimes, she reminds me of the guards in England who wear tall black hats and don't move, no matter how much tourists taunt them. I've never been there, so I can't say how true that is, but I've heard enough references to it that I imagine it has to be real.

After four weeks of spending three-plus hours a day together, she's given up nothing about herself beyond her name—not willingly, that is. It's felt like the moment a glimmer of her personality shows through, she gets this regretful look on her face, like she's wishing she could take the tiny piece back and bury it in whatever deep, dark hole she hides herself in.

Most teenage girls are more than happy to talk about themselves. It's not their fault. Being self-centered and egotistical comes with the territory at that age. It's the awkward and annoying stage in life that we all go through where we think the world revolves around us, and everybody we know spends all their time thinking about us.

At that age, kids haven't realized that most other people don't care to think about them nearly as often as they believe. People are far too busy being wrapped up in their own lives for that. But that's not Maddie. She seems to prefer sawing off her arm to talking about herself.

Now, I regret pointing out her little slip because her face instantly changes. The mood in the room had finally lightened up; she cracked a small smile at my joke, which failed miserably, but all that progress flies right out the window.

I watch her for another moment, drumming my fingers against my thigh as the thoughts play out behind her eyes. They may be hidden, but I can tell they are there, moving across her face one by one. I'd be willing to bet that if she knew how expressive her eyes are, she would walk around in sunglasses.

I hold my breath as she opens her mouth to speak, closes it, reconsiders her words, and then goes through that same sequence three more times.

She seems to channel all her courage in one long breath and then lets it all word vomit out. "Look, I don't mean to be...well, whatever I am. A bitch. Cold. Closed off. Take your pick; I know people have said it all. I don't know how to get out of my head. I don't know how to relate to people or make meaningless conversations. It all feels so fucking inconsequential, you know?" Her chin rests in her hand as she stares out the window, watching fat drops of rain dance down the glass.

"I spent so much of my life filtering every word that came from my mouth, guarding most of myself away from anybody and everybody and keeping this huge secret. I got so exhausted from the effort that one day, I decided it was easier not to try at all. If I didn't talk about myself, I didn't have to try so hard to ensure the wrong thing didn't slip.

"Then, by the time I didn't have to do that anymore, the rumors had already started, and people made up their minds about me, so again, what was the point? Plus, by then, everything that was important to the few friends I still had left felt stupid and pointless. I couldn't fake it all the time."

She stops speaking momentarily, still trying to piece her words together. I notice a slight tinge of blood pooling at the bed of her fingernails, where she is picking at little pieces of skin. Her jaw is clenched and her eyes pinch shut.

"I guess what I'm trying to say is that I'm sorry." She stops again, sighs, runs her hands down her face and looks up at me for the first time. Directly into my eyes with this pleading desperation. "I wasn't always like this, you know? I don't know how to get back to that person. I don't think she exists anymore. It feels like I got cheated out of the chance to figure everything out. Isn't that what middle and high school are supposed to be for? Figuring out who you are, exploring and trying on different hats to help find your place in the world. Deciding what kind of person you want to be. Nobody has it all figured out by eighteen, but at least they've had the chance to give it a shot. I never got that. And the worst part is, I don't even know who to hate for it."

She laughs, but it's one of those short, humorless laughs. "I appreciate you trying to get to know me and pull me out of my shell. You're a good person, I think. You seem to care, and that says a lot. But I mean this in the nicest way possible: please stop. I'm not a person you want to know or care about, for that matter. Give up. Focus your energy on somebody who deserves it."

I'm left speechless. I can understand why Wyatt is so dead set on helping her. I can't recall ever meeting somebody who hated themselves as much as Maddie seems to.

I stay silent, carefully forming the words in my head before speaking. I need to get whatever I say next right. It feels like one of those make-or-break moments where I either gain her trust or shatter it. Somebody needs to prove to her that no matter how ugly of a past she might have, her voice deserves to be heard.

"Try me."

It's nothing profound, but it's the only thing that seems to fit. It's the only thing I can think of that will show her that I'm not afraid of her ugly parts. I've seen ugly, lived through ugly, and have plenty of my own ugly. I'm not scared of hers.

Somebody needs to care enough to listen.

CHAPTER ELEVEN

I DON'T CARE WHAT people think about me. Not anymore.

Or, at least that is what I tell myself. In truth, I think I care more than I like to admit. Otherwise, why would I be spending so much time caring about what Mr. James thinks of me? But it does bother me and so I have to face the reality that I might care, just a little.

The guy has been nothing but kind to me from the start. I can't imagine he was thrilled about this arrangement, but he did it anyway to help me out. He's gone out of his way to make small talk and try to get to know me, even after I kept shutting him down. Without being pushy or overbearing, he's given me space to chat if I want to but left me alone when it's clear I didn't have any interest in talking.

I shouldn't be surprised by his comment, but something about it bothers me. I hate the idea of him thinking I am just being a jerk for the sake of being a jerk.

Would it be the worst thing in the world to let him in? Even just a little. I've pushed people away plenty over the last year and a half. Hell, I've been pushing people away for the last six years, if I'm honest. Wyatt is the only other person who has pushed back, and that's because it's his damn job.

Every time I look up, he's there, waiting patiently while I sort through all the messy crap bogging down my mind. Those steel-gray eyes seem to hold a pain of their own. The way he looks at me is like he understands what it is like to suffer, and something about that is comforting.

I can't believe I'm seriously considering this. What in the actual hell is wrong with me? I don't open up to people, especially not virtual strangers. Even my best friend hasn't been able to pry much information from me apart from the basic details, though that's all on me. She would be there for me if I let her in, and I've considered it. Ultimately, I haven't been able to open up the way she wants me to.

It's too tainted, especially for a bright, cheery person like Kenna. Plus, I can't stand the thought of her looking at me differently once she sees the broken ugliness inside my head.

After this year, I'll never see Mr. James again. I hardly know him, which is both good and bad in this situation. I can't imagine he thinks much of me. Or I can only assume he doesn't, anyway. Apart from these three hours a day together, he has no role in my life.

So again, pro and con.

On the one hand, what does he care about how messed up I am, and on the other, is that the impression I want to leave? What if I need letters of recommendation in the next few months? I could get them from other teachers, but would they mean as much as coming from my English teacher, depending on my major? Plus, how much more awkward will these three hours get once he can barely stand to look at me?

I need his classes—all three of them—to graduate. I can't simply drop once things get weird, and while I don't think he can kick me out of his class for no reason, I'd rather not risk it.

He seems to care, and that's messing with my head. Usually, when I tell people I don't want to talk about my crap, they drop it. I seek him out again, allowing my eyes to lock on his for the slightest glimmer of a moment. It's long enough to catch a glimpse of something that looks an awful lot like his own black cloud of pain.

Nothing about Mr. James makes any sense and the way he makes me feel like I can trust him makes even less sense.

This guy all but challenged me. Who does that?

And why do I keep getting the sense that he won't judge my darkness?

It's similar to how I felt immediately with Wyatt, but also distinctly different.

I have a shitty sense of character, given that the last man I trusted, well, that's what landed me here in the first place. So, nope, I don't trust myself at all.

Fuck, why am I still thinking about this?

"I'm sure you have heard some interesting stories about me by now. Some true. Many far from it." I don't want to look him in the eye, but I want to get a read on how he reacts. People lie, but their faces don't do it nearly as well as their words.

The sudden movement of his chair gliding backward into the wall as he gets up from behind his desk startles me. What the hell is he doing?

Stop, no, abort! Why is he coming closer?

Nope, that is not how this works. *Please go stand in a corner with your back to me!*

If he can see the panic on my face, he does well to ignore it and parks his tight, fine ass in the chair right next to mine, then looks me dead in the eye.

He is far too close, and holy shit, that smell!

It's like bourbon, maybe, mixed with something warm—vanilla, I think. It's subtle enough that it takes me a moment to notice. It's not strong enough to be cologne, more like body wash or shampoo or something.

Don't you dare sniff this man, Maddie!

It takes him long enough to answer that I almost forget what I said.

"I actually know little to nothing. It didn't feel right to ask anybody or look it up. It's your life, and the way I figure, if you want to share any of that, you will. If not, there's probably a reason. What kind of person would it make me to invade anybody's privacy like that?" He pauses, carefully choosing his next words. "I've pieced a few things together on my own, but it's pure speculation based on what I've seen. Ball's in your court, Madalynn. Your story is yours to tell, however and with whomever you see fit. Nobody else gets to decide that for you."

He rubs the back of his neck and looks down, contradicting the confident delivery of his words. Well, I wasn't expecting that kind of answer.

"Oh." Yeah, that was eloquent.

I can't say I have ever had anybody show me that level of respect.

My voice is shaking when I muster up the courage to speak again, which pisses me off. I don't want to cry, so I detach myself from my words.

It's a method I picked up on quickly after days of going over the same story over and over. I ran out of tears, then anger, then even apathy, after the first week. Which left me a shell of a person so sick of saying the same words to different groups of people that I couldn't feel anymore. I might as well have been reciting the numbers of pi, but it hadn't taken long for me to realize the benefit of that. From there on, it became less of a default and more of a saving grace for my sanity.

"I entered foster care when I was eleven, then bounced around a few places for months until I finally landed in this house that I thought was going to be a great home. It was the perfect fit at first. The foster parents were this super nice couple in their late thirties who had tried having kids on their own for years and couldn't, so they decided to foster in hopes of adopting." An unwelcome, painful image of Andrew holding a baby pops into my head like a punch to the gut. It takes everything I have to shake it away and focus on the facts again.

"I was the longest placement they had ever had. Mrs. Garrison, Kelly, got this promotion a few weeks after I moved in, though, and I guess her new job required a lot of travel. It started as a day here and there and then built up to a week and sometimes two weeks at a time. She was gone more than she was home, but it never bothered me. I was always closer to her husband, Andrew, so it didn't matter whether she was there.

"It was like we bonded right away. He was more involved, and I got the feeling that fostering was his idea, not hers. She was nice, but a lot more reserved and hesitant to 'get attached,' I think." I shrug, trying to convince myself just as much as him that it didn't hurt.

"Everything was good and normal for a while, but I was young, and he was the first man that ever paid me any attention. I didn't have a father or a brother or anything like that, so I didn't know how to handle the relationship. Looking back, I realize I was pathetically desperate for his approval."

My cheeks burn with shame at the way I acted. Rolling up my shorts as high as they could go, forgetting to wear underwear, basking in the smallest bit of praise. "I soaked in every moment of attention.

"Somewhere along the way, it sort of turned into this crush, and that's where it all got complicated. I don't know how to explain it all, though." I pause, fighting the lump forming over what comes next. I still haven't found a "good" way of saying it. It tastes like acid, no matter what words I choose.

"I was twelve the first time anything happened between us. I, um..." I clear my throat and go for it, the words all coming out in a string that runs together so fast you can't tell where one word ends and the next begins. "The uh, police report or charges or whatever…hewaschargedwithsexualassaultofaminor."

There. I didn't say it well, but I said it. Sort of.

I have yet to look up as I talk, afraid of what I might find staring back at me. Instead, I focus on my lap, where I continue picking at my nails.

"I never told anybody or said anything. I was too weak—too much of a coward. The only reason it stopped was because a teacher saw something they weren't supposed to outside of school hours and reported it. I was sixteen by that time.

"He had taken me to a concert out of town. We were two hours away from here, and I suppose he figured that in a crowd that big and that far away, we wouldn't run into anybody who knew us. I've always looked older than I am. I guess he wasn't worried about it." By now, my voice is trembling and all that effort to keep my mask on fails. I replay that day over and over in my mind, wondering what might have happened if we had stayed home that day instead. Would I still be with him?

I want to say no. I want so, so badly to say no. I want to believe I would have been strong enough to see what was happening and walk away. To stand up for myself. But how can I believe that when I still don't even know how I feel about any of it?

"So yeah, she was there and saw him…acting like I was his girlfriend." Telling my teacher that Andrew had his hands all over me the whole time, my ass pressed into his front, kissing my neck…yeah, probably not the best idea, so we'll stick with that explanation.

"Things got pretty ugly pretty fast after that." Mr. James still hasn't made a sound. If it wasn't for that vanilla bourbon scent and the warm heat of his body pressing in on me from all sides, I'd question if he was still there.

My stomach churns, flipping itself into knots until I'm fighting not to vomit. It's a good thing I haven't eaten today.

As much as I would love to avoid it, I force myself to look up and gauge Mr. James' reaction. Of all the things I was expecting to see—disgust, pity, detachment, discomfort—what I couldn't have predicted was rage.

In the twenty or more times I have had to tell this same story, the reactions I've gotten have differed from one person to the next, depending on who I was talking to. The people who deal with messed up shit every day were always good at remaining neutral and unaffected by my words. They were never rude or dismissive, but I think they had to detach to maintain sanity.

I recall being asked in one of my first interviews to use the proper biological terms for things. Something about making sure it was clear and direct since different words mean different things to people, and they needed specifics.

Lucky me.

It made sense, and yet I had to wonder if part of the reason was to help them maintain distance, to keep things clinical and detached and to remove the emotion from the fact. It was easier to stomach that way, I think.

I adapted the method quickly. The sticking to the facts part. You couldn't pay me money ever to use the term *penis* again.

The contrast in Mr. James' reaction takes my breath away.

I'm used to the clinical responses. I had come to expect them, in fact. Considering that the only people who got to hear the "real story," or at least the parts I had to share, were all in the same professional field, I wasn't prepared for this.

Wyatt teared up but tried to hide it. It wasn't out of pity but more out of anger, sadness for the childhood that was taken from me, heartbroken over, I don't know what. It helped me trust him, though. But that's irrelevant because it's not remotely close to the reaction I'm seeing right now.

Looking at Mr. James' face is like watching a pot of water boil. At first, a few bubbles rise to the surface as he processes my words. He's hot, ready to inflict pain, but not at full capacity, at least not yet.

His jaw clenches beneath the short, neat beard along his face. His fists are clenched like he is moments from throwing a punch, his legs shake violently, and his nostrils flare like an angry bull.

The deep breaths he appears to be taking seem completely ineffective. The longer he sits, the hotter he gets until those bubbles are furiously popping, spilling over the top, and hitting the surface with loud hissing noises.

The moment he reaches his boiling point comes when he hurls his body out of the chair, sending it skidding backward with enough force that it slams into the table behind us. The table rattles.

I'm frozen as he picks up the nearest object, which happens to be my stainless-steel water bottle, and flings it with uninhibited force toward the back of the room.

It smashes into the brick wall, scattering small chunks around the room in a cloud of dust before it drops to the floor.

My ears are still ringing when Mrs. Perkins comes flying through the door.

Mr. James is pacing back and forth, hands clasped on his head, trying to control his anger. I have to tear my eyes away from him toward the woman I greatly admire, to find her confused and concerned face watching him, too.

One look at me, and somehow, she seems to understand what's happening, which is baffling when even I don't understand, despite sitting right here. I expect some form of reprimand for the grown man who caused a considerable commotion, lost his shit in front of a student and disrupted who knows how many surrounding classes.

Instead, my respect for her only grows when she nods with understanding, gives me a slight smile, confirms that I'm okay, and walks back out the door, pulling it closed behind her without a word.

CHAPTER TWELVE

R AGE.

Fury.

Red hot, blinding, fucking anger.

It's consuming me. My skin is burning. Every muscle inside me is tense, waiting to burst. I'm vibrating with the desperate attempt to contain it when all I want to do is lash out, punch the living shit out of this man until his blood stains my fists.

It's taking everything in me to not let her see me go postal, at least not any more than I already have. Lord knows she has been through enough as it is; I don't need to add to it.

Twelve.

Fucking twelve?

My stomach rolls at the same time as surges of adrenaline burst and pop in my veins. She's staring at me like a wild animal set free from its cage.

Shit! I've scared her.

I can only imagine she's got to be afraid of me at this point. I would be. Hell, scratch that, I am scared of me and this is exactly the reason why. I can't seem to get a grip over the haze holding my humanity hostage. I'm like the damn Hulk. All I want to do is smash, even if innocent people get hurt in the process. I'm just like—

Fuck! No! This is about Maddie.

I need to be here for Maddie. She is what matters, not my past.

Walking around the room, hands folded on the top of my head, allowing deep inhales of stale air to fill my lungs, helps. I feel the blood that's running hot throughout my body slowly cool with each exhale.

In my pacing, I notice the chair I had been sitting in is now tipped over a few feet away, so I walk over, pick it up, and set it back in its rightful place while also straightening the table I disrupted and then walk over to pick up Maddie's water bottle which is dented and scuffed as hell from smashing into the wall.

I spin the thing over in my hands, finally locating a brand name on the bottom and noting the color and design to ensure I replace it for her—it's the least I can do.

With one more deep breath, I pull out the chair again and retake my seat next to her. Looking straight into those piercing, pale green eyes, I apologize.

"That was completely inappropriate, and I should have had better control over my emotions. I didn't mean to scare you."

Her eyebrows shoot so high that I worry they might get lost in her hairline. A million thoughts pass over her expressive face. She raises her brows, then tips her chin and squints at me, scrunching up her nose, assessing me. That pinched look makes it seem like she doesn't believe my words.

"You're sorry?" she questions.

"I, uh, yeah. I mean, I don't know the right thing to say here. It all feels wrong, and I know anything would fall short of what you deserve to hear. I want to be able to come up with something meaningful, but I'm so angry right now that I can't think straight." I pound my fist on the table, rattling the legs against the tile floor.

Maddie looks terrified, making me want to turn all that rage around on myself. I worked my ass off to get a handle on my anger. Every stupid class, every therapy session, all for it to go right out the window when I need it the most. Here I am, promising to be a safe space for her to talk, just to lose control.

At the same time, how was I supposed to respond to something like that? I can't imagine any decent human could hear her story and not want to rip the head off of the person who could do that to a child.

When Maddie speaks again, her voice is small and timid. Not at all what I have come to expect from her. I hate it. "I knew I shouldn't have said anything. Can we please forget about this and go back to the whole weird silence thing? We were getting so good at it. I wasn't trying to piss you off!"

Hold the damn phone. What did she just say? Is this girl really trying to apologize to me?

"What the hell are you talking about? You think I'm angry with you?"

The way she averts her gaze says it all.

"Maddie, no! How could I be mad at you for that?" My fingers itch to reach out and turn her chin back toward me. To make her look me in the eye. I want to know that she hears me.

"I'm grateful you felt you could trust me enough to share, and I'm angry at myself for reacting so poorly. And angry doesn't begin to explain how I feel about this sick asshole."

Asshole is probably the wrong language to be using in front of a student, but with Maddie's potty mouth, I don't think she cares.

An ear-splitting ring breaks the heavy silence in the room as the bell announces the end of the period. Despite the interruption, neither of us intends to walk away from this conversation. Whatever it is Maddie needs to say, I'm staying right here, no matter how badly I want to track down this Andrew fucker and beat the living shit out of him.

"It wasn't like that." Her voice is so muted that it takes me a minute to register her words.

"I'm not sure I understand." I try to keep my tone free from judgment, but every word that leaves my mouth feels inept. I'm saying all the same wrong things that everybody said to me all those years ago.

Maddie continues to fidget before me, pulling at the skin around her fingernails, chipping away at the small amount of black nail polish that remains intact, and biting at her lip—anything to avoid looking at me. I count six times that she opens her mouth to speak, then stops. Whatever she's about to tell me is either too hard to say, or she can't find the right words to explain.

Maddie's shaking, whispered voice interrupts my train of thought. I have to lean in to hear the words that tumble from her mouth in rapid succession. "I know I was rap—um, you know. Sorry, I can't say that word. Anyways, I know that is technically what happened according to the law or whatever, but it doesn't feel like what I went through. I don't know how to explain it." Her voice quivers and her body shakes. If I knew it wouldn't be inappropriate as hell, I'd pull her into a hug.

"When you hear that word, you think of this big, scary man creeping into a little girl's room at night and forcing them to do things. That's not what happened. I didn't cry or scream. It wasn't this back alley behind a bar with a man wearing a mask. I didn't even ask him to stop or say no. I lo—" She stops herself from whatever she was about to say and runs a hand through her hair, tips her head back, and pinches her eyes closed once again.

"How can I compare myself to women and kids who are legitimately assaulted, held at gunpoint, beaten, forced, and violated? How am I supposed to sit in a courtroom and tell a group of strangers that I was assaulted when—" Again, she stops herself.

I can't expect to have earned whatever those innermost thoughts might be. As curious as I am, I won't pry any more from her than she is willing to give.

"It's unfair to group me in the same category as those people. What happened to me didn't get bad until other people found out about it. That was the worst part of it all. How messed up is that? There are girls out there being trafficked and sold to actual monsters—women who die at the hands of abusive men. And then there is me…

"Monsters don't take you out for ice cream and hold you and tell you that you're beautiful after a day filled with girls calling you fat and ugly and unlovable. They don't remember your favorite book then read it to learn why you love it so much. They don't shower you with affection, attention, and praise." Maddie's voice grows louder as she speaks until she's screaming. When she looks up, tears stream down her face.

The room falls silent again. She slumps back down in the seat next to me and whispers again. "So, how the hell can I call myself a victim? I'm as messed up as him."

I imagine this is the part where I'm supposed to tell her it's normal to feel that way. Where I am supposed to reassure her that her feelings are valid and despite how she might feel, she isn't sick and broken. Those things might be true, but hearing it doesn't help. I would know.

So instead, I pull myself to my feet and move until we are toe to toe and she can't help but look at me. "Maddie, I can't pretend to understand what that has been like. I can't imagine going through something like that and the mess of emotions and thoughts and God knows what else that goes through your head."

I close my eyes for just a second and take another mustering breath. "What I can say is I know what it's like to feel responsible for something that, from the outside, doesn't appear to be your fault."

Maddie holds my eyes without blinking. I don't even think she's taken a single breath of air. "I know what it feels like to wake up every day and wonder 'if only this had been different' or 'if only I had said this instead of that'. To question how your actions impacted the most insignificant moments and if one small change could have made a difference. I know what it feels like to feel tainted and broken and ugly." My teeth grind as I talk. Every word that leaves my mouth has me fighting to keep back all the feelings and beliefs that I've held for myself for so long. I thought I had moved on from this. I thought I had healed, but now I realize that isn't as true as I made myself believe.

"I could sit here and tell you that what you believe about yourself isn't true because it's not. You are not broken. You are not sick or ugly or disgusting. But, I know those words mean nothing until you figure that part out for yourself."

What I don't say is that the "figuring it out" is the hardest damn job in the world. One I clearly haven't pulled off myself.

Chapter Thirteen

B RIGHT BLUE WALLS PLASTERED with butterflies and an ABC banner cutting through the middle. Toys and books stacked in a corner. It's all so innocent and welcoming... for a six-year-old. That idea alone makes me shudder.

I don't want to be here.

The whole space feels like it's mocking me. On the one hand, it infuriates me that I'm being treated like a kid. I'm almost seventeen, not seven. On the other, the idea that there is an office like this dedicated to kids is fucking sick. With that comes pity for these poor people who have to give *rape kits to kids for a living. What kind of world do we live in?*

Entering the exam room feels surreal. Everybody is so kind. They treat it like any old doctor's visit, smiling and making small talk. They ask me to undress, give me a little gown, lay back on the table, and they will be back. What's the point in leaving the room if they're about to be all up in my business, anyway?

I do as I'm told, settling my head against the flat, plastic pillow and laugh.

An adorable little kitten poster is tacked to the ceiling above my head. Is that supposed to make this easier? Here, look at this sweet little kitten and forget about the trauma of having strangers take pictures and swabs from my lady parts.

The last few days' events swirl through my mind like a fierce and unrelenting tornado, destroying everything in its path.

The cops took my phone a few days ago, the day I was called to the office. No phone meant no communication, but that only mattered when it came to Kenna. She had to be losing her mind. It's been years since we went more than a day or two without talking, and now it's been a week of radio silence from me. She doesn't know why I'm not at school, so I can only imagine she's been freaking out.

Andrew is the only person besides her who probably cares enough to question where I disappeared to. I try not to think about him, but I can't help it. Like it or not, he's been the center of my universe for the better part of four years. Does he know yet that the cops know? Has he been arrested, or is he sitting at home wondering where I am?

I have to assume he knows that something is up by now. Would he dare reach out to Jackie? It would be bold, that's for sure, but bold is how Andrew operates.

I don't want to care. Everything has gotten so messed up and confusing these last few days. One moment, I'm wracked with guilt for ruining his life and the next, I hate him as much as these people keep telling me I should. From their perspective, I get it. I was twelve the first time anything happened between us. Most people would see that as a kid, but they don't know me. I had been taking care of myself for years. By the age of eight, I had learned to pay bills and balance a budget better than most adults. And now, I'm only a year away from legally being an adult. Doesn't that mean anything?

The questions and thoughts continue barreling through my brain. One minute, I'm crying over the memory of Sunday night movies and Chinese food, and then the next, I'm getting a headache from the tension in my jaw remembering all the things I missed out on.

How many times had we fought over me wanting to go to a bonfire with friends or check out my first high school football game?

The resentment that came every Monday morning when all around me, I was subjected to stories of all the core memories that were supposed to make up this period of my life that I would never get to be part of.

The only positive side to the whirlwind in my brain is that it tunes out the strange women shoving cotton swabs up my hoo-ha.

Hours later, still feeling violated, my caseworker kindly calls to tell me the STD panel I didn't know they had run came back clean. I think it was supposed to make me feel better.

It didn't.

"Maddie?"

I'm pulled from my trip down memory lane by the strong, firm hand that lands on top of mine with a gentle squeeze. It's gone in an instant.

"Sorry, I—" I what? What can I say? *Sorry, my doomsday brain took over and hurled me into a super fun PTSD flashback. Sorry, I unloaded a heaping pile of shit that is my life on you.*

"Please stop saying that. I want you to know that wherever your head was just now, you can tell me if it helps. You don't have to keep dealing with all of this alone."

I nod, drumming my fingers on my thighs, still unsure what to say.

"If you would rather, I can go get Wyatt. Or maybe you want to call Kenna?" Mr. James asks, leaning forward in his chair next to me with his elbows resting on his knees.

I shake my head.

"Please don't treat me like a China doll or a bomb that's about to explode the next time you look at me. I'm not unstable, though it might sometimes look like it. I'm struggling through a lot, and yeah, my brain is a hot mess pretty much constantly, but I'm dealing with it the best I can. I'm not going to go nuclear. So please, don't start doing what everybody else does: guarding your words, letting me slack off, or avoiding me altogether. That's the one thing I can't handle. I wouldn't be here if I didn't think I could handle it, and I wouldn't be talking to you if—" I stop mid-sentence, unsure what words were about to come out of my mouth.

I might have almost said *trust*, but that's a bit too crazy, even for me. What reason would I have to trust somebody I barely know with things I haven't told my shrink or whatever Wyatt is?

For all I know, dear Mr. James here has severed thumbs stashed inside peanut butter jars in his basement. Honestly, that would be my luck, too. Trust somebody for the first time in years, and bam, they turn out to be a psycho. I don't mean to, but the snort leaves my mouth before I can rein it in, making me laugh a little too hard.

Mr. James meets my eye with a look that reads, *What the hell was that?*

Since the weirdness is already there, nothing stops me from voicing my ridiculous thoughts. "You don't happen to have dismantled body parts in your basement, do you? Or attic, garage, anywhere for that matter?"

A wide grin turns into laughter that makes my cheeks hurt and fills the room as Mr. James surprises me with a raised eyebrow, quickly followed by a wink. "If I did, I certainly couldn't tell you...yet."

Tears fill my eyes for an entirely different reason this time. I want to hug him. Whether he meant to or not, the tension in the room dissipates, leaving me feeling like maybe Mr. James is one of the good guys after all.

From there, we fall into an easy conversation, like two old friends reunited as if no time has passed. It's a strange phenomenon for somebody like me.

Wyatt had me do this personality test once that analyzed top strengths. One of the strengths was called "woo." Stupid name if you ask me, but that's beside the point. There was a little book that explained each one, including "woo," which is apparently a trait some people have that gives them an annoying ability to walk into a room and make friends with anybody. They're the life of the party type people, the people anybody would go up and strike up a random conversation with.

People like Kenna.

Out of thirty-four traits, woo came in dead last for me.

It must be high up for Mr. James, though, because we sit there and chat for so long that I lose track of time. So much time that when my phone starts blaring through the room, I can't begin to fathom who could be calling.

I snatch it from my bag and see Bea's name light up the little screen.

"Hey, Bea, what's up?" I mouth *sorry* to Mr. James, feeling rude for answering. My boss never calls me, though.

"Are you okay? Where the hell are you?" Her words come out urgent and direct, but not angry.

"What do you mean? I'm at school."

"Maddie, it's 4:45. You were supposed to be here almost an hour ago. Did something happen today? Why are you still there?"

"Wait, what!?" I pull the phone away and glance at the screen, waiting for it to light up and show me the time. Holy shit, she's right!

"Fuck, I'm so sorry! I will be there as soon as I can!"

I've never been late for work. Ever.

During a time when I'm supposed to be maintaining focus, working my ass off, and keeping my head down, I sure seem to be messing up left and right.

I quickly gather my things, throw out a half-assed apology and rush out the door, down a stupid number of stairs, across the building, and finally out into the student parking lot toward my car, praying as I go that it starts on the first try.

The old beast has a habit of throwing a security error that prevents me from starting it. Wyatt checked it out for me one time and claims it's a common issue in this make and model. I've dealt with it knowing I can't afford to get it fixed, but I'm really regretting not picking up some extra shifts to make that happen as I throw open the mismatched red door on my white car and send a silent prayer to the universe that it starts.

If I had time to revel in it, my body would sag with relief when she roars to life right away. I don't have time to even be thankful as I press the pedal to the floor and race out of the empty parking lot.

By the time I get clocked in, it's nearing five-thirty, and I feel like complete crap for letting Bea down like this. The diner is packed like it always is this time of evening, and she's running around trying to juggle the entire front of the house alone.

Even with the twenty-minute drive, my heart is still racing as I fight to catch my breath from the scramble. I feel so out of shape that the brief thought of taking a page from Mr. James' book to start running crosses my mind. I'd rather shove toothpicks under my fingernails, so the idea passes in an instant.

Despite the rush demanding her attention and the crappy situation I have left my boss in, she drops every-thing the moment she sees me and rushes over.

"Hey, is everything okay?" Her hands land on my upper arms and then pull right back.

I know she's only asking because it's not like me to be late. I'm a strict, "if you aren't ten minutes early, you're late" kind of person. I love Kenna dearly, but unlike with her, when Bridget asks, there is no hidden meaning.

"I'm so sorry. I lost track of time. I was...going over an assignment. It won't happen again." I don't know why I lie. It just comes out, and once it does, it feels more awkward to correct myself, so I leave it be.

I blame the fact that my thoughts are still caught up in the events of the last few hours. I'm still surprised at myself for sharing the little that I did with Mr. James but more than that, I'm stuck on the little he shared in return. He has a past of his own, that much is pretty obvious.

I can't stop wondering what demons are hiding and how they compare to my own. He looked so hurt talking about it but at the same time, the anger that was woven into that was just as apparent.

"Okay, you're sure?"

"Yup! Now, where do you need me?"

Chapter Fourteen

M^{Y FEET HIT THE} dried, hard dirt path while my lungs burn with every breath in the cooling fall air. I've run more in the past few days than I have in months. The busier my mind gets, the more my body craves the release that comes with being out here on the trails, music blasting through my ears, drowning out the noise of the world.

I'm three miles in, deep in thought over last week's conversation with Maddie, when my music stops abruptly, replaced by my phone's default ringtone. I slow my pace, pull the device from my armband, and glance at the screen. Seeing my father's face grinning up at me from the assigned contact photo, a smile takes over.

I miss them more than I want to admit.

"Hey Dad, how's it going?" I exhale, trying to catch my breath. I keep moving while I talk, slowing it down to a brisk walk that allows me to talk without falling on my face.

"Harrison, I'm good. How are you, son? How's the new job treating you?"

"I'm good, Dad."

I could fill him in on Maddie and how her uncanny resemblance to Fallon has left me fighting for sleep and constantly on edge. I want to talk to him about it but I hold back. I don't need to pull my parents back into the past alongside me. Those few years almost broke my family.

They *did* break my family.

I can still hear my mother's sobs for weeks on end. The fighting. The slammed doors. My little sister crawling into my bed at night, not feeling safe in her own home.

I won't risk dredging all that up for them again. Their marriage barely survived it back then. Who knows what unresolved issues lie beneath the surface. They are doing so well now and I won't be the one to taint that.

"The job is good too. It's been an adjustment from middle school but not an unwelcome one. Some of the kids are jerks, some are funny, and a lot of them are pretty darn smart. I have a few that are working their asses off and still can't seem to get it, but I think those are the kids I enjoy working with the most.

"I wanted to teach the honors courses and don't get me wrong," I shrug. "I love that too, but I don't know.

Something about these few keeps calling to me. I get such a high from working day in and day out and then getting to witness the moment it clicks. There is such an innocent pride there that I'm honored to be part of."

"That's great to hear. I'm glad you like it, though it makes the reason for my call feel a little silly. Perhaps not, though." Dad sounds hesitant. There is a hint of hopefulness in his tone, but it's dominated by what sounds like doubt.

"Okay..." I wait, confused about what he is getting at. It's enough to make me stop, throw my hands on top of my head as I take slow, deep breaths.

"Well, you know your mom and I started playing pickleball with Emerson Young, right? He's on the school board and happened to mention an opening next year in their English department. It's a much smaller school, though. A lot smaller. I think he said their average class size is around seven to nine kids. It's not a big town to begin with, so I don't know if you would be interested in looking into somewhere so small, but, well, son, your ma and I miss you. When he brought it up, I had to at least mention it."

My dad's typically jolly voice cracks at the end, bringing with it the realization that he might miss me as much as I miss them. A lump that sits heavy in my throat.

They aren't getting any younger, and this is the first time we've lived more than two hours apart. It's not so easy to jump in the car and drive home to see them for the weekend anymore, and the distance has been getting to me. I think my sister feels the same way. She's brought up going for a visit more than a few times lately, but now that school has started up again, the nine-hour drive isn't so easy to make.

"That's an interesting offer, Pops. I promise I'll give it some serious consideration."

He seems happy that I haven't immediately dismissed the idea. It's not only for his benefit, either. A small school is pretty appealing.

It's the one thing I have been most frustrated by since the start of my career. I don't get enough individual time with any of my students. Even the kids I just told him about who have been struggling have to make time to come in and see me outside of class because there isn't enough time for them all. I know that the limitation stops some from getting the extra help they need.

So, if I consider that and add the close distance to my family, I'd be crazy not to give it at least some thought. In the same breath, I'd be uprooting not just myself but my sister as well since she moved in with me a few months back.

Not only that, but Wyatt put his neck on the line to get me this job, so to walk away after only a year feels like I'm betraying him.

I shift the conversation back to my parents. We talk about pickleball. I can't help but imagine my mother, who has as much grace as a baby sloth, flailing around a court twice a week.

I chat with my dad for a few more minutes as he fills me in on his life as a retired man until my mother snatches the phone out of his hand and takes over.

"Harrison, sweetie! How are you?"

"I'm good, Ma," I repeat. A couple jogging together passes me as I stroll. They smile and wave, to which I return the gesture even as a pang of jealousy hits me.

"Well, good. Meet anybody new lately?"

I shake my head, smiling, though still slightly annoyed. It took her less than ten seconds to bring up my love life.

It's been six years since I ended things with Zoe, and I've had zero interest in plunging back into the dating world since. The way things ended didn't leave me too eager to open myself up again, just to have all my biggest insecurities thrown in my face. Something my mom doesn't seem to understand.

"Nobody worth mentioning."

I swear I hear her sigh. "You're such a good man, Harrison. Don't worry; the time will come when you least expect it. Life has a funny way of working out in the last ways you might imagine."

"Not likely, Ma. But thanks anyway." I rub a hand over my face, wiping away more sweat and regretting answering my phone at this point.

I love my mom, but times like this, she drives me insane. Is it really that hard for her to understand my hesitations? The first girl I ever loved died in my arms as a teenager without even knowing how I felt about her. It took me a long ass time to put myself out there after that.

When I finally did, I met Zoe, and things with us were great. At least at first.

Until she learned about the demons hiding in my closet and I overheard her talking to her sister about how she didn't know if she could be with somebody like me. How she wasn't sure she could ever feel safe with me. I don't blame her. It's a valid concern and one I think about far too often. Often enough to keep me from putting myself back into the dating pool.

But of course, Mom doesn't get it.

"I talked to your brother—" Mom starts, but I'm quick to bring that topic of conversation to a screeching halt. I can only take so fucking much.

"Don't." There is a harshness in my tone I hate using, but she knows better. I don't have a brother.

From the background, I hear my dad cut her off at the same time I do. At least he understands. Mom always tries to play this "mother's love" card and claims that she loves all her children equally, no matter what, even when she doesn't agree with their choices.

Screw that. I don't care if he is her son, my brother, or the damn Pope. He's been dead to me for a lifetime and nothing is ever going to change that.

"I gotta go, Mom." I can't deal with this right now. Talk about bad timing. I don't wait for a response and hang up the phone, then shove it back into my armband.

I had been ready to head back toward home before Dad called, but now, the fire in my veins is raging once again and I know exercise is the best way to tame it.

The sun has set, bringing the temperature down, but the humidity still sticks to my skin. Breathing feels like trying to inhale glue, but I don't stop. I let my music invade my body and take over. I lose myself in the heavy beat for another four miles.

By the time my street comes into view, I'm too exhausted to think, which is exactly the point. I welcome the silence and slow myself to a leisurely walk, fingers intertwined on top of my head as I cool down.

Inside the house, I beeline straight for the shower.

With my skin no longer coated in a thick layer of sweat, I find myself in my office, pacing. The calmness my run had granted me was only a momentary reprieve.

A stack of papers sits on the desk, calling my name.

I ignore it.

Back and forth, again and again, as thoughts race around, playing chase inside my head. I latch on to one, only for it to sprint off and tag in another. It's maddening.

In my pacing, I find myself considering the surrounding space. If I decide to move, I will lose this office that I love so much, which would be a shame. But it's nothing that can't be rebuilt, possibly expanded upon. I'm close to running out of shelf space for all my books anyway, so maybe that's something to add to the pro list.

My home office is the only place in the house that I put any effort into. The rest of the house is bare, with tan walls and basic furniture that was picked solely for comfort and not remotely for style. I poured all the care that the other rooms lack into this space, where I spend the majority of my time.

It all started to come together based on this vintage, dark-brown leather armchair with its matching footstool I found a few years ago at a rummage sale with my mom.

At the time, she thought I was working too hard and needed a break. Her idea of fun turned out to be dragging me to a field full of old people's even older junk. I went, rather unwillingly, but because I love my mom, I sucked it up with a fake smile on my face that lasted maybe ten minutes before I found it to be pretty neat. Old people collect some incredible things.

When I saw the chair, it took me right back to my child-hood, when I sat in an almost identical one that belonged to my grandfather while we read for hours. Story after story, I begged for more, and he never turned me down.

Seeing it brought back all of these warm, happy memories, which served as a visual reminder of why I became a teacher—at least, that's part of the reason. I knew it had to come home with me, no matter the cost.

Sitting in it, I could practically smell his sandalwood cologne and the tickle of his whiskers against my cheek. I brought it home that afternoon, placed it into a bare, empty room, and everything fell into place after that—with a bit of added help from my sister.

Harleigh picked out a deep, moody evergreen paint for the walls and then, together, we put up these thin wood strips on the walls that made them appear like giant, empty picture frames. She found some old, but distinctly not creepy, artwork in elegant gold frames and then mounted matching gold museum-style spotlights above each frame.

The desk was all me. I designed and built it from scratch, and while it took forever, I loved every minute.

The wood is a light, natural ash on top with smooth planks and a picture frame border around the edge. I kept the legs simple with an H-style design, angled slightly on either side. When it was all said and done, the result felt masculine and industrial but still homey and warm, fitting the room perfectly.

Harleigh added what she called a jute rug, which was basically made of twine and rope-like material. The desk sits right on it and itches my feet, forcing me to wear socks anytime I work, but I can't complain too much because she was right about how nice it looks.

The final piece that brings the space together and took up as much, if not more, of my time than the desk is the floor-to-ceiling bookshelves that run the entire south wall. The bottom portion is made of cabinets for hidden storage, but the top two-thirds is open shelving framed with slim pieces of wood. All of it was painted the same color as the wall, making it blend in, as if it is a wall in itself.

The moment I step into this room, the stress of the day drops at the door. Something about it clears my mind as if all the bad, lousy parts of the day can't get through the door frame.

As I stand, admiring the space for the hundredth time, I imagine one of the many Sunday afternoons I have spent lounging in my chair with the rain pattering against the windows while I read.

The thought itself is entirely mundane and typical until the image morphs into Maddie, sitting at my desk, tapping away on the keys of her laptop, writing some beautifully tragic tale that her mind weaves together.

That should send me reeling, and it does, but only because of the way my heart warms at the idea. I force it away in disgust, then wonder where in the hell it came from and why. I want to scrub the image from my mind as shame washes over me.

Chapter Fifteen

I FEEL LIGHTER. THE weight of my secret still looms in the shadows, ensuring the threat remains and that I never forget it could pop out at any given moment. Yet, it's far enough away for the time being, that I can go about my day with a small sense of relief.

Having at least one person to talk to, well, it feels good. I've been carrying around this perception that the minute I told anybody even a partial truth, they would run for the hills, avoid me like I was infected with the plague, be disgusted by me—any or all of the above.

So, I've taken to keeping people away, keeping my mouth shut and learning to be okay with solitude.

But it's fucking lonely.

I may not have told Mr. James everything, far from it, but with the little I did share, I expected judgment or, at the very least, pity. I figured he would start treating me like everybody else did.

I know I'm putting far too much thought and hope into one silly little interaction, but I can't seem to help myself. The seed has been planted, burrowing its little roots inside my head that might one day turn into something akin to hope.

I might consider Mr. James a friend in a weird way. But I'm also fully aware that he likely hasn't thought twice about it. Or me. And that's fine too. If nothing else, I think he is at least an ally. Every time I looked in his eyes, all I found was understanding. His words from the other day have played over and over in my head. He gets it. I genuinely believe that, at least to an extent, he understands. I hate that for him, but I kind of love it for me.

I've also been obsessing over what his past must hold. He implied he is broken like me and I can't help but feel desperate to know and see into that side of him. I can't begin to understand my obsession, but it's the same way I flock to all these dark romance novels all the time. Kenna doesn't think it's healthy. I just don't know how to make her understand that I find peace and comfort there. Seeing other people's darkness makes mine feel a little less suffocating. Even when it's not real.

Either way, things have gotten more comfortable since my little unplanned word vomit. Instead of sitting in an empty room together in awkward silence, we joke, chat, and laugh. He doesn't push me to share, but is there if I want or need to. I no longer dread the three hours a day I have to spend in his classes.

"What will it take for you to go to Homecoming with me?" Kenna asks as we walk toward English together.

I roll my eyes. "Pigs to fly. Backward."

She groans and stomps her foot. "Come on, Maddie! It's our senior year! You haven't been to a single dance. It's a rite of passage. *Paahhllease!*"

"I'm telling you, it is not happening. Don't act like you don't have plenty of choices in the dating department." I know for a fact that four different guys have asked her to go. She's turned them all down in the politest way possible.

"Maybe, but none of them are my best friend," she pouts.

We enter Mr. James' class, still arguing, but are stopped short by the empty room and waving arms as he ushers us right back out the door we just came through.

"Senior assembly in the gym today," he explains, closing the door and locking it behind us while I take the opportunity to appreciate the dark wash jeans perfectly molded to his amazing ass. Kenna elbows me and smirks when I look up, red-faced over getting caught.

With the rest of the class ahead of us, Mr. James falls into step with Kenna and I. Fellow seniors file out from their various rooms as we walk. A few of them wave hi to either Kenna or Mr. James and ignore me completely.

Like I care.

"So," Kenna asks, "what's this assembly about?"

"Not a clue." Mr. James shrugs in response. "They sent an email this morning about bringing you hooligans down at one, so that's what I'm doing. I figured if anybody knew, it would be Miss Class President."

Kenna grins, proud of her new title. I roll my eyes, but the corners of my mouth pull up despite myself. I'm just as proud of her, knowing how much hard work and the extensive hours she poured into her campaign. I might not understand her desire to run, but I understand how badly she wanted to win. Dork.

"So, I couldn't help but overhear you guys talking about homecoming. What's this about you not going, Maddie?" Mr. James questions as we walk.

I roll my eyes in his direction. "You're joking right? Do I seem like the school dance type to you?"

Kenna snorts next to me. Her hand flies up over her mouth and she mutters an embarrassed apology.

Mr. James chuckles, but then turns back to me. "Not at all. But that doesn't mean you shouldn't give it a chance. Who knows, maybe school dances are totally your thing?" He wiggles his eyebrows and says *totally* in a stereotypical preppy teenage girl voice that makes me laugh.

"Yes! Thank you Mr. James! That's what I've tried telling her. See Maddie, now you know I'm right." I roll my eyes at Kenna but am lost in my own thoughts, not really paying attention to her.

I can't compare the two for obvious reasons, but it's odd hearing somebody other than my best friend encouraging me to participate in events. The very mention of a dance or sporting event with Andrew would have resulted in a fight. He'd get offended that I didn't want to spend time with him, saying he had a nice night planned and was going to cook me dinner or take me out. I would try to be reasonable and ask if we could do that the following night.

Inevitably, that would lead to a huge blow up where I would be accused of sleeping around with any guy that looked in my direction. By the time he would insist that I "just go" because "what did he care," my mood would be ruined and instead of having a nice normal night being a fifteen-year-old girl, I would lay in bed and cry myself to sleep.

I'm pulled from my thoughts by an elbow nudging me in the side. Kenna is still chattering away happily about all her ideas for decorating the gym for the dance and somehow, Mr. James and I are walking side by side.

I peer over, wondering if the contact was intentional, to find Mr. James's eyebrows pinched and his head tipped, silently questioning if I'm okay.

I sort of like that he recognizes when I get lost in my head.

I nod and give a small smile, then shake myself out of the past. Doing so leaves my brain with nowhere else to latch onto but the tall, handsome man at my side.

Despite it being the very last place my feelings should be going, I have to admit that I'm drawn to him, and the more time we spend together, the worse it gets.

Students flow and chatter all around us, all headed to the same location. A bolt shoots through me when my fingers accidentally graze his.

I expect him to recoil, yank his hand away or at the very least, step to the side, increasing the distance to avoid further contact, but he doesn't do any of that. Instead, while I watch from the corner of my eye, trying to make it seem like I hadn't noticed, his gaze travels down to our hands, brows drawn together, mouth pulled tight. He stares at my hand like he just watched it morph into a tentacle or something equally ridiculous.

Given that minor but terribly awkward incident, I do a double take when Mr. James settles into the chair directly next to mine as we reach the auditorium. These small theater-style chairs are all linked together, giving each occupant little personal space. The result—one large, muscular thigh pressing firmly against mine.

Is it stuffy in here?

For the next forty-five minutes, my entire awareness is on my body, especially the parts that keep gently grazing Mr. James. His thigh never budges; if anything, he spreads his legs wider, increasing our contact. Or maybe that's all in my head.

We fight over the joint armrest. The thick blonde hair of his arm brushes against mine. Then his fingers. Our shoulders bump here and there.

It's maddening.

He doesn't seem to have the same issue with the girl to his left. I would know; I've been watching her like a sniper from the corner of my eye, to be sure.

By the time Vice Principal Gill and Wyatt finish talking, I'm squirming in my seat with the female equivalent of blue balls. I'm sweaty and achy, and I think I need to run home to change my pants. Seriously, it's a damn good thing these seats are cloth; otherwise, I can't guarantee there won't be a visible wet mark on the seat when I get up. How fucking embarrassing.

I'm so lost in my thoughts, both the dirty ones where I picture being bent over Mr. James's desk after class with a classic schoolgirl skirt flipped up over my ass and the ones where I berate myself for that deliciously dirty mental image, that I don't realize the room has started to empty.

"You coming, Maddie?"

Almost.

The husky, low tone in his voice makes me wonder if, somehow, he could have been thinking the same things as I was.

"Oh, um, yeah." I scramble to get up and gather my things, only to realize Kenna has already moved on to her next class.

"So, care to fill me in?" I ask on the walk back to his classroom.

"On the assembly?"

"Yeah, I spaced off and missed...pretty much everything." As I talk, I keep my head down, hoping he won't notice how my cheeks are stained crimson.

Mr. James chuckles and rubs his hand along the back of his neck. "I was a little distracted myself," he admits. I want to scream and beg him to tell me why.

"It seemed like the gist of it was the counselors are overloaded and don't have time to go through and help every single senior with college planning this year, so I assume we have our dear friend Wyatt to thank for this; they asked that each student finds a faculty advisor to work with. Collaborate and share ideas and experiences, review admissions essays, and write letters of recommendation. That sort of thing, I suppose."

"Oh, well, I guess that isn't too bad. Do we pick the advisor ourselves?"

"Huh?" He appears only to be half-listening. "Oh, um, yeah. You do."

His mood makes me hesitate, but I can't imagine asking anybody else. Perhaps Mrs. Perkins, but I don't have any classes with her this year, so that might be a wrong choice for practicality's sake.

"So, how about it?" I try to sound as nonchalant as I can.

"How about what?"

Dammit. So much for making that easy. "Oh, well, I figured that since we are already working together with me as your TA and all, it might be easy if you were also my advisor. I won't ask for much from you, if anything. I have most of it figured out and prepared myself, but I could use somebody to read over my admission essays. If not, though, that's okay too. I'm sure you are plenty busy. Not to mention sick of dealing with me as it is." I fold, then unfold my arms, then wave a hand through the air. "You know what, forget I asked. I'll find somebody else. I shouldn't have bothered you with it."

So much for sounding confident.

"Easy there. I would be happy to help you. Let's chat about it more this afternoon, okay?" He sounds back to his usual self, laughing at my ridiculous muttering.

"Are you sure?"

"Definitely."

"Thank you. I do appreciate it. This is pretty important to me, so I promise I'll take it seriously and not waste your time." As we walk, I fidget with my fingers, wishing I was wearing a hoodie that I could stuff my hands into. Why are hands so awkward? I never know what to do with the damn things.

"I wouldn't have expected anything different. If you don't mind me asking, why is it so important? What's your end goal? I see you working tirelessly toward college but you've never said what you want to go for?"

His question throws me off. To the point that I can't come up with an answer right away.

It takes a minute, but I decide to just go with the truth. "I remember sitting in the clinic one day, waiting on, well, it doesn't matter. But anyway, there was this pamphlet that talked about the statistics for abuse victims. It basically said I had no chance and was most likely to end up addicted to drugs, becoming a prostitute, dropping out, recreating the cycle of abuse, or something equally awful, and that was if I didn't kill myself first." I notice a visible flinch from Mr. James as the insensitive words fly from my mouth. I probably could have worded that better.

"As soon as I read that, it was like I had this moment of clarity and maybe some of it was anger and this determination to prove that statistic wrong. Whatever the reason, and it's probably dumb of me to even think I can go through with it. Hell, I'm probably working toward this goal that will never pan out and all my hard work will be for nothing but at this point, I think if I stop, I'll crawl into bed and never leave again and I just can't stand that idea." I visibly shudder at the thought.

"So what's the idea?"

"Huh?"

"The goal. The plan. The thing you think for some dumb reason, you won't be able to do. What is it?" Mr. James urges.

"Oh, um, well. It probably sounds stupid. It's not like I'm trying to cure cancer." I tuck a loose curl behind my ear and wish I had just kept my mouth shut.

"Maddie." Mr. James's tone makes me pause and look at him. His eyebrows are raised, waiting for me to answer the question. Urging me to stop rambling and tell him.

I groan. "I think I want to be a social worker."

Mr. James stops again, putting a hand out to bring me to a stop as well. Then he turns so we are face to face. "What about that is stupid?"

Why did I ever open my mouth?

"Uh, because they will never let somebody like me be in charge of helping other people. That's like the blind leading the blind!" I throw my hands up, annoyed that I have to explain something so obvious.

Mr. James' eyes darken. "Want to know why I became a teacher?"

I blink. "Um, sure."

"Books saved my life. When I was at my lowest point in life and felt like I was completely alone and had nothing left, I started reading like I had done when I was a kid."

If he is aware of the stream of people filtering all around us, shooting dirty looks at the clog in traffic, he doesn't seem to care.

"Getting lost in those pages and the desire to know what happens next, was about the only thing that kept me going. It gave me an escape from the real world and it saved my life." His eyes bore into me. If it weren't for the heavy topic, I would have a hard time not getting lost in the sparkling gray pools.

"It took some time and some healing, but I eventually came to the decision that I wanted to teach and to help foster and inspire that in other people. To teach kids the power that books hold. Does that sound stupid to you, Maddie?"

I can't tell if that's meant as a rhetorical question or not. Of course that isn't stupid. It's the exact same reason I read and I love knowing somebody else understands that.

He keeps staring at me, so I realize he actually wants an answer. "Not at all." I lick my lips, which feel cracked and dry all of the sudden.

"Then tell me how it's any different from your dream?"

I scowl, realizing he just called me out, and I walked right into it. Fair enough. I don't want to give him the satisfaction of admitting that he is right, so I just turn and keep walking. He falls into step beside me again with the slightest smirk on his face that I want to be annoyed over, but God is it hot.

What is it about this man that makes me keep spilling my guts?

After a few more moments of silence, Mr. James reaches over and holds his hand out in front of me. At my confused and dumbfounded expression, he explains. "Give me your phone."

"Um, okay?" I question.

"I'll give you my number so you can reach me while working on those college applications or whatever else."

"Oh."

At my usual loss for words, I fish my phone from my back pocket and hand it over. He casually grabs it, taps his large fingers across the screen and hands it back like I'm not feeling utterly childish about this right now. My heart is racing. The phone feels heavier as he hands it back, like his phone number carries an invisible weight with it, one full of temptation and sin.

I've always been annoyed by the kinds of girls who think any person that shows a morsel of kindness toward them is flirting or wants to get in their pants. Equally annoying are the ones who fall for anyone who breathes in their remote direction. I'm not one of those girls. I can't be. They're stupid and vapid and ridiculous.

But that's precisely how I feel right now. I refuse to be anymore cliché than I already am.

I need to remember that Mr. James is not remotely interested in me. And the fact that I'm not interested in him, no matter how many dirty fantasies I have about the guy. That's all it is: attraction and an appreciation for a nice ass. I think I can allow myself that. It sort of feels good to have a normal teenage crush for the first time in my life. Isn't it a high school rite of passage to have a crush on a teacher?

Yup, that's all this is, and I won't feel bad about it.

Except, whatever I'm feeling toward Mr. James is unlike anything I've felt before, which isn't great, but it isn't all bad either. The contrast helps me see that whatever happened with Andrew wasn't real.

I'm not saying this crush is anything real either, but the feelings there were so different.

Andrew made me feel confused and dirty. With him, I had no future. Even in the midst of smiles and laughter and moments when I felt loved and cherished, it was always obsessive and even suffocating.

I feel guilty about the silly little butterflies I get from Mr. James that comes with the desperate desire to always be near him, but it also feels innocent. He gives me hope that there are good, kind men out there, and maybe one day, I might be normal enough to deserve one of them.

"So, at this point, you know significantly more about me than I would like and far more than almost anybody else. It seems fair that I get to know a little, too. Am I allowed to ask how old you are?"

Perfect, straight white teeth flash beneath large, pillowy lips. "I don't see any harm in that. I'm twenty-eight." I pretend to wince, and he laughs. "Excuse me?"

"I would have guessed mid-forties. You're not aging well there, buddy." I find myself smiling, forgetting how good it feels to share in a light-hearted conversation with somebody.

"Ouch, I think that was below the belt there, Miss Klein." Mr. James clenches his hand over his heart and flinches as if I have wounded him.

His charade is interrupted by a distinct buzzing from his front pocket. I have to fight against the desire to be nosey and peek over at his phone screen as he taps away with a grumble. I'm trying so hard not to look, I end up tripping over my feet and stumbling forward, catching myself at the last second and narrowly avoiding face-planting into the dirty linoleum floor.

I'm pretty sure I look like a newborn horse stumbling around, and lucky for me, it's enough to gain some snickers and annoyed stares. Mr. James' attention is pulled from his device and back on me. His raised eyebrows question me, so I shoot back a pathetic thumbs up.

The phone buzzes once again; this time, his groan is loud and unmistakable. "Everything okay over there, Teach?"

He growls. "Just peachy."

Having regained my footing, I fall back into stride beside him as we near his classroom. The vibrant buzz of the hallway has started to wind down as kids make their way to their respective rooms, abandoning each other outside doors with promises to continue their meaningless conversations later. As much as I hate it, I also can't help but have moments where I wish I got to be part of it all. I would give up a lot to be an ordinary teenage girl.

"Tell that to your face." I return to my conversation with Mr. James and try to recapture that light-hearted feeling from a few moments ago.

He takes a deep breath, rubs the back of his neck, and throws his head back with a long sigh. "I love my mother and I know she means well."

I consider his words, wondering how it would feel to have a mom like that. "I can't speak much from experience, but I think you can still love somebody and occasionally be annoyed by them, especially a parent."

He quickly removes the surprised expression from his face, just not quickly enough for me to miss it. I don't know how to feel about it, so I decide to let it go. "I suppose that is true. "

"So, what'd she do?"

"Huh?"

"To annoy you," I add.

"Oh," he rubs the back of his neck once more. "It's nothing. She's trying to not so subtly send me the phone number of her friend's daughter. Her match-making efforts know no bounds."

Saved by the bell. Literally. The piercing noise rattles my eardrums, bringing my attention to the time and surroundings. We've made it back to Mr. James' classroom and have been standing outside the door chatting in a now-empty hall. The noise is enough to bring our chat to a halt before I can dive any deeper into that. I tuck the little tidbit away in my brain to obsess over when I am alone. I'm not sure I needed to know he was single.

Mr. James holds the door open, motioning me through so we can resume our rightful roles as student and teacher. With the change, all feelings of friendship dissolve and fizzle at my feet.

Figures one of the first people I've been able to feel like a real person with has to be somebody I'm not even allowed to be friends with.

My life is such a joke.

CHAPTER SIXTEEN

"Oooooo, Harry!"

I look up from the mountain of essays littering my desk. Any other time, I might be annoyed by the interruption, but I have been moments from stabbing my thigh with a pencil just to stay awake. Overall, I like freshmen, but like them or not, their essays suck. While it might be my job to help them with that, it doesn't mean the start of that process isn't painful.

"I swear, if you don't stop calling me Harry, I will kick you out!" She knows the nickname drives me insane, which is precisely why she enjoys using it so often.

The first thing I see is honey-blonde hair as her head pops through my office doorway, a cheeky grin plastered across her face. She's lucky I love her annoying ass.

"What are you up to, big brother?"

I grumble, irritated more with myself than her, but irritated nonetheless. I've been poring over these crappy papers for hours and getting nowhere. My mind seems stuck on one person and one person only, no matter how hard I try to convince it to stop. I went for a seven-mile run earlier trying to escape her and still, flashes of silky brown hair and piercing green eyes wait for me every time I close my eyes.

"Alrighty then..." The unmistakable raise of her brow has me fumbling around the desk for something to throw at her.

Harleigh turns to leave the room but, for some stupid reason, stops and turns back to me. "You need to get out of the house, and I know for damn sure that I do. I found this super cool little diner about two blocks away. The coffee is heavenly. The food too. Do you remember that burger place we went to on vacation forever ago? Shoot, what was the name of that place?" She leans against the doorframe of my office, tapping a finger on her chin.

I wait, kicking back in my chair, arms folded behind my head, and give her a chance to come up with it on her own. When it's clear she's not going to, I pipe up. "Chicago. I'm pretty sure I was about sixteen, so you would have been eight. How do you remember a single burger from twelve years ago?"

"*Yaaassss!*" I roll my eyes as she jumps and claps. "That's the place. Okay, so remember how amazing those burgers were? Also, come on, don't question my powers regarding food." She pats her stomach like an old Texas cowboy walking into a barbeque joint.

The eye roll I get is over the top, but I can't argue because she's not wrong. My sister might be long and lean, but she can out-eat a grown man any day.

"Anyway, take that place times ten. Plus, it has this cool vibe where it's all eclectic and bookwormy but not at all snobby. You'll love it, I promise!"

Part of me wants to decline so I can sit here being a moody asshole all by myself, but that part is outweighed by the thought of her continuing to badger me until I relent. I might as well skip that part.

"You know what," I push myself up and out of my chair. "I do think I need to get out of here for a bit. Lead the way."

My sister squeals, jumps up and down, and claps like a four-year-old. I can't do anything but shake my head and follow her through the house.

"I have a hard time believing you about this burger situation, though. I'm willing to try it but to claim it's better than Jimmy's feels like a crime. What's the milkshake situation?"

She throws one more knowing grin over her shoulder, silently answering my question, and darts off toward the basement to grab her shoes and bag.

While I wait, I throw on a hoodie and tennis shoes, trying to think about anything but Maddie. I've been intrigued by the girl since she walked into my classroom in that ridiculous green dress, which I still don't know the story behind. My suspicions over the oddity of the outfit were confirmed within the first week or two of school, when she showed up in some form of jeans or leggings and an old t-shirt every day after. I need to remember to ask her about it one of these days.

The more I get to know Madalynn Klein, the more my initial intrigue has grown and mixed with—I don't know what. I feel weird calling her my friend, but it's the only word I can think that sort of fits.

It seems like she's never far from my mind; the slightest thing makes me think of her. *God, why does that sound so creepy?*

At first, it was all because of Fallon. I felt obsessed over the way she looked just like her. Anytime I glanced in her direction, it was like seeing my unrequited love from high school staring back at me. It fucking hurt.

But as I have gotten to know Maddie, I see less and less of Fallon. She was my friend. I loved her, but she's gone and while there are significant similarities between the two, there are also stark differences.

Maddie has a fierceness in her that Fallon never did. Where Fal was happy to go with the flow of others and be a follower, Maddie screams leader, something I doubt she sees in herself, but is pretty obvious if you pay attention. She thinks for herself, forms her own opinions, and is fighting for a better future for herself when it would be so easy to just give up.

I need to stop this train of thought immediately, so I turn my attention back to my sister, who has rejoined me and now walks by my side down the sidewalk toward this little diner. I find it odd that I haven't noticed it, given how close she claims it is, but I don't eat out often, so I suppose it makes sense.

"I talked with Mom and Dad a couple weeks ago. You should probably give them a call tomorrow if you can."

"I know, I know." She shoves her hands deep into her jacket pockets, looking down to avoid my gaze.

I haven't asked what she's running from or why she came to live with me. Everything about it was completely out of the blue, but she made it clear at the time that she wasn't ready to talk about it. Now, here we are six months later, and she still hasn't made a peep about it. For the most part, she seems like herself, so I've tried respecting her and not pushing, but at some point, she's going to have to give me something.

"You ever going to tell me what the deal is with that? What did they do that you are avoiding them?"

Harleigh's brows draw in, confused by my question. "I'm not avoiding them. Coming to live with you had nothing to do with them, really. I just knew if I moved back home, Mom would be on my case about why and I wasn't ready to face that yet. I'm still not sure I am ready to talk about it." She sighs and dips her head, avoiding meeting my eye.

Several questions sit on my tongue, but I swallow them to avoid ruining the night. Besides, I know my sister. Harleigh is stubborn as a mule and until she's ready, she's keeping her mouth shut.

The mention of moving and our parents has me circling back to the job in Georgia. It's been looming in the back of my mind ever since Dad brought it up last week. Every time I feel confident about my decision to at least schedule the interview, something stops me.

I can lie and tell myself it's because I don't want to reflect badly on Wyatt, who went out of his way to get me this job but, I don't think I really believe that.

He wouldn't care. Not about that aspect, anyway.

In the same breath, I can't figure out what my hang up is. In theory, everything about the prospect is appealing. It's smaller so I can focus on more individualized attention, it's a hell of a lot warmer and considering how much I hate the cold, that alone should be enough to make me say yes. If not that, then being close to my family again should definitely tip the scales. And it does. Sort of.

Ridge Valley is my home. I was born and raised right here and aside from college, I've never lived anywhere else. My roots are here. My life is here. But if my family is no longer here, is it really still my home?

Our walk grows silent, each of us lost in our respective thoughts. Thankfully, it's not far because the silence grants my mind too much freedom to wander and neither place I keep ending up is helping my sanity right now.

Harleigh and I approach a nondescript building where my sister's big "ta-da" is the only thing that clues me into our destination. No wonder I never realized it was here. The only signage present is a small logo on the door that simply says *Bea's* in curly black lettering with a small coffee cup logo. I would have missed it even if I had been explicitly looking.

I can't help but raise an eyebrow, immediately suspicious that such a place could be as unique as she has hyped it up to be.

"Just trust me!" Harleigh rolls her eyes, opens the door, and ushers me inside.

CHAPTER SEVENTEEN

TUESDAYS ARE MY FAVORITE night of the week. Bea's is almost always a ghost town after about seven anyway, but on Tuesdays, for whatever reason, once six hits, I could bet my right elbow that I won't see another soul except for Bea and her four-year-old son Caden.

Tuesday is also Pauly's night off. He always goes out and has dinner with his mom, which I find adorable. Not that I can or would tell him that. The only reason I know is because Bea told me.

So, my boss covers for him. It's not needed, but I'm pretty sure she knows that if somebody did come in and I was forced to cook, well, the diner would be a burned-up hockey puck by morning. I don't cook.

It all works out though, because I get to spend the night with my favorite little man, and Bea gets to catch up on paperwork, inventory, ordering, and all that other owner nonsense.

Caden isn't your average kid. He's smarter than shit, but he doesn't talk, at least not much. If you listen closely, he might whisper something so softly that nobody can hear it, but that's exactly why I make sure I'm always listening.

The kid is hilarious.

Every once in a while, he will randomly start yelling at the top of his lungs for no apparent reason. It about knocks my damn socks off. The first time it happened, I almost pissed my pants. That was about the time Bea filled me in on Caden's autism. I can't recall exactly what she said about it, but there was something about a type. Two, I think. Or maybe it's level two.

Either way, it doesn't mean a whole hell of a lot to me. He's a kid, and my buddy, and that's all I care to know.

For some completely bizarre reason, the kid glued himself to my side within hours of meeting.

So, Tuesday nights have become our night. Bea makes spaghetti for dinner—the mere suggestion of something different will end in a major meltdown—so spaghetti it is.

After dinner, he helps me clean the table...and the floor...sometimes the walls, because, man, is that little dude a messy eater. Then we get him hosed down and changed into his pajamas, which are always the same because it's Tuesday, obviously.

Each night has a different pair, and my night is a set of navy-blue button-up ones with little yellow construction vehicles all over. Once his little body is covered in bulldozers, cement mixers, and backhoes, we settle into a giant beanbag chair that Bridget brought in just for this purpose.

The routine never changes; another reason I always work on Tuesdays.

Like every other night, I get him all set in his PJs, settle myself into the beanbag while he waits, and then he walks, which is more of a stomp, over to me, spins around so his back is to me, shimmies himself backward like a skunk trying to spray a predator and then he plops down into my lap with his head resting against my chest and my chin on the top of his little head.

These nights might be part of his routine and how he likes things done, but I'm convinced he knows I need them as much as he does. Sitting in our little slice of the world drowns out everything else. Even my darkness can't reach us here. It's all about Caden, and I wouldn't have it any other way.

As we get into position, I pull this kick-ass weighted blanket from my side and cover us up, ready to spend the next two hours reading. Two hours of reading children's books might have sounded grueling at first, but I wouldn't trade it for the world. Plus, I learn so much from it. I'm pretty sure I could name every single truck known to man, but I've still got nothing on my man, Caden.

I would not be the least bit surprised to learn he could disassemble any vehicle you put in front of him down to nothing but bolts and washers and then have it put back together within a matter of hours. It's unreal how smart he is.

As we are finishing up book number eight of the night, our peace and quiet is interrupted by the chime from the diner's main entrance. The unexpected noise has my heart beating faster than the race cars in the book we just finished. I can see the clock out of the corner of my eye.

8:29.

Whoever the hell is walking in is damn lucky that they are coming in right at Caden's bedtime. If I had to jump ship to help them, he would not be a happy camper, and nobody wants to deal with an angry Caden.

I don't have the chance to go into full freak-out mode as Bea comes out right on schedule to collect our little guy. Her eyebrows go up, her head tilting slightly over her shoulder toward the people who walked in. She's as surprised by them as I am.

"Say goodnight to Maddie, bud."

My heart swells, almost feeling whole again as he nuzzles his face into my neck and mutters, "Night Mads," just loud enough for me to hear.

"Goodnight, sweet boy." I kiss the top of his head and pass him back to his mom, who scoops him up and retreats to her office to settle him.

Once they disappear, I quickly straighten the bean bag chair and gently place all of Caden's books back into his bag so that none of the pages get folded, crumpled, or damaged in any possible way. Those books are his prized possessions.

After that is done, I'm able to turn my attention toward the door and finally acknowledge the pair that has come in.

Hippie Girl has come in a few times over the last two months, so I'm not surprised to see her walk in. The man next to her, though, has all my attention. Mr. James' eyes land on mine, noticing me at the exact moment I do him with bugged out eyes and raised brows that match my own.

But why is he with her? Holy shit, is Hippie Girl dating my teacher?

What are the odds of that, and why does it bother me so much?

The man is young and annoyingly attractive. Obviously, he has a girlfriend. Or maybe a wife? A fiancée? Except, didn't he just say something about his mom trying to set him up?

Of course, he has to walk in here looking ridiculously hot. His messy hair, that's always unruly by the end of the day from the way he runs his fingers through it. A pair of black athletic shorts show off the sexiest calves I've ever seen and are paired with black sneakers and a deep-red Ridge Valley Raven's hoodie. The mascot is stretched across his broad chest and has never looked so good.

Damn him. He's not even trying, and he still looks hotter than sin. Meanwhile, I can't begin to imagine the hot mess I must be. I can feel strands of my hair hitting my neck from where they always seem to escape my bun. The sweat dripping down the center of my back during dinner earlier has long since dried, but that slimy, makes-my-skin-crawl feeling still lingers. I could use a nice cold shower.

"Maddie, how's it going!?" Harleigh comes bouncing over to me with the energy of a small child and pulls me in for an unexpected hug. I force my body to relax so it's not weird, but I'm not sure how well it works. "This is my big brother, Harrison. Harrison, this is Maddie. She's pretty kick-ass."

Thankfully, Hippie Girl releases me from her tight hold quickly. It takes a moment for my focus to shift away from the contact and register her words.

Did she say brother?

"Yup, he's a major pain in my ass, but I'm kind of stuck with him, so we make the best of it. Especially since I decided to crash at his place while I figure my shit out." She laughs at herself, brushing off whatever her baggage is.

Wait, shit. I didn't mean to say that out loud. I need to find something to make this less awkward, but words and polite conversation fail me. Not a single damn thought is coming to mind, so instead of easing the tension, I'm making it worse as we stand here...staring at each other.

I rock back on my heels, swing my hands together, anything to avoid meeting Mr. James' eye. Harrison: The name fits. I like it.

This stupid crush I have developed is getting ridiculous. The more time we spend together, the worse it gets. The first time we met, I brushed him off as arrogant based on nothing but his looks, which was completely unfair of me.

It hasn't taken long to learn that I was way off-base with that judgment. I find myself wishing I could undo the "getting to know you" shit that's made me actually like the guy. This would be so much easier if I could go back to those first impressions.

As much as I want to deny it, something about the man calls to me. I might be jaded and cynical, but I'm also a closet romance junkie and have read enough love stories to hold on to this tiny bit of hope that the kind of love I read about might really exist.

Not to say I love him.

That would be insane, and while I might be toeing the edge, I'm not full-blown bonkers yet. But still crazy enough to be crushing hard on a man who is completely unobtainable, out of the question, forbidden, and might as well have a big fat *NO* stamped across his head. Which, come to think of it, might be a helpful reminder. Somehow, I don't think he would be on board with the idea.

What is wrong with me that I can't be attracted to a regular guy my own age for once? Probably because guys my age tend to be immature assholes.

But that's beside the point.

I need to hurry up and get out of this damn town already. Every day feels like death by a thousand paper cuts. I don't care where I end up so long as it's somewhere new where I can walk down the grocery store aisle or go for a walk around town and not be bombarded with painful memories. I'm sick of looking over my shoulder everywhere I go or resisting the urge to go for a drive only to wind up sitting in my car staring up at the very house that tricked me into thinking it was a safe and happy place, only to shatter me to pieces.

"Maddie, I'm sorry, but he's not going down for me. He only wants you. Do you mind? I can get these guys seated and drinks going while you tuck him in." Bea emerges from her office, opening the door to a whimpering, sad little boy.

Saved by the bell.

Thank you, Caden, and thank you, Bea.

CHAPTER EIGHTEEN

THIS CERTAINLY ISN'T HOW I was expecting my night to go. I left the house with the intent and hope of getting a certain person out of my head and end up walking right into their place of employment, mere blocks from where I live.

What are the odds?

And how could my sister have failed to mention that the new waitress she's become friends with looks just like Wyatt's little sister? Even though Harleigh is a few years younger than Fallon, they were friends. She had to see the similarities. I'm a little more than pissed she didn't warn me, but I'll save that conversation for later.

I'm also not so sure I like knowing Maddie's place of employment is so close to my house. The temptation of knowing Maddie is this close, and I can come down here anytime I want, is concerning. I shouldn't have thoughts like that, but I can't seem to stop them.

Being around Maddie feels strange, to say the least. It's the same feeling I get during Christmas when my family is together, laughing and playing games around the dining room table.

No matter how many times I have tried to figure it out, I can't seem to make sense of how a person I don't know that well can give me the same happy, warm feeling that I get being around the people I love most. It's part of the reason I can't seem to get her out of my head.

I know some of it comes from the desire to help her. Witnessing that panic attack and then having her open up and share some of her most vulnerable thoughts invoked this strong protective instinct in me. But then, as we have talked more, and I have gotten to see those rare moments when she lets her guard down and lets me see the real her, I don't know how to explain it.

She's kind in a way I couldn't have predicted. Just a few days ago, she shared that she hopes to become a foster parent one day. After how horrible her experience with the system has been, I would have expected her to want nothing to do with it ever again. Instead, she told me that was the very reason she wanted to. According to Maddie, one person may not change the system, but it could change the lives of at least one or two kids. She claims they need more decent people to step up who legitimately want to help—her words, not mine.

I've never been more in awe of a person than I was right then. The strength it takes for a young woman to see something broken and, despite being hurt by it, want to help, is rare.

The more bombs like that she drops on me, the more my feelings change.

Our conversations flow naturally; we can easily jump from movies to books to music and anything in between. Even the moments of silence have shifted from awkward to comfortable and easy. I'm fighting like hell to stop the wrecking ball that is getting closer and closer to my heart as things I can't dare to say aloud emerge. The thought alone makes me feel like a monster.

I follow Harleigh, who trails behind a purple-haired young woman. I can't tell if they know each other or not. My sister will talk to almost anybody as if they have been friends for years, even if she just met them, so it's hard to say.

Our seating choices are wide open in the empty space. It makes me once again question how good a completely deserted place can be, but I'll find out soon enough.

The woman leads us to a booth near the back, right next to a little reading-type nook that houses the bean bag chair Maddie had been in when we first arrived. The little boy on her lap had been snuggled into her while she gently stroked the top of his head and read him a book, varying her voice with each character and making *vroom* noises that made him giggle. His little eyes were fighting to stay open, but neither appeared to be in any hurry to wrap things up.

Maddie might want the world to think she hates everyone in it, but moments like that make it clear that it is nothing but a defense mechanism—one I can't blame her for, given all that she has lived through.

Harleigh settles into the booth across from me, boarding on drooling over the burger she's about to order.

"What can I start you guys out with?" the waitress asks, pen hovering over her little notepad, ready to jot down our drinks.

"Coffee and a water please."

"Same." It's far too late to drink coffee, but I'm about certain I won't be sleeping tonight, anyway.

"You got it. I'll let your waitress know. She should be right back to get your orders."

Harleigh and I thank her as she turns on her heel and heads back to what must be the kitchen.

"I told you this place was cool."

She's right. It's relaxed and comfortable with book-themed decorations, warm wood tones in the furniture and original brick walls. My favorite area is the little book corner, with a few different couches, chairs, and bookshelves lining the walls. I notice a small sign on one of the shelves claiming that a children's book is donated to the elementary school for every book purchased. The books lining the shelves are all used, and it makes me wonder if there is some kind of story there.

The waitress comes back and must notice me studying them. "Maddie's idea. The waitress I stole away from you guys. I used to keep a few books for people to read as they came in and drank coffee or hung out, but not long after she started, she came to me with the idea of selling the books and donating the kids ones. She picks them all out herself, too. God only knows where that girl finds the time, but every week, she comes in with a new stack to replace the ones that got sold, and then she picks out the ones that get donated, too. Delivers them to the school herself."

"Wow, that's amazing. I knew Maddie was awesome!" My sister isn't wrong. Maddie is a hell of a person. Too bad she can't see that.

Movement catches my eye from the opposite wall to a partly opened door. It's far enough away that I can't hear anything, but I can see directly into it where that same brown-haired boy is lying on a small cot, buried in a blanket covered with pictures of little trucks. Enough stuffed animals surround him to fill an entire toy box. I have to respect the little dude's ability to get cozy.

As cute as he is, my focus gravitates back toward Maddie, stroking his hair while she talks to him. The boy gives her a few small smiles and rubs his sleepy eyes again.

She seems to be singing to him or maybe reading something as she taps a different part of his body every few moments, which makes him scrunch up and smile again. They're in their own little world over there, and I can't help but wish I could be part of it.

Before I gave up on the idea of settling down, I had always wanted a large family. Our house was a revolving door of cousins, aunts, uncles, friends, and grandparents. Anybody and everybody seemed to flock our way, resulting in a dining room table that was never empty. Even as a kid, I appreciated being the house everybody ran to. Mom always kept this huge basket of snacks on a low shelf of the pantry so everyone, down to the smallest kids in the neighborhood, could reach it when they were over.

Anytime somebody had a sick kid or lost a loved one, my mom was right there with a warm meal and a shoulder to cry on. She was the go-to town babysitter, served on every volunteer committee and brought the absolute best cookies to every bake sale. To this day, she still knows the names of every one of my friends and colleagues.

My dad was and still is, just as great. He's got this deep, jolly laugh that ensured him the part of Santa at every Christmas celebration downtown, long before he had the gray hair to suit the role. He's never once left the house without a simple peck on my mom's cheek, and it's the first thing he does when he comes home each day.

They are, from what I know, rock solid now but that doesn't mean it wasn't rough for a few years. There was a time when it would have been easy to throw in the towel; most marriages don't ever recover from a pain and tragedy like what our family went through. Wyatt's parents are a prime example of that.

But despite the odds, my parents refused to give up on one another. It took years of therapy, hard work, and a couple of short separations, but eventually, we all fell back into a new kind of normal and apart from the occasional arguments, mostly over Hudson, we are all pretty close. My parent's marriage is stronger than ever from what I can see and I respect the hell out of them for that.

"So, what all did Mom and Dad have to say?"

"The usual. Mom's trying to set me up again, and Dad's got a friend with a job offer for me down there." I run my fingers through my hair and down my face, stressed about the idea of making such a difficult decision.

Harleigh's coffee cup hits the table with a loud thud. "Wait, back up. A job offer, Harry? That's a big deal!"

I shrug, taking a sip of my coffee. Holy shit, she wasn't wrong; this is amazing. "It's not so much of an offer as the possibility of an offer. There is an opening that he wants me to check out. That doesn't mean I'll get it. Or that I even want to. I don't know, Lee."

Harleigh falls silent. She gathers a chunk of her long hair and studies the ends, occasionally pulling at a piece and snapping it off. Each time she tugs one free, I wince. The anxious habit makes me feel like an ass. I should have mentioned the job right away.

"I miss them." My sister's somber voice reflects exactly how I feel about it.

"Me too, kid. Me too."

A tender smile passes over her face, and she looks up and laughs while wiping a tear from the corner of her eye. "I'm trying to teach Dad to video call."

I share in her laughter at the very idea. The thought of a wireless mouse freaks out Dad. How she talked him into trying a video call is beyond me.

"Yikes, I can't imagine that's going well."

"Nope." She smiles but looks back at her coffee, swirling the spoon around the cup. "They're happy down there, aren't they?"

"They are, Lee."

She looks back up at me again, another tear still sitting in the corner of her eye, but manages a half-hearted smile. "So, what are you going to do about the job?"

"Honestly, I have no idea. I haven't decided if I'm going to even call the guy yet," I admit, toying with the rim of my coffee mug. My mind has been too preoccupied with other things to think about it—or rather, preoccupied with a certain student.

I can't help but look back toward the little office where Maddie is still putting the boy to bed. He appears fast asleep now, and Maddie creeps backward, closing the door slowly as she backs out of the small room.

Once it silently clicks into place, her hand falls from the knob, but she drops her forehead against the door and stands there, her body rising and falling with deep, slow breaths. After a few moments, she straightens, reaches up and tugs either side of her bun, pulling it tight against her head. She squares her shoulders, does a little shake and then turns around, nothing but pure determination plastered over her soft features.

Her eyes land directly on mine, locking into place, but I can't seem to look away. Thousands of words swirl unspoken in the air between us. It's the moment that confirms that whatever connection I'm feeling between us, she feels it too.

I don't know what to do about that.

Chapter Nineteen

T HERE IS THIS MOMENT in basically every single cheesy romance movie where the two characters lock eyes, and the world fades away to some equally corny love song. That scene always makes me gag.

Ironically, I'm now living it.

Or, at least, it feels that way, except the movies and books always describe this electric feeling of sparks flying and a racing heart. Looking into Harrison's eyes, I feel the opposite. It's more like coming home after a long day, collapsing on the couch, or pulling out my favorite oversized sweatshirt and fuzzy cabin socks on the first snowfall of the year. It's not electric or sizzling hot. It's warm and safe and peaceful.

I could stay here, staring into his soothing gray eyes for a dangerously long time. That scares the shit out of me.

Harrison quiets my brain. When I'm with him, even when we aren't talking, all the loud, intrusive thoughts disappear. The memories, doubt, and self-loathing fall away and I can be myself. I didn't think I knew who that was anymore, but talking to him makes it feel like there are parts of me that I didn't lose after all.

I have to force myself to look away when he runs his thumb over his bottom lip, eyes still locked on mine, filled with something I might identify as heat, if I didn't know better.

In my effort to look somewhere else, I find a different set of the same gray eyes on me. I can't believe I hadn't noticed the similarities in the matching color.

I approach them and then stand in weird silence as we all take turns looking around, waiting for somebody to talk. It might be one of the strangest encounters I have had in a long time, which is enough to make nervous laughter spill from my mouth. This is too weird, and I'm both embarrassed and amused, and very overtired. Within seconds, they join in on my laughter, though I'm fairly certain none of us knows why it is we are laughing.

"So, I'm guessing you two know each other?" Hippie Girl asks once we get ahold of ourselves long enough to return to awkward silence.

"Harry, I thought you said you haven't been here before?" she questions. "Oh shit, please tell me you guys had a one-night stand or blind date and ghosted or something? That would be hilarious but also so awful!"

Mr. James coughs, making me recoil. *Wow, is the idea of going out with me that horrible?*

"Um, no, Harleigh, but thank you for that. Maddie is my student." He places an unmistakable emphasis on the last word. "She's also my TA."

Harrison rubs his hand along the back of his neck, then up through his hair. The fingers of his other hand drum nervously against the tabletop. I can't say I blame him for wanting to get the hell out of here as fast as possible.

"So, how exactly do you two know each other?" He motions between his sister and me.

"Oh, we go *waaaayyyy* back to, what, about two months ago?" She turns to me and winks while I nod and play along. "I wandered in, in need of a good cup of Joe, and bam, our lovely friend Maddie here helped me out. We hit it off, and we're practically best friends now."

That's news to me. I like this girl but didn't realize we had reached friend status. I think I'd like to be friends with a girl like her though, so the title makes me smile.

Harleigh grins back at her brother in a way that makes me jealous of their relationship. As far as I know, I don't have any siblings, but the idea of having a brother or sister has always been something I've longed for. Being an only child sucks. It's boring and lonely, and when life kicks you in the ass, there isn't anybody obligated to stick around and deal with your sorry ass.

I may not have a sibling, but I suppose I do have Kenna, and she's about as close as I think I will ever get to one. She's got my back, and I've got hers, in the same way it seems these two do. It might not be quite the same, but I've got to take my wins where I can get them.

"Yup, that's about right. Except I don't even know your name. I've been calling you Hippie Girl in my head for weeks now. Now that I say that out loud, it sounds like I've been thinking about you in a creepy way. I haven't. Thought about you. I mean, I have, but not—I'm going to shut up now." My cheeks are burning. I think I can crawl in a hole now and never come out.

Mr. James seems to have forgotten about being disgusted by the notion of us together for a moment and bursts into laughter. "Shit, that's funny. It fits, too! Sorry, sis. Anyway, Maddie, this is my annoying little sister, Harleigh."

"Harrison and Harleigh? Cute. Is there a Henry or Haley out there setting the world on fire, too?"

My comment is meant as a joke, but a dark, loaded gaze travels between the siblings that makes me squirm. I just unknowingly stuck my foot into a deep pile of shit.

Typical me.

"We have a brother as well. Hudson," Harleigh says. Her voice is quiet, almost sad. Did he die or something? "He's actually Harrison's twin."

My eyes go wide with this news. Holy shit, a twin?

"He's a piece of shit and is rotting in prison where he belongs," Harrison barks out through gritted teeth. Dark storm clouds hang over his head. I've never seen the guy look so angry. Not that I know him that well, clearly. But damn.

"Harrison," Harleigh starts but stops when her brother holds up a hand.

Harleigh turns back to me and winces in a way that says she's sorry for the awkward family drama. "Sore subject. Obviously," she says.

Then, as if wiping the slate clean, she perks back up into her usual smile. "Anyways, our parents are Hank and Harriet. So, yes, in case you were wondering, they do have a creepy obsession over the letter H."

I give her a small, fake laugh and steal another glance at Harrison, who has his head buried in his hands, elbows propped on the table. I wish I knew what I could say to erase the tension of the moment.

"Shit. Waitress of the year over here. I'm so sorry. Did you guys want to order something to eat?"

They each order a burger dressed the same and a side of fries. I jot down the details and scurry off before I can say something else stupid. I need to work on my social skills.

As soon as I hand the order over to Bea, I sidestep to the nearest empty corner, crumble to the floor, hide my face in my hands, and try to clear my head.

If I had known this was what was in store for me tonight, I would have called in.

Liar!

Even as I think it, I know it's not true. I wouldn't have missed the chance to see Harrison. How pathetic am I?

"So, who's the hottie?" My boss interrupts my thoughts with her blunt question. Her lack of filter amuses me any other time, but it's pretty damn annoying when she's using it against me.

"You don't want to know." My words come out muffled from behind my hands.

"Oh, trust me, I really do. Unless it's a kid, you rarely do more than grunt at people. This smoke show comes in, and the two of you look ready to rip each other's clothes off. So, spill."

Yup, that has my attention. I jerk my head up and glare. "You're delusional!"

I've always been in awe of Bridget. She's twenty-four, owns a kickass diner by herself, and does well, as far as I know. And she does it all as a single parent. This is the first time I have ever questioned her sanity.

"Oh please," she rolls her eyes, "I might not be getting much action these days, but I know 'fuck me eyes' when I see them."

I gape back at her, ignoring the little surge of hope that she's right. "I'm serious; it's not like that. He's my teacher!"

She takes that revelation in stride, scrunching up her nose as she considers the implications of the news, bops her head from side to side and looks me dead in the eye. "Doesn't change what I saw."

What is happening right now? Is she serious?

"He really fucked with your head, huh?"

"Who, Harrison?"

"That's the teacher?"

I nod.

"No, not him. I know we don't talk about it, but I'm not blind, hun. You had a wall built around you taller than Mt. Everest the first night you walked in here. It wasn't hard to tell that there was a story there. I've done my best to respect your privacy and not pry, but I've put enough pieces together to know that somebody hurt you. Bad. You wear that armor like a second-skin, kid and don't get me wrong, you wear it well." Bea flips burgers, shakes the fry basket, and continues working like she isn't flaying me open like a dead fish.

"You're strong as hell, Maddie and I admire that in you. Do you know you're the only person besides me that Caden speaks to? He's never uttered a single word to his grandparents, aunts, cousins, anybody. Except for you. If there was anything I needed to know about you, that alone tells me everything. You've got a huge, loving heart, but it seems like you have done your best to rip it out of your chest and bury it so deeply that nobody will ever be able to find it, including you."

Bea sets down the plates in her hands and looks directly at me, leaning forward on the counter with an expression I can't read. "I don't blame you, hun, I don't. But take it from somebody who has been there in their own way: don't let whoever he was ruin your future. Happiness is only available to those brave enough to reach out and take it for themselves. Besides, the guy that hurt you... fuck him. Seriously, don't let him win. He doesn't have the right to have that kind of power over your life anymore.

"If you find a good thing, take it and run like hell. Don't let something like that go—teacher or not. I've seen enough people come through here day in and day out to have gotten pretty good at weeding out the good from the bad. I'm pretty sure those two out there are good stuff. Don't let me tell you what to do, but I'm just saying, if I were you, I would give the guy a chance."

With that, she picks up the plates, walks out of the kitchen, and leaves me shattered on the floor.

Chapter Twenty

"So, Maddie?" The meaning in my sister's words couldn't be more clear.

Harleigh and I are walking home after one of the strangest nights I can remember. The air has cooled significantly as fall drags us deeper into changing leaves and brisk winds. The chill and threat of winter bring my parents and Georgia to mind.

Even though I know better, I still try to act like I don't know what she means. "What about her? Or are you referring to the fact that she looks just like Fallon and you didn't think that was worth a heads up?"

Harleigh stops walking, waiting for me to turn around and face her. "You think?" Her eyes dart up and to the left, like she's recalling Maddie's face and comparing it to her old friend. "Hmm, I suppose they do kind of look alike."

When her eyes return to mine, they are filled with a familiar pain that I can relate all too well to. "So, is that what this is about?"

"I don't follow."

This time, she shoots me a look that says, cut the bullshit. "Oh please, don't play dumb with me big brother. There's a connection there and you and I both know it. That little boy could probably feel the energy between you two even when he was fast asleep. What I'm asking is, is Fallon the reason? She might have been dating Hudson, but it didn't take a rocket scientist to see that you were the one who was in love with her."

I haven't figured it out myself, so how can I explain it all to her?

But I suppose maybe getting an outside perspective might not hurt, and I sure as shit can't talk to Wyatt about this. He would wring my damn neck.

"Cone of Silence?"

She nods and allows me to talk through this. With my hands crammed in my hoodie pocket, we continue walking as I try verbally processing where my head is at.

"I don't know where to start. Yes, at first, she reminded me of Fallon, and it drew me in. Made me feel like I needed to know her and then, somewhere along the way that changed and I sort of forgot about Fal and it became entirely Maddie that captivated me." Harleigh nods along, listening and processing the words that come out without interrupting.

"I feel like we are both in this strange place. Maddie's not just a student to me anymore, but I don't know what to do about that. We've moved into this place that feels more like a friendship, but that still doesn't quite describe it—" I trail off because, once again, none of the words feel right. For a guy in love with language, it sure seems to be doing a good job failing me lately.

"I feel like such an idiot saying this, but it feels like we have this connection bigger than anything we get a say in. Like the universe is pushing us together. Two puzzle pieces that don't fit anywhere but together. Man, that sounds more ridiculous out loud than it did in my head."

My sister remains quiet beside me as we slowly walk down the deserted sidewalk, nothing but the wind howling around us. She hasn't knocked my teeth in yet or stopped to tell me what a monster I am. I take that as my sign that I can continue.

"She's been through so much already, and given the nature of her past, I feel that much worse for having these feelings. I want to kick my own ass." I laugh at my own expense. "I don't know how to deal with any of this. I think it's mutual, at least some of it. You saw it, right?" I need her to confirm that I'm not completely losing it.

She nods, and I exhale a sigh—albeit small—in relief.

The confession that's spilled from me feels good to release. It's everything I have been bottling and shoving deeper and deeper for weeks, so if for no other reason, it feels good to get some of that pressure off myself.

Harleigh has never been one to shy away from calling me on my shit. She is the first person to speak up in a room, the kind that always tells you if your fly is undone or you have toilet paper spilling from the back of your pants. She doesn't believe in filtering herself. It's probably why I knew she was the right person to talk to about this. If I'm in the wrong, my little sister will have no problem telling me, no holds barred.

I wait with bated breath for her to say something. Anything. But she sighs and remains silent for at least half a block. I shouldn't be surprised that she carefully considers my words, mulling them over in her head instead of giving me a knee jerk reaction. My baby sister has grown up a lot lately, and while she's still her same wild self, she's far from the rebellious teenager she was not that long ago.

When our mom called and asked if she could move in with me, a big fat "not a chance" sat perched and ready to charge right out of my mouth. Harleigh is my opposite in so many ways. Where I'm neat and tidy, she is chaotic and messy. She carries a cloud of disarray wherever she goes. All that considered, having her come in and mar up my peaceful home was the last thing I wanted. Sadly, I've never been able to tell my mother no.

A week later, the girl who showed up at my doorstep wasn't the unhinged teenager I expected. She had grown into a woman in the short time since I had last seen her, and now, looking back, all I can say is that I'm glad I didn't turn her away. The time spent living together has brought us closer than ever. Even if it means dealing with her eighty-seven plants.

It took some getting used to after years of living alone and yet, I'm now faced with worrying about what happens when she moves on. Or I do.

Returning to a quiet, lonely house makes my skin itch over my entire body. The only thought worse than that is that of rejoining the dating world.

My small, cozy home comes into view as Harleigh breaks her silence. "You love her."

That's it. That is all she says: no accusation or judgment. There is no disgust in her tone or hidden meaning. It's a simple statement that punches me in the gut.

Every hair on my body stands at attention, and my shoulders tense. "Jesus, of course, I don't love her."

"Harry, stop lying to yourself. Maybe you don't, but I think you owe it to yourself to explore it as a possibility because from the outside looking in, it sure as hell seems like you do." I bring us both to a halt on the sidewalk outside my house.

This conversation feels too heavy to carry inside. I don't want to taint the walls with the turmoil swirling inside over the possibility of being in love with my eighteen-year-old student. The cold, quiet night feels much more fitting for something like this.

In a way, it feels like anything I might admit will be picked up by the wind and carried off as if it never happened—wrapped up in tumbleweed, bouncing down the cement, barreling over piles of leaves, cracks in the sidewalk, and peacefully sleepy homes. I can imagine watching it long after it disappears beyond the horizon, out of sight until nothing is left to prove it was ever there. The darkness would help wash it away and clean the slate for tomorrow's rising sun.

My dad's voice breaks through that refreshing thought, reminding me there is no way out of a problem but to charge through it. The man is pretty smart and has yet to steer me wrong, so I've always been inclined to believe him.

"Lee, if I admit to feeling that way about her, how am I any better than the fucking sick monster who—" I stop myself, knowing Maddie's story isn't mine to tell. I respect her too much to betray that trust, even with my sister.

"God, I swear I would never hurt her. I don't know what the hell is wrong with me. Why her? Of all people, why does it have to be her?" I throw my hands in the air, pacing back and forth over my browning lawn. "Even putting her past aside, what about mine? I'm not good enough for her. I'm not good enough for anybody. I'm dangerous, Lee. I have poison running through my veins that I can't risk getting anywhere near Maddie. But here's the thing, I've never come close to finding somebody that made me consider a future. And then Maddie barges into my life, cursing like a sailor, haunting me with those fucking eyes, and I can't get her out of my head. I can't picture a future that doesn't have her in it. And for so many reasons, she's the one person I can never have!!"

I want to kick and scream like a two-year-old who didn't get their way. I've never hated my brother more than I do right now. And that's saying something.

"Alright, I'm going to stop you right there, Harrison James. You are not a damn monster. You might be Hudson's twin, but you are not him. You walk around carrying the weight of his sins on your shoulders like you were right there pulling the trigger with him. He made those choices. You are not more tainted than I am. He's my brother too, you know. I have his blood just like you do. And do you see me that way? Am I a monster too, Harry?"

Her words ring out, echoing against the empty night and bouncing around in my head like a racquetball.

"Now, I may not know Maddie's history, but I've gotten to know her well enough to see that she's smart, strong, and capable of making her own decisions. She's more mature than most of my friends. And yours too, honestly. Besides, technically, Maddie is eighteen and trust me, she's as into you as you are her. You two being together wouldn't hurt anybody; it's not illegal either, even if it's frowned upon."

Harleigh runs her fingers through her long hair, pops a hip to the side and locks her familiar gray eyes on mine. "Look, Harry, you really are a great guy, and you will make whatever woman you end up with incredibly happy. It's not in you to be anything less than a loving man, husband, partner, or whatever when the time comes. Is it fair of you to deny Maddie the chance at the kind of happiness you both deserve? She at least should have a say in the matter. You have a mountain of obstacles and complications in your way, and maybe that's enough to make you both walk away, but I can't see that being the case.

"I can't tell you what to do here. It's a shitty situation, but you know what? Sometimes the best things come from the worst places, so if you want my advice, talk to the girl. Spend some time as friends, get to know each other, and confirm what you already know is there. Then, give her a say in any choices you think you need to make. Don't throw something away before it has a chance to get started. Just do so carefully, at least for now."

I stare in silent awe. When did my baby sister, with little space buns in her hair, skirts covered in mud, and a temper the size of a rocket ship, turn into the wise, grown woman in front of me who just knocked me on my ass?

She cocks her hip like she can read the thoughts running through my mind before turning on her heel and marching her way up the front steps.

"Oh," she stops and turns back toward me. "I also feel like I should remind you that you have a best friend who has a degree in this kind of thing, so why in the hell are you asking me about it and not him?"

The reminder is enough to make me scoff. "Uh, because he works for the administration team that writes my paychecks and would fire me without hesitation if they knew anything I said. That, and he's basically the Hulk, so getting my ass kicked by him would hurt far worse than if you do it."

My joke makes her laugh, but only briefly before she gets serious with me again. "You don't really believe that, do you? After everything you did for him when Fallon died, do you think he would turn his back on you like that?"

Except, what I did for him is so insignificant compared to what I didn't do. Despite my own beliefs, I know that Wyatt doesn't see it that way and so, for that reason, she is probably right.

CHAPTER TWENTY-ONE

My alarm blares, unaware that I've been awake for hours. According to my Apple watch, an over-the-top gift Kenna gave me last Christmas, I generally average four hours of sleep per night. I'll have to check later to be sure, but I would estimate that I got no more than two hours last night.

I should be grateful it wasn't my regular nightmares and dark, depressing dreams haunting me from the shadows that kept me awake this time. Instead, I tossed and turned, my body burning up with desire. Every damn time I closed my eyes, all I saw was Harrison. The later it got into the dark of night, the fewer clothes my imaginary version of him seemed to be wearing.

Sometime around three-thirty, I had to take a cold shower. I'm not entirely sure where that idea originated, but it doesn't do jack shit. By five, my resolve had shattered. I gave in and dug out the small mint green vibrator that sat in a tote buried under my bed. I hadn't touched the thing in, well, ever maybe. I ordered it online one night around two in the morning when lack of sleep was making me delirious and apparently a bit desperate.

In a matter of minutes, the little device, paired with images of Harrison's naked, toned, tanned body straining over me, had me screaming out his name while thrashing around in my bed.

The moment my heart rate dropped to normal, the guilt and shame I felt over the whole thing settled back in. Then the reminder that I had to face the man today smacked me across the face, and I've been laying here dreading that obnoxious tune telling me to wake up ever since.

I have at least ten minutes before I need to get up, fifteen if I push it and beg Kenna to bring me coffee, which I know she will. She knows I turn rabid without my caffeine fix. With that in mind, I pick up my phone and scroll through random apps before landing on my email. I check my school and personal account, hoping to have some response from the few colleges I've applied to waiting for me.

But, of course, I don't because it's far too early for any decision to be made. I only started sending them last week, far ahead of the deadlines. I can't imagine hearing anything until January at the earliest. The wait might kill me.

Every day that passes makes the urgency to get away from here grow. It's about to drive me mad once and for all. Memories lurk all around me, taunting me until I slowly get crazier. I haven't been able to let my guard down in almost two years, something far more exhausting than I could have imagined.

I can't allow myself to even think about the trial. I haven't heard anything about it or when that could happen, but I imagine that day is not too far off. It has to happen at some point. It's already been a year and a half since he was arrested so I have to think the clock is ticking. I assume they can only draw that sort of thing out so long.

I should probably stop avoiding my lawyer and see if she's heard anything. Maybe knowing when that dreaded day is going to come will at least alleviate the anxiety of the unknown.

God, what are they going to ask me? How am I supposed to face him and—

No, I seriously cannot let myself go there. I might vomit, and then I will definitely be late.

With nothing in my phone to distract me, I drag my tired body from the thin, scratchy bedding and force myself to start the day. The dread of it all has me longing for the days I was excited about school. I still love the academic side, but I stopped feeling like I was being challenged all of last year, which sucked the little joy I could cling to right out.

Today, that dread has gained a new name, knowing I have to face Harrison after last night. I'm desperate to talk to Kenna about this, but something keeps stopping me. I don't know why that girl puts up with me to begin with, so the idea of telling her anything that would make me seem worse than I already am is entirely unappealing. This is just one more thing to add to the heaping bucket of shit I can't tell my only friend to ensure she doesn't start to hate me.

Wyatt is the only other person I can think of who can help me process these dangerous feelings, but I obviously can't do that either. So, like everything else in my life, I suppose I'm left to face this on my own.

By the time I'm walking to my second class, I'm already exhausted, and the day has hardly begun.

"Maddie! Maddie, wait up!"

As much as I want to avoid Kenna, she's the one person I can't bring myself to be an asshole to, so I step off to the side, allowing the flow of foot traffic to carry on through the halls without me. I lean against the closest bank of lockers and wait for Kenna to politely push through the sardine-packed space to get to me.

She finally emerges from the herd, lips pinched, and her nostrils slightly flared. I start to pick at the raw skin around my nails and can't seem to look her in the eye. She deserves a far better friend than me.

"What's the deal with you today? I waited for you this morning." Her tone is as accusatory as it can be for someone like Kenna.

"Oh, uh, yeah. Sorry about that. Was running late." She knows I'm lying through my teeth. I don't have to look up to feel her eyes boring into me. "Alright, fine!" I throw my hands up. "I was avoiding you, okay?"

Her head jerks back, and her eyes widen, filling up with tears. "Wow, okay. Ouch. Care to explain?"

"No. But yes. And also, still no."

Hurt quickly changes to a flicker of annoyance. "Not gonna work with me. Spill." Kenna folds her arms and attempts to look serious, tapping her foot and everything. It's enough to make me laugh, breaking the tension between us.

"Alright, alright. When I was working last night, Mr. James came into the diner with his sister. She's super cool actually, we've met before. I didn't know who she was before last night, but then they came in together, and at first, I thought they were together-together, but then she said he was her brother, and yeah, her name is Harleigh. You would like her! I should introduce you sometime if we can continue to be friends. That might be weird now." I'm completely rambling.

"Okay, chill for a second. Way to bury the lede there! But what does any of that have to do with me? What the heck did I do?"

That's a fair point. I shrug and hope she lets it go, but I should know better. After thirteen years of friendship, Kenna knows me better than I know myself most of the time.

"Holy crap! You have a crush on him, don't you? Aww, did Maddie have a dirty dream about the hot teacher?" She's teasing me, I know that. Too bad trauma is a raging bitch and doesn't catch the memo. It doesn't care about logical thought or bad timing. Her comment is meant as a joke and not an incorrect one, and yet, it strikes something in my head that plunges me into a spiral of memories.

My lungs start to burn as I fight for each breath. My skin gets cold and clammy but also overheats with the exertion from my racing heart. The hard metal of a padlock digs into my vertebra as I fall against the lockers.

Kenna is utterly unaware of how her words have affected me, so she keeps talking, but the ringing in my ears makes it hard to determine what she's saying. I blink past the black dots dancing in my vision, trying to find something to focus on.

I can't see anything clearly, so I try turning to what I can feel instead.

The seam of my sock is slightly misaligned, making it dig into my pinky toe. Everything in the hallway has grown significantly quieter, so class must have started by now. A few stragglers giggle in the distance. A locker slams.

The spots behind my eyes start to fade, letting me take in the dirty, worn tile floor that presses against the ball of my foot. The gray color has faded with time, worn down until uneven dips and grooves have formed, unlike the smooth, flat surface that shines in the newer wing of the school.

Two large hands wrap around my forearms, bringing the dancing black dots back. I'm instantly tense again, my muscles locking up like hardened cement as I inhale, disgusted by the scent of Irish Spring soap.

Except, wait, that's not what I'm smelling.

There is a stark difference in what I'm anticipating compared to the warm, inviting scent that's forcing its way through the fog. Something isn't adding up.

Opening my eyes, I realize that the person holding me isn't who my brain is lying to me about. Steel-gray greets me, full of care and concern. The eyes staring back at me are gentle and soft. A warm blanket in the middle of a harsh cold.

His voice breaks through the ringing in my ears. It's quiet, meant for my ears only. Calloused fingers lightly stroke my arm, infusing a sense of serenity into my skin. The sensations feel like happiness and home and everything I've never had.

I can't figure out what I'm supposed to do with that.

Hope fills me, sending my heart soaring, wanting to hold on to this moment forever.

It fills my head with dangerous thoughts like maybe things can get better, maybe life doesn't always have to suck, and maybe Harrison James is the person who can help me learn how to make that come true. Maybe he is the one person in this messed up world capable of taking all the disgusting, broken parts of me and finding a way to make them whole again.

"Maddie? Can you hear me?" His resonant voice flows through my brain like silk, smoothing everything in its path.

I'm not sure I'm ready to let this moment go. It's fake and constructed solely in my mind, but it's so perfect and peaceful, and damn, it sure smells good. I know it will shatter to the ground the moment I move my eyes away from Harrison, so yes, I can hear him, but I'm not ready to acknowledge that yet.

It takes everything in me to pull my gaze from Harrison and those beautiful eyes that fill my dreams, taking all the nightmares away with him. Harrison picks up on my return to reality and leans into my ear to whisper. His hot breath against my sensitive flesh makes me tremble. "We need to stop meeting like this," he says, winking at me.

The moment passes before I can get a firm grasp on it. In its place, Harrison has transformed back into professional mode right before my eyes.

"You good, Maddie?"

"Yup, all good over here. Just another day in the life of your favorite freak show. Gotta do something to get some attention around here, don't I?" I pry my attention away for a moment to seek out Kenna who is standing a few feet away, staring at us with wide eyes. My cheeks heat at the idea of what she might be thinking.

I get a clear, "we are talking about this later" look from her before she spins on her heel and darts off to class.

"That mouth of yours doesn't get enough attention as it is?" Harrison winks again, but his eyes drop toward my lips, which have grown bone dry.

"Have to keep things interesting."

He grins. "That doesn't seem to be an issue with you."

A smile that matches his pulls at my lips. "Only when you're around."

"Lucky me."

I can't think of a response anymore. All my attention has zeroed in on the distance, or lack of, between us. I can feel each word he speaks on my face, hitting me with the sweet butterscotch scent on his breath. I wonder if I could taste it on him. I would barely have to lean forward to find out.

Is he thinking the same thing? He slowly leans in, but shifts to whisper in my ear at the last moment. "Get to class, Maddie." His voice is husky and quiet. His words tickle the shell of my ear. My legs wobble.

How does he expect me to move after whatever the hell that was?

I somehow manage, floating down the hallway, dazed and weightless, unaware I'm walking in the completely wrong direction.

Chapter Twenty-Two

MADDIE HAS AVOIDED EYE contact with me through both classes today. Two full hours of studying her shoes, picking at the corner of her desk, doodling in her notebook without so much as a single glance in my direction.

Our little hallway encounter earlier had been entirely unintentional, but even with her avoidance, I can't say I regret it. That simple touch was enough to confirm what I had suspected to be true: Maddie is attracted to me, at the very least. As soon as she realized it was me, her breath hitched, her pupils dilated, and her body re-acted to my presence.

Seeing her trapped by her own mind was not something that got easier, no matter how often I saw it happen. It tore me in two to know that she had demons living up there, taunting her with no means of escape except, apparently, me.

I acted without knowing what I was doing, and somehow, it worked. There is an irrational side of me that revels in knowing I have the ability to affect her in that way. To bring peace and safety in the storm.

Despite that, it was risky. Wyatt warned me not to touch her, which I ignored and acted on instinct instead, but I did at least remember the part he told me about helping her breathe and did my best to stay there until she felt safe again. Out of that trap. At least that was something I could relate to.

I realize now that anybody could have witnessed what happened in that hallway. But at that moment, all I could see was Maddie. I can't feel sorry for that, no matter the potential fallout. She smelled like watermelon and summer, a combination that shouldn't suit her, yet, somehow, it does.

My fingers still tingle, remembering the softness of her skin. And then there was the desire that flooded those expressive green eyes. I've been stuck hiding the effect she has on me behind my desk ever since.

"Alright, class. That's all I have for you today. If any questions come up as you work through the assignment, feel free to email me." The bell rings right as I finish talking, dismissing the class on my behalf. They all file out, leaving Maddie and me alone in silence.

Moments like these make me wish I could see inside her beautiful mind. Her eyes might give away a lot of her emotions, but that only works if she looks at me, and right now, she's doing anything but.

"Look, about this morning—"

She interrupts me mid-sentence, head still down, picking away at her fingers. "Yeah, I'm sorry about that."

"That was supposed to be my line."

Finally, she looks up at me, squinting with her nose scrunched up the way I love. "You're sorry that I'm a nutcase?"

I will do whatever it takes to get her to stop talking about herself like that. The more she does it, the angrier I get. "Maddie, you are not a nutcase. Cut yourself some slack now and again, would you? From what I've seen, you are handling your situation much better than you give yourself credit for. I don't think there is a person in this world that could live through what you have and not carry a few demons around with them."

She purses her lips and nods, not believing a word I say.

"You know what?" I smack the lid of my laptop shut and shove aside the papers on my desk. "I don't feel much like working today. It's been a long week, and it's only Wednesday. Let's talk."

She rolls her eyes while crossing her legs and tucking her hands into the pocket of her hoodie, visually shutting me out. "How about we don't."

"Humor me." I smile when the most ridiculous idea comes to mind. "Would you rather...spend your time inside or out?"

Maddie looks up at me like I'm crazy. I half expect her to get up and walk out of the room. She's not obligated to stay here.

"Outside." I'm surprised she's playing along. "Would you rather not shower for a week or not brush your teeth?"

"Sick. Not shower. Would you rather be blind or deaf?"

"Blind. I like music too much to be deaf. Would you rather go shirtless or pantsless?" She asks this with a playful eyebrow wiggle. I get a tiny bit of satisfaction at the idea of her picturing me without either.

"Shirtless," I answer with a wink. A pink blush crawls up her neck and fills her pale cheeks. "Comedy or thriller?"

"Thriller. Pizza or Chinese?"

"Oh, come on, You can't expect me to choose!" I protest.

"Tick-tock, Harrison." She taps her wrist.

My real name coming from her plump lips pulls my attention. It's a sound I would love to hear over and over again. "Fine, pizza. Skydiving or mountain climbing?"

"Hmm, skydiving. Can you imagine what that would feel like? Weightless and so free, falling through the air with nothing to stop you." Her eyes light up as she pictures it. I'm far more of a feet firmly on the ground kind of guy, but for Maddie, I would jump out of a plane to see that wonder and excitement painted across her face.

She gets lost in her daydream, tipping her head back with her arms stretched out to either side. It's the first glimpse I've gotten to see into what a carefree, unburdened Maddie looks like—the first time I can see through the trauma to the girl beneath it all. The world falls away, her problems fade, and she smiles as she pictures flinging her body from a plane.

One moment, she's lost to the imaginary sensation, and then, remembering where she is, her arms drop, and she tilts her head back down, catching my eye. She gives me a small, shy smile and looks away when she sees me staring. "Book or movie?" she asks.

"Oh, that's cheating! You already know the answer."

She shrugs and looks back at me again, giving me a cheeky smile. I shake my head, unable to wipe my grin off my face.

"Books. Coffee or tea?"

"Oh my God, coffee. That's cheating, too. When have you ever seen me without a coffee in my hand?"

"You started it," I counter.

"Alright, fine then. If that's how we are going to play this. Favorite author?"

Chapter Twenty-Three

"**C**OME ON, YOU CAN do better than that. Harper Lee, F. Scott Fitzgerald, Melville. Remember, English teacher? I'm a cliché; what do you want from me? Your turn."

Well, shit. Walked right into that one, didn't I?

My hand flies to my forehead and covers my eyes. I don't want to answer this question. "Alright, so, as a fellow book lover, I know I should be saying the same kind of thing. I don't mind *To Kill a Mockingbird* or Gatsby, but come on, *Grapes of Wrath*? Hated it. *Dante's Inferno*, awful!

I'm not a classics kind of girl. Don't get me wrong, I want to like them, but I can't do it. Now, before you give me the whole song and dance, I know, I have heard it many times. I can't be a true book lover if I hate Jane Austen. I get it."

Crickets.

He says nothing, forcing me to look up from behind my hiding place. The man is laughing. His eyes are lit up with amusement, shoulders shaking, perfect teeth on full display.

"Hey, no judgment here. Not everybody is a classic lit fan. That doesn't make you any less of a reader. I can devour a good genre fiction book as fast as the next person." It's the first time I have heard him sound nerdy. It's cute.

"I suppose. But I have to say, I hate that expectation. Like, because I don't like poetry and long, drawn-out prose that says a lot but means nothing or these vague, ambiguous scenes that leave me wondering what the fuck I just read, and not in a good way, shouldn't be grounds for automatic dismissal from the reader club. Don't get me started on the implications as a writer. I'm not looking to write the next great American novel or invent a damn word like Shake-speare. I want to tell a story that people like and that helps them escape the bullshit of the real world for a while!

"Is there a reason I have to describe how each blade of grass is kissed with dew that glimmers in the light of the sun to be a good writer? Can't I leave it at 'fuck, the grass is wet, and now I'm going to have stinky socks all day?' So what if my favorite novels come from B-list authors who self-publish and write smut, fan fiction, or whatever else it is?"

End rant.

And now I'm completely mortified that I said that out loud. It spilled out before I could reign it all in. I have some pent-up feelings about the matter I might need to deal with.

Harrison busts out in full belly laughter. I can't tell if I'm annoyed or relieved, so I shoot him my best glare, which only comes out half-hearted.

"Sorry, I don't mean to laugh. It's not you, I promise. You unknowingly stumbled into one of the most heated debates in the literary world. Trust me, come college, you will spend far more time down that rabbit hole than you care to."

As I look up, I find his eyes locked on me again.

It's something that happens a lot.

I will be working or reading in class and feel those steel-gray eyes on me. It's never creepy; more comforting. But as soon as I look up, he's always quick to look away. I can't say much though because I find myself doing the same.

Anytime we are in the same room, my eyes seek him out. It's like there is some weird invisible magnet between us, pulling us together. It makes me wonder if the universe knows something we don't.

Even when we aren't together, my body buzzes with the need to be near him. We don't have to talk or even be alone; his presence is enough to wash away the worst thoughts from my head and blanket me in a safe, warm cocoon of quiet.

How can a person I barely know feel like home?

I feel stupid thinking it. I've never believed in anything spiritual or religious. I don't think there is some magical force in the world that has this overarching power over us little people. If I did, I'd be inclined to believe it hated me. But now that I think about it, is that what this is all about? Dangle somebody in front of my face who checks all the right boxes only to rip it all away.

If I were smart, I would keep my head down, my mouth shut, and focus on getting through the next two months. Then, repeat the process next semester and walk away from this place once and for all.

"It doesn't get any better, does it?" I mutter out loud, though I'm not expecting an answer. Looking like that, I doubt Harrison struggled with fitting in.

"What? Life?" He leans back in his chair, arms folded over his lower stomach, gray eyes locked on my green ones.

"I suppose, yeah. I keep waiting and hoping that things are going to start getting easier, but they never do. The moment I feel like I might be able to breathe again, it all comes crashing back down. That might have been my biggest mistake with Andrew." I bury my face in my hands while Harrison rounds his desk to take a seat next to me.

"I was so desperate for things to be good that I ignored all of the bad. I got tricked into thinking moving in with him and his wife was going to be this big turning point. Things finally seemed like they were going to start looking up. I had finally found a family and a place in the world. I felt loved and seen and cared for. It was the first time I felt like I could explore who I wanted to be, test my boundaries, or challenge my thoughts. No matter how hard I pushed, he never budged. He still loved me. Or so I thought. How fucking stupid was I to believe that?"

Tears fill my eyes, realizing how stupid I had been. "That hope was the hook, I suppose. I wanted it to be real so badly that I dismissed the red flags. I fought and fought to keep everything in this perfect little shape so I could finally feel normal. I wanted to matter. I wanted to be loved, cared for, seen." My body shakes as the words pour from my soul, admitting to all my biggest mistakes.

"I wanted it so bad that I lied to myself, mistook it for love despite the cost. I lied to myself for so long that I started believing it was true. And now, all I'm left with are these memories of how gullible and pathetic I am. How immature and desperate." I swallow, trying to keep it all in check, but the hot tears continue spilling down my face, landing on my shirt in fat, ugly drops.

Harrison doesn't say a word, but he's out of his seat, pulling me up and wrapping his solid arms around me instantly. He doesn't lie and tell me it will get better. He doesn't say sorry or look at me with pity, sadness, or disgust. He doesn't throw out meaningless words to break the tension of the moment.

He seems to understand that no words will fix this.

He holds me and absorbs my pain.

For the first time in a long time, my shoulders drop, the tension falls off me, and I cry into his arms. My tears and eyeliner paint his baby-blue button-down, but he never once tries to pull away. I know I need to, but standing here in his arms, there is nothing to worry about or do, nobody looming in the shadows. I get to be here, in this moment, with him.

It's a feeling I could get addicted to, and that is a dangerous thought.

CHAPTER TWENTY-FOUR

I'M FALLING FOR MADDIE.

The more time we spend together, the harder that becomes to deny. I don't know how to get off this road I seem to be racing down. I don't know that I want to.

Each day, I toe the line a little closer, knowing that crossing it feels unavoidable. I hate myself for that.

I breathe in the sweet watermelon scent of Maddie's hair and revel in the warmth filling my chest as I hold her. She bathes me in a feeling of hope that I haven't experienced in a very, very long time. Holding her makes me believe in a future. Our future.

How can that be?

I force myself to pull away, finding a similar guilty look staring back at me. She's feeling it, too.

We overstepped.

I don't regret it.

"I, uh, should probably get going. I gotta get to work."

"Have a good night, Maddie."

I'm a coward.

Chapter Twenty-Five

THE DINER'S BEEN EMPTY for a few hours now. Long enough for me to have finished all my homework, submitted a few more scholarship applications, and tried and then given up on reading. I'm sitting in Caden's beanbag chair, kicking my feet, unsure what to do with myself.

I'm getting better at figuring out how to be okay with my own company, but nights like tonight, when I can't get my head to stop spinning, are a little too much. I find myself wishing I had somebody to talk to. Kenna went to bed hours ago, and she's my only friend, so the list ends with her.

The quiet moments are when Andrew's voice filters through the cracks. I find myself scrolling through old emails, searching for social media pages that were deleted months ago, and checking Google for any news updates on his case. It's a sick form of self-torture. If Wyatt knew about it, he would rip me a new one.

I don't know why I look.

Part of me hopes to see posts and articles filled with horrible things about him. Anything that shows people see the sick monster behind that charming, fake mask he wears so well. But if anybody knows he is in jail, they aren't saying anything.

I often find myself wondering what his family and friends think. They have to know, right? Kelly does, but sometimes self-preservation can be a strong force to reckon with. Maybe she tells herself I'm the monster. I tricked him. I lied. I manipulated the situation. It's probably an easier story to believe that the broken foster kid fucked up than it is to see the middle class man who volunteers at the local veterans hospital and goes to block parties is the messed up one.

Thinking of Kelly fills me with a hollow, painful wound right in my chest. I truly believe she didn't know what was happening in her own home, but I also haven't heard a peep from her since this whole thing began. We might not have been super close, but after four years of taking care of me and having me call her Mom, you would think that I would have gotten at least a phone call.

Would she testify for him at the trial? Maybe that doesn't happen in real life like it does on television. I guess I'm going to find out at some point.

Regardless, seeing the little relationship status that shows *married* on her social media profile feels like twisting the knife. I can't understand how she can continue to claim that man. What about me? Did she ever care about me at all?

Okay, Maddie, this is not productive. It's in the past and doesn't matter now. Move forward.

I have nothing to distract me from digging deeper and deeper down that hole. It's a compulsion at this point, and I still haven't figured out how to get control over it.

I pull out my phone, desperate to find something to keep me busy. A game or something on Pinterest. I open my notes app, then my photos, then YouTube, then my contacts, where I aimlessly scroll through the list as if the name of somebody to talk to might magically appear.

Harrison James.

The name has been taunting me from my pocket for months now. I've opened a message to him a dozen times but have never known what to say.

Our recent conversations have been messing with my head. Every time we talk, that feeling grows. I've never connected with anybody where the conversation has flowed so freely. I don't have to think back after the fact and dissect my words, wondering if I said too much or too little. I don't worry about how I sounded or if my laugh was weird. It's all so easy.

My broken, cynical brain tries to interject any thought I have that he might care for me, with reminders of my many shortcomings. Where Harrison is sexy, kind, intelligent, funny, charismatic, and well-liked, I am over-weight, chock-full of self-esteem and mental health issues, have crippling shame, awful social skills, and am avoided like a foul odor.

I hover over his name, those thoughts of doubt swirling around as I stare at it.

With one big middle finger to those voices in my head, I go for it. I can always claim temporary insanity when this blows up in my face later. I am mentally unstable, after all.

Maddie: Would you rather get up early or sleep in late?

I send the text and stare at the phone, not daring to so much as blink. My eyes start to burn and water, but I still don't look away. Within seconds, three little dots appear on the screen.

Harrison: Get up early. Fight a bear or a lion?

Holy shit. He actually responded. I don't think I was expecting that. I figured it would just stay on read and I would be left hanging, but at least then I would have my answer as to where we stand.

Maddie: Lion, 100%. Cook dinner or do the dishes?

Harrison: Dishes. I'm a shamefully lousy cook.

Maddie: Duly noted. I guess we would both starve together then. Quiet or fancy dinner?

Harrison: Have you eaten today? You seem hungry.

Maddie: Hamburger and fries. Dinner of champions. Answer the question.

Harrison: Okay bossy. Spend time with family or friends?

Harrison: Shit, that was a bad question. I'm sorry!

Maddie: It's okay. If I had either one, I wouldn't want to pick. Friends can be family; it's about the relationship not the title.

I'm surprised that I actually believe that.

Kenna is the only family I have. When I was with Andrew, if you can call it that, I was adamant that I would never get married or have kids. Looking back, I can see that I wanted it but knew I could never have it. Now, I'm scared to admit that I might want both someday.

Harrison: You never fail to amaze me, Madalynn Klein.

Maddie: I'm going to take that as a compliment.

I type a winky face and then delete it. Then I type it again and delete it one more time before pressing send.

Harrison: It was

Maddie: Sweatpants or jeans?

Harrison: Jeans. Camping or a resort?

Maddie: Never done either, but I think camping. Maybe in the mountains?

Harrison: My kind of girl.

Okay, I need to not read into that too much. *Be cool, Maddie.*

Something about the distance texting provides gives me the courage to push the boundaries just a tad.

Maddie: Would you rather be seen naked or have somebody read all your texts?

Harrison: Depends on who it is

Maddie. Not how the game works.

Harrison: Fine, read my texts. Back massage or foot massage?

Maddie: Feet are nasty. Back. Love somebody you can't have or love somebody who doesn't love you back.

Those three little dots dance across the screen. Then disappear. And reappear. It's a good two minutes before I get a reply, but it feels like an hour. I wish I could be a fly on the wall to what he is thinking right now.

Harrison: Love somebody who doesn't love me back. Would be better for me to suffer alone that way

Harrison: Would you rather be the first to admit your feelings for somebody or have them say it first?

This is so far from where I expected this conversation to go when I first typed that innocent little message. I wanted to talk to somebody, but we have ventured into heavy territory. At least, it feels like we have. I may be reading more into what is being said than I should be.

I can't begin to think of how to respond. The more intimate things get with Harrison, the more that inner demon calls at me not to ruin the life of yet another person. However, this other voice has been gaining some confidence and seems to be learning to speak up and dismiss thoughts like that. That voice tells me that Andrew was a grown-ass man who made his own shitty choices. I can't control the actions of others, and I'm not going to keep taking on the guilt and weight of their mistakes.

Maddie: I would want them to confess to them first. I suppose I'm a little old-fashioned in that way.

Maddie: ...you feel this too, right?

Harrison: Yeah, Maddie. I feel it.

Maddie: So where does that leave us?

I wait. And wait. And wait. Not even the little dots appear this time. I might have fucked up. I pushed too far, put my foot in my mouth, said the wrong thing. The phone drops to the table as it vibrates in my hand, notifying me of an incoming video call. It's Harrison. What is he thinking? This conversation was so much easier behind a screen!

I glance at my reflection blown up on the screen in my hand. The little bit of mascara I put on this morning has melted, giving me raccoon eyes. My hair is springing up out of my bun all over the place. I'm not the kind of waitress who dresses cute and spends extra time on my hair and makeup for tips. You get what you get with me, and that's not anything fancy. I've never cared before this very moment when I wish I looked a little less like Beetlejuice.

With trembling fingers, I swipe the little button across the screen, allowing Harrison's face to take over.

God, he is sexy. His hair is tousled and slightly damp. I don't need the image of him in the shower in my head right now.

The royal blue of his Belton Buckeyes t-shirt brings out some of the blue in his usually gray eyes. He looks like he belongs on the cover of a *GQ* magazine, and I look like a drowned rat. Lovely.

"Hi." My voice comes out quiet and shaky.

"Hi." His voice is low and throaty in a way I've never heard. It sends tingles throughout my body. "Am I allowed to tell you you look beautiful?"

I snort. Loudly.

"Probably not, but I wouldn't believe you if you did. I'm disgusting."

"You're stunning, Maddie. I like seeing you in any state. Right now, I imagine this is what you look like at the end of a long day when nobody else is around but you. It's intimate, I suppose. I know that sounds strange, but it feels like I'm getting to see you in a way nobody else does. I like it."

"Oh." This man. He makes me question every negative thing I have ever thought about myself. I don't know how to begin to feel about that.

Harrison gives me a lazy smile. "I hope it's okay that I called. Having this talk through a text didn't feel right. And I needed to see your face." His lips curl up in a gentle smile, but he turns serious, leveling me with an intense gaze. "You asked where this leaves us but I can't make that call as much as I want to. I can tell you how I feel and what I want. I can tell you where I want it to go and what I want the future to hold for us. But it's not up to me alone."

Harrison shifts on the bed, changing the angle of the camera so that the soft lamplight highlights the sharp line of his jaw against the dark room. "We need to make this and any other decisions together. It's not as simple as I wish it could be, and there are some serious implications. You gotta talk to me here, babe."

Speechless.

Harrison James leaves me utterly and completely speechless.

"How are you so perfect? What's the catch?" I wonder out loud.

Harrison falls silent, then sighs and rubs at the back of his neck again. It makes me nervous.

Whatever he is thinking about feels big. I knew there had to be some kind of catch. I give him a minute to gather his thoughts and try not to jump to conclusions. He's given me the benefit of the doubt more times than I can count, so the least I can do is return the favor.

I kick off my shoes while I wait, shift around in the beanbag to get comfortable, and pick at a loose thread on the seam of my shirt.

Finally, he looks back up at me. "You are so worried about being the broken one here, Maddie but you have it all wrong. If I was a good man, I'd be the one pushing you away. I'm rotten. From the inside out, I am tainted. Corrupt. Damaged. And the thought of dragging you down, of hurting you, makes me want to sink to the bottom of the ocean." Harrison pinches the bridge of his nose, squeezes his eyes shut and goes quiet again, caught up in whatever storm is raging behind those beautiful gray eyes.

"I suppose Wyatt would be okay with me sharing this. It's about as much my story as it is his. He avoids looking me in the eye as tears well behind his lashes. "I loved her, Maddie. Was in love with her. Fallon. Wyatt's sister. She was my best friend but she didn't see me that way. Instead, she ended up dating my brother, Hudson." Harrison's eyes track into the distance, staring off as he fights against the shaking in his voice and the tightness of his jaw.

"Hudson and I weren't like most twins you see in movies. There was never that telepathy thing or even a strong bond between us. Most of the time, we were more enemies than friends. We fought constantly. And not just bickered like most siblings. Hudson was cruel. Where I was shy and nerdy, he was outgoing and loud. He was daring and rebellious and I just wanted to keep to myself and stay out of the way."

I note the way Harrison talks about his brother like he's dead. But from the hatred in his tone when Harleigh brought Hudson up the other night, I suppose maybe he is in Harrison's eyes.

"I was so bitter when he started dating Fallon. Everybody thought it was such a beautiful match. Our families were close, we had all grown up together and had been best friends practically our entire lives. I was the only one who wasn't so thrilled. But then again, I was the only one who got to see the worst side of Hudson. He was so good at hiding it from the world, but not me."

Harrison turns his head and looks at the camera once again. His eyes have turned that dark stormy color, buried under furrowed brows. "The night Fallon died was such a fucking mess, Maddie. Hudson dragged her to a party she didn't want to go to in the first place. I think they were fighting but Hudson didn't care. Everything they did was always on his terms. Anyways, she called me shortly after midnight, crying. Begged me to come get her. The music was so loud and people were screaming. I couldn't make out much of what she was trying to tell me just that she wanted to go home." He runs a hand down his face, stopping the movement just below his neck where his hand lands and rests against his heart. Like it physically hurts to think about.

I'm pinned to my seat, hanging on to every word he says, terrified about what is coming.

"When I got there, the party was out of control. People passed out on the lawn, doing drugs right out in the open. I counted at least three fights while pushing my way through the crowd trying to find Fallon."

Tears start to fall from Harrison's eyes. I'm too stunned to speak.

"I was too late. I couldn't save her. I don't know what even happened. Some sort of fight. It must have been bad. Fuck, obviously it was bad. When I finally found them in a bedroom upstairs, I walked in and Hudson was standing just a few feet from Fallon. Gun in his hand, pointed right between her eyes." I suck in a breath. My eyes bug out at the same time as Harrison's fall closed.

"One minute she's looking at me, more terrified than I had ever seen in my entire life and the next, she's falling to the floor in my arms, blood spilling down her face into my hands. Hudson stared right into my eyes as he pulled the trigger. Like he wanted me to know that he was doing it because of me."

I want to wrap my arms around him and hold him while tears continue to fall down his face. I don't think he knows they are there. I've never seen somebody look so broken before. As he talks, the words fall out soft and shattered. It's like he is choking over every syllable.

"Hudson didn't even have the decency to look sorry. He just chucked the gun to the floor and walked out of the room like he was in the fucking mafia or some shit. We found out later he was high on a cocktail of garbage. But it wasn't the drugs that made him do it. He's a fucking monster, Maddie. The worst goddamn waste of human flesh."

"Oh my God, Harrison. I don't even know what to say. I—" I truly am at a loss for words.

"That's not the worst part. I mean, it is, but it isn't. All I saw was red. I'd never known anger like that before. I lost it. I lost control, left Fallon lying there in a cold pool of blood on the floor and tracked Hudson down. He didn't even run. I found him downstairs, about to snort something up his nose." Shame and a heat that can only be described as intense hatred simmer across his face.

"The next thing I knew, I had people all around me, pulling me off my brother. I couldn't stop. I just slammed my fists into his face over and over. My hands were covered in blood, some of it mine, some Hudson's. So much of Fallon's.

"Afterward, they found all kinds of emails and notes from Hudson to her. Telling her she should kill herself. Bragging about times he pimped her out to his lowlife fucking friends. He used her. Broke her. Destroyed her. And then he killed her. I wanted to do the same to him. I tried. If four other people hadn't pried me off of him, I would have done it. He spent weeks in the hospital. Broken ribs, swelling in his brain."

I know better than most that in times like this, words are meaningless. It's better to stay silent than fumble around and make somebody feel worse. So, I sit and let him deal with all the emotions that telling me this story has brought up.

"I left her, Maddie. How could I have just left her like that? What I did to Hudson wasn't worth it. Even if I had killed him, it wouldn't have been enough. It wouldn't have brought her back."

I imagine some people would hear this and immediately see Harrison as some kind of monster. Most people assume they would never be capable of that kind of violence, even in the worst situations. But, a lot of people think in black and white only and believe that no matter what, there is either good or there is bad.

Not me—I live in the gray.

The regret he has over his actions is abundantly clear. Harrison is no monster. A person who feels big things and loves hard, yes. Violent for the sake of being violent, no.

I trust him.

I feel safe with him.

Nothing he shared changes any of that. If anything, it makes me trust him more.

When Harrison looks up at me again, his eyes are red and puffy, but his tears have dried. I stare back at him, refusing to look away. He needs to know that I'm not scared.

"I'm not going anywhere," I tell him.

For the first time since meeting, Harrison looks angry. At me. "Jesus, Maddie, you don't get it! He is my twin. We are two halves of the same fucking whole. Everything that he is, so am I. If he is venom, I am too. If he could hurt somebody like that, what makes me any different? We all have our demons, Maddie. He is mine and I have to live with that. You've seen me lose control. I get angry. More angry than I would like. I want to be with you, Maddie. I want this to work, us to work. But I won't put you in danger!"

"Nope." I shake my head. "I refuse to accept that. I've seen real evil, Harrison and it's not you. You of all people should know that. You are not your brother. Shared DNA or not. Don't let him have that kind of power over you."

Harrison might not see it, but he is far from the villain in this story.

Chapter Twenty-Six

M Y SOUL FEELS LIKE it's been ripped out of my body and laid bare at Maddie's feet.

The memory of Fallon's lifeless body is burned into my vision. It took me years to stop reliving that moment over and over again, and in seconds, it all comes flooding back. I feel the need to go shower for the second time tonight. Scrub every inch of my skin until it bleeds, washing away the horrible thoughts.

I get so caught up in the past that I forget Maddie is still staring at me through the phone. Her tranquil voice breaks through the restlessness that burns its way through me. "Are you home?"

I nod, meeting her pale green eyes filled with nothing but warmth and an openness that shocks me.

Everything about tonight has been surreal. Between getting that text from her out of the blue to somehow ending up here, having shared the darkest moment of my life, then praying to God it doesn't scare her away. While also praying that it does. I'd gladly let Maddie be my ruin, but I don't have it in me to be hers.

"The diner closes in about an hour. I can't exactly leave before then, but you can come here if you want." I can't fathom how she isn't running as far from me as she can get right now. She wants to see me? After that confession?

Part of me wants to be alone and wallow in my memories. Part of me knows I need to stay the hell away from her. But, the idea of seeing Maddie outside of a classroom is too appealing to say no to.

I'm a weak man.

Glancing down, I consider my faded plaid sweatpants and t-shirt and decide it's good enough for a short walk in the middle of the night. I don't have the energy to change.

"Okay," I answer.

We hang up, and I snag a hoodie from its hanger and cram my feet into an old pair of sneakers before heading out the door in under a minute.

The air outside freezes my breath, creating little clouds that dance alongside me as I walk. Winter is officially here, arriving fast and brutal without enough respect to allow fall to fade softly away. It's hard to believe it's already the beginning of December. My cheeks are red and numb, and I think my toes might have frostbite by the time I make it to the diner.

Walking in and seeing Maddie makes it all worth it. She takes my breath away. Tonight, she's wearing a pair of skin-tight black leggings with intentional rips going up and down each leg, showing tiny slivers of her pale, creamy skin. The leggings are paired with a faded tan Red Hot Chili Peppers t-shirt, and her feet are bare except for a pair of black socks with a hole in the toe.

I smile at the shirt and a small part of me hopes she bought it after I told her class it's my favorite band. I'm sure that's not the case, but I like my version better than reality, so I stick to it.

Maddie appraises me like she's suddenly seeing me in a new light, but not in a bad way, like I would expect. She's not looking at me like a teacher, stranger, or acquaintance. Or a monster. Her eyes shine with something I can't put a name on.

As soon as I'm through the door and halfway over to her little reading corner, she's charging across the diner in a few long strides, not stopping until her socked toes are pressed against the tips of my shoes. She's got this determined look full of bold, unashamed confidence flaming in her bright green eyes. It's by far my favorite look on her.

I'm still holding my breath when she pops up onto her tiptoes and slams her lips against mine.

Kissing Maddie is like waking up on a mountain to watch the sunrise or sinking your toes into the warm, sun-kissed sand at the beach. It's peaceful, calm, and exhilarating all at once. Kissing Maddie washes away all the bad, ugly things in my head and replaces them with happiness, hope, and everything I shouldn't want. My future flashes before me, and I like what I see as long as she is there.

Maddie is my future.

My home.

I'm pretty damn sure she's my soulmate and holy hell, does that scare me.

Her lips seal my resolve not to let anything get in the way of giving us a chance. I'm not sure what that means for our future, but I can't find it in me to care. As long as I don't have to face it alone. I can't entertain a single doubt that it's what she wants, too. I can feel it. Her soul speaks to mine at a level words could never touch.

If she's so easily willing to accept the worst parts of myself and not for one moment waiver in her confidence over who I am, then maybe I can learn to do the same.

I run my fingers slowly up her sides and then cup her cheeks between my hands. My thumbs stroke against her perfect, freckled cheeks as her lips explore mine. Her mouth is plump and pillowy soft. She tastes like butterscotch disks—my favorite candy.

I fight to memorize every detail of this moment.

Her watermelon shampoo fills my senses, and her small hands travel between the back of my neck and my chest, stroking along the short stubble that lines my jaw. Her body presses forward into mine, mirroring every ounce of desire that fills me. The most perfect gasp fills the silence between us when she presses her hips forward. The effect she has on me isn't something I can hide, especially not in a thin pair of sweatpants.

Maddie pulls back, breaking us apart only to press her forehead against mine. She's standing on her tiptoes; her hot breath mingles with mine. "You're freezing," she giggles, running her fingers along my ice-cold cheeks. Her mouth is swollen and red where my facial hair has scratched and scraped against the delicate skin of her mouth.

"Sorry." I'm not. "It's brutal out there."

As if we needed the reminder, the wind howls outside the door, making the lights flicker for barely a moment.

"I like it."

"You taste like butterscotch."

Her cheeks turn a deeper shade of red and then she buries her face into my chest. I barely make out her murmured words, muffled by the fabric. "It was the closest I could get to tasting you."

My God, what is this girl doing to me?

I can't help myself. I need more of the perfect, sugary combination that makes up Maddie.

In all this time I've spent isolating myself from the world and believing that the ugly parts of me were more than any person would be able to take, I now realize what it was all for.

I was waiting for Maddie.

With nothing left to hold me back, I pour everything into this kiss and pray it isn't the last one we ever have. I could spend a lifetime kissing Maddie and still not get enough.

My tongue sweeps over her bottom lip, begging for access. She meets my movement with a sigh and parts her sweet lips. Our tongues dance, never getting enough. I memorize everything that makes her wiggle or moan.

I catalog the feel of her body as my hands roam over her skin, under her shirt, and over the velvet expanse of her back. She shudders in response to my fingers trailing softly down her spine.

Maddie responds beautifully to every single one of my touches.

First kisses are usually weird. There always seems to be some fumbling awkwardness as you figure each other out. That doesn't happen with us, though. We are perfectly in sync; just one more reason to believe she and I are made for each other.

Besides, what would an epic love story be without a few hurdles to overcome along the way? Our hurdle might come in the form of a mountain, but mountains were made to be climbed, and I'm up for the challenge.

CHAPTER TWENTY-SEVEN

M Y BRAIN SHOULD BE screaming at me with objections right now. The risk is too high. It's too complicated. I'm not anywhere near ready for a relationship. None of those thoughts would be wrong, but even if they were circling my negative brain right now, I wouldn't care. For every negative thought, I'm armed and ready with a positive one.

Harrison is a good man—a far better man than I deserve.

He quiets the anger and sadness. He bathes me in peace and serenity. He understands my shattered pieces and makes all the bad times before feel worth it to have brought me to this very moment in time. I want to hold on to it. To live in this happiness for as long as I possibly can. Harrison makes that feel possible.

For now, the world can stay the hell away.

His kiss feels like it's breathing life into me. He's awakening this light inside me that I haven't felt or seen in years. It's fucking addictive.

Everywhere he touches feels like little zaps of electricity. They burn a trail over my body that I wish would leave a permanent mark, one that would claim me as his and let the world know I am off limits to anybody but Harrison James.

Deft fingers dig into the flesh of my ass.

Every word that has floated between us but left unsaid pours from his mouth to mine and mine to his. It's not one of those kisses you know is a prelude to something more. The kiss is enough in itself; it doesn't need more. It's the kind of kiss you pray can last a lifetime. The type that ignites your soul, binds you to another person, and tries to explain everything that words can never be enough to say. It's the kind of kiss that ends in a promise.

Harrison ends our kiss but pulls me into a hug. His massive arms wrap around my body, making me feel small in the best way. "Maddie, baby. What are you doing to me?" His words come out in a husky growl that makes me think I might need a cold shower as soon as I get home. I should probably run out and take a dip into a snowbank.

"Back at you there, Mr. James."

His body stiffens at the accidental use of his title. Whoops. I suppose I should wait to tell him I think it's kind of sexy.

"Sorry," I whisper instead.

Harrison plants another peck on the top of my head, grabs my hand, and leads us toward the little couch in the reading nook. He sits first before pulling me down next to him sideways, with my legs swinging over his thighs.

"We should talk."

I groan. He's right, but talking feels like it will ruin this moment.

It will make it more real and less dream-like. No, thank you. "Do we have to?"

His fingers run along the gaps in my leggings, stroking my bare skin with his rough, calloused pads. It's distracting as hell.

"I'm serious about this, Maddie," he stops to gesture between us. "Whatever this is. I need you to know that. I don't want to be on two different pages so if you aren't, I need to know that right now."

It's hard not to be offended by his words. "I wouldn't be here if I wasn't serious, Harrison. I know what's at stake for you, and I would never put that at risk over something I didn't know without a doubt I wanted. I know I'm young, but I'm not a kid. I know what I want in my life, or at least I'm figuring that part out, but still. I've lived through too much bullshit to waste time entertaining anymore of it. I'm not the kind of person who sleeps around.

I haven't exactly figured out how to put everything into words, at least not yet, but I've never felt this before, and sure, most people my age haven't, but most people my age haven't had the same kind of life as me.

"If there is one positive thing that has come out of everything, it's that I have become incredibly self-aware. I have a shitload of learning and growing and healing left to do, but who doesn't have some things they need to work on, despite their age? So yeah, if you are asking if I'm serious, the answer is yes. But I also know that you have far more to lose than me in this situation, and so, with that said, I need you to be the one to call the shots right now. I can't be responsible for that."

"Not a chance in hell. That's not how this works, babe. We are in this together and that means we both call the shots. All decisions are made equally, you got it?" I nod. "I want you to know I refuse to keep you my dirty little secret. You deserve so much more than that; I can't bring myself to do it. But with that comes some big decisions, which I know it feels early for, and I don't want to have to do it like this, but given everything, it's unavoidable."

He's making perfect sense, though I'm still having a hard time keeping focus with him so close, his fingers lightly brushing over my thighs, and my body still buzzing from that kiss.

It's also past midnight now, and after a long day, long night, and an equally, if not longer, day tomorrow, I think this might need to be a conversation we save for another day. I can't handle any big decisions right now, and I need time to process them with a clear head.

"Can we sleep on things?"

"That's probably a wise choice. I assume you need to close up here. How can I help?"

Without any patrons, there isn't much left to do. Say goodnight to Pauly, lock up, and close out the register.

"Nothing much. I'll be done in a few minutes, so you can go ahead and head out. I appreciate the offer, though."

The day's emotional, mental, and physical toll is starting to hit me hard and fast. I want to get home and crash into a deep, dreamless sleep.

One more week until winter break. If only I didn't still have another entire semester to go.

Harrison doesn't seem to be in a hurry to head out, so I hold up a finger while I pop into the back office to lock the register drawer in the safe and shut things down. After that, I peek through the back door to let Pauly know I'm heading out for the night. He grunts in response without turning in my direction, oblivious to anything but his little radio. I don't know why, but it makes me smile. With anybody else, I would find it rude, but since it's Pauly, it's endearing.

He means well.

I think.

After I finish, I snatch my hoodie up, slip it over my head, and cram my feet into my shoes.

"Alright, all set. I'll, um, talk to you tomorrow then?" Everything suddenly feels awkward. I don't know if I'm supposed to wave and say see you later or give him a hug or another kiss. I certainly know which I would prefer, but it feels weird.

"I'll follow you out. Where are you parked?" He glances around the empty street, searching for a car he won't find.

"Don't worry about it, I walked. It's not worth the gas when it's not that far. The cold helps keep me awake anyway."

Harrison growls. Like actually fucking growls. It would be hot if it didn't piss me off. "It's not my place to tell you what to do," he forces out through gritted teeth, "but that idea makes me pretty damn unhappy. It's cold as hell out here, Maddie. Not to mention it's the middle of the damn night, and you are a beautiful woman. Do you have any idea—" He stops himself, which is a damn good thing.

I close my eyes and inhale deeply, burning my lungs in the process. My nostrils stick together from the cold. I force myself to unclench my fists and remember that he cares and is concerned. I shouldn't be annoyed or angry about that.

And yet, given everything, having my judgment called into question followed by a reminder of what could happen to me? It hits a nerve. I've been taking care of myself almost my entire life. Every decision I make is done so with the thoughts of "what if" followed by every worst possible scenario, whispering doubt and worry into my ear. I don't make choices lightly. Walking home from work in the middle of the night might not be the safest choice, but to assume I haven't already considered that makes me more angry than it should.

But that's my issue and not his. He obviously understood the implications of what he was about to say and stopped, which is more than I would expect.

"Sorry, that was wrong of me to say. Can I at least walk you home? It would make me feel better even though I know you can take care of yourself." Harrison reads me like a book.

"Sure, that would be nice. If it's not too much trouble. It is pretty damn cold out here." *See, I can compromise.*

"Not at all."

We walk in silence for a few moments. I imagine he's as lost in thought about the night's craziness as I am.

With my hands twisting together to stay warm in the pocket of my sweatshirt, I try to think of anything to bring the subject to something a little lighter.

"So, tell me more about your family." *My God Maddie, really? I am a moron.*

Harrison's head jerks back, surprised by my stupidly insensitive question. But instead of berating me over it, he thinks for a moment and chooses to answer the question in a normal way. By pretending his psycho killer twin doesn't exist. Fine by me.

"Hmm, what's there to tell? You already met my crazy sister, Harleigh. She lives with me and is determined to fill my house with so many plants that I might get eaten by them one day." He chuckles. "As for my parents, they've been married forty-five years now and seem to be happier than they've been in..." The unspoken words linger between us, frozen in the air. "A long time," he finishes.

"They were both seniors in high school when they met, but my dad was about six months older than Ma and had just turned eighteen. I think that's the only reason they waited the four months; the day after Ma turned eighteen, they were in line at the courthouse saying *I do*. It's a cool story, the way they met."

Harrison chuckles again and I'm happy to see him smile after earlier. A grin takes over his face as he shares their love story. "My mom went to this wrestling meet to watch her new boyfriend compete. My dad went to the same match to cheer on his brother. It turned out they were both there for the same guy, my Uncle Nick. Nick introduced them, thinking nothing of it. Naturally, they sat together for the match, and well, I suppose the rest is history."

"You're kidding! How did your uncle take that?"

Harrison laughs again. God, that sound is addictive. "Oh, he was pissed at first. They didn't cheat, but once they got to talking and hit it off, Ma quickly realized that she and Uncle Nick weren't that compatible, and she and Dad were. I don't think it took Nick long to see how perfect and in love they were together, so he came around pretty quickly. They got over it and are all great friends now."

I know Harrison didn't have it easy by any means based on the shit he endured with his brother, but aside from that, I can only imagine what it must have been like to grow up in a household with two loving parents like that.

By the time Harrison drops me off at my apartment and I'm snapping the deadbolts into place, I realize I made it the entire walk home without looking over my shoulder a single time. I'd like to think that's because Harrison makes me feel safe, but maybe I should be more worried about him making me careless and stupid.

"Have you gotten all of your applications in yet? " Kenna questions as she sucks down the last of her strawberry milkshake.

Ah, the one topic I would love to avoid. Just the mention of it has my blood pressure rising. "I think so. I've also applied for no less than a hundred different scholarships."

She smiles back at me with her usual sunshine grin. "Don't stress. I'm sure it's all going to work out!"

"You know, I actually kind of think it might," I reply.

I chuckle at the shocked look on Kenna's face, but before she can say anything, Bea walks up to our table and slides in next to me. Without any other tables to wait on, she apparently has time to chat.

"Seriously, Maddie. You don't spend enough time here when you're on the clock?" She nudges my arm playfully.

"That's what I said!" Kenna shakes her head at me.

"Better here than at home," I reply with a shrug. I didn't intend for my words to bring the mood down, but the table falls silent around me. "Anyway, Bea, where's Caden tonight?" I ask, trying to get the attention on anything but myself.

"With my brother. They were doing a family game night and asked if they could steal him for the night. Joke's on them though. Caden will destroy them in Uno," Bea explains with a soft smile, saved only for Caden.

I chuckle in return. Man, I love that kid.

"What are you girls up to tonight?"

"Avoiding life," Kenna answers. I raise my eyebrows at her, not used to such negative comments from my always optimistic best friend.

"Parent drama again?" I question.

Kenna huffs and drops her forehead onto the table top. Bea shoots me a questioning look and I just shake my head. Having no parents isn't all that great but, sometimes, I think I am better off than Kenna in that way. I'd rather be an orphan than have to live with the Kamp family.

"The usual, 'why can't you be more like Brayden and Tori? Look how successful they are. Tori never sleeps in, she wakes up at four every morning to work out. You need to be more like her, you're getting a little flabby'." Kenna mocks her mother's condescending tone.

"Hold the damn phone. Your mother called *you* flabby?" Bea's eyes about bug out of her head.

Kenna's lip tighten and she raises her eyebrows in response.

"God, they suck," I mutter. It still blows my mind that perfect, always on time, always follows the rules, literally took her shoes and socks off her feet to give to a homeless woman once, Kenna, is the black sheep of her family. No wonder her parents hate me so much. Her dad once tried to pay me off to stop being her friend.

I was eight.

"Can we talk about something other than college? Or the future. Please?" Kenna pleads.

"Sure! I bet Maddie has something interesting she might like to share." Bea rolls her head in an exaggerated way toward me with a devious smirk. I narrow my eyes, trying to figure out what she means by that.

She answers my unspoken question with a ridiculous grin. "I don't normally check the security cameras but the other night, an alert popped up pretty late at night and I was worried."

My eyes fly to hers, horrified at the idea of what she might have seen. She has to be referring to when Harrison showed up. What else could it be? Fuck!

I shift my attention to my empty coffee cup. Perfect, just the excuse I need to get far, far away from this conversation. Bea and Kenna aren't letting me get away with it, though. As I try to push my way out of the booth, making a strong point to avoid their eyes, Bea makes it clear she has zero intention of letting me up.

"Somebody clue me in here!" Kenna demands.

I look to Bea with the intention of letting her tell Kenna what she saw, but again, no such luck. These two really won't give a girl a break, will they?

I settle back into the booth, slumping down as far as I can without sliding to the floor. I still can't believe Bea saw that. Talk about embarrassing!

I bury my face in my hands and mutter words I was not planning to utter aloud anytime soon. "I kissed Harri—I mean, Mr. James." Wincing as I look up, I find Kenna's wide blue eyes bugged out, gaping at me.

"WHAT?"

"Shhh! Holy shit, Kenna!"

Bea cackles next to me. Traitor.

"Okay, I need a heck of a lot more details than that! How did this happen? When did this happen?"

"Fine, I will tell you everything but only if you let me up first. I need coffee if we are going to do this."

Bea graciously slides out of the booth and allows me to get up. "We need snacks for this. Fries anyone?" Bea asks.

"Oh yes, please!" Kenna chirps.

"I suppose," I grumble and head toward the coffee pots for a much-needed refill.

Once we are all settled back into our quiet table in an otherwise empty diner, I go through everything that has happened, which isn't the most exciting given that I don't even know how last night came to be. It was a gradual slide down an unsuspecting hill that I don't think either

Harrison or I ever intended to be on. The last thing either of us needs is messy and yet, messy is exactly what we have plunged ourselves into.

Aside from the shitstorm in my brain over that, on top of everything else, I have to admit to myself that it feels good not to keep this a secret. At least not entirely. Filling Kenna and Bea in on something and having them be understanding and encouraging is a far cry from what I've been used to these last years with Andrew. It's just one more nail in the coffin that helps me see how, even though Harrison is similar as far as being off-limits, this relationship is nothing like my last race down taboo lane.

CHAPTER TWENTY-EIGHT

"I APPRECIATE YOU TAKING the time to meet with me. As far as I'm concerned, the job is yours if you want it. I'll email you over an official offer letter later today. Think it over and get back to me once you've made your decision." Emerson Young looks up from the notepad he's periodically been scribbling on over the last hour and flashes me a brilliant white smile. I never would have guessed the guy was in his late forties if my dad hadn't already mentioned his age. Apart from the smattering of gray sprinkled throughout his dark hair and beard, he appears only a few years older than me.

"Thank you, Mr. Young, I will let you know as soon as possible." I return his warm smile with one of my own, my finger hovering over the *End Call* button of our video conference.

"Tell your dad I say hi too, will you?"

"Of course. Talk to you soon." With that, I click the little red button and collapse back into my chair. With the official offer on the table, I'm facing a heaping pile of hard decisions. I know what I would like to have happen, and yet that involves so many factors and variables, almost all of which are outside my control.

I spend the rest of my lunch mulling over my options, listing out the pros and cons on a scrap of paper from my desk drawer. On paper, the decision looks obvious. The pros far outweigh the cons. Reality isn't quite as clean cut, so my decision isn't as easy as I wish it could be.

The one factor I don't know how to count is Maddie. It's far too soon to be including her in a decision like this, but how can I not?

I spend the rest of the day caught up in my thoughts and being a shit teacher. I can't focus, so I give each of my remaining classes time to read their assigned novels just to get some quiet time to think.

At the end of the day, I'm no closer to an answer and more confused than ever about this Maddie situation.

I'm moments from ripping my hair out when I realize I need to call in a professional. As scared as I might be of that, it's my only option.

I scramble to shove the discarded papers from my desk into my bag, throw my laptop in and race out the door in hopes of catching Wyatt before he leaves.

His office is down the hall from mine, so I make it there in several long strides, swinging the door open as he shuffles his things into his bag.

If he's startled by my loud arrival, he doesn't show it. "Hey, buddy. What's up?"

"Got a few? I need to talk, and I don't think it can wait." Wyatt continues stuffing shit into his messenger bag, not even bothering to look up.

"Sure, wanna grab a beer?"

I can count on one hand the number of times I have willingly asked to talk about my feelings, yet Wyatt seems entirely unaffected by my request. "Sure, but let's skip the beer and make it whiskey." That, at least, earns me a grunt.

We walk silently down two flights of stairs and toward the staff parking lot, where we part ways. He heads off toward his massive black pickup to our left while I angle right to my metallic-gray Rav4. I keep the radio off as I drive, preferring the quiet as I attempt to gather my thoughts, bracing myself for the conversation ahead. I hate dragging my friend into this mess, but I need his advice. Remembering what my sister told me about Wyatt helps ease some of the nerves.

By the time I pull into the deserted parking lot, I've sweated through my shirt. I pull the soaked material off and swipe a plain black t-shirt from the backseat. Wyatt got stuck behind a train that I just barely missed, so I take advantage of his delay and consider what I'm going to say. Nothing sounds right and no amount of sitting here is getting me closer to figuring it out, so I give up and head inside.

The bar hasn't changed in all the years we've been coming here. The long-standing tradition must have started when I was just starting college, as Wyatt was finishing his undergrad. Any holiday break or long weekend that we were both home, there was an unspoken rule that we would meet up here first, share a couple of beers, and commemorate over classes, shitty professors, and the like. The bar itself wasn't anything particularly special, but the memories and tradition kept us coming back.

The door swinging closed behind me is all it takes for the familiar setting and nostalgic atmosphere to take a bit of the edge off. Wood planks line the ceiling, black vinyl-topped barstools with metal legs and round veneer tables are scattered around. A few pool tables and dart boards sit off to the left. In the summer, they host a weekly bags league on the patio out back. The floor is simple, bare concrete marred with stains, scuffs, and chips.

The bar itself is wrapped in the same cedar planks as the ceiling. The most remarkable thing here is actually the bar top. It's made up of hundreds of small sticky notes in various colors, with drawings, notes, and scribbles penned on each one. They laid them all out and then sealed with some sort of resin. There are beer tops, defaced dollar bills, some gum wrappers with little doodles and a few business cards sprinkled throughout, making it a visual testament to the history of anybody who has come and gone from this place.

I love coming here just to sit and read all the little notes, laugh at the drawings, and wonder about the lives of all the people who have written their thoughts, hopes, and dreams down to share with whoever took the time to look. I would love for tonight to be one of those casual days where I can sit and ponder over the scraps of paper.

Instead, I find a booth tucked in the far back corner, away from the eyes and ears of the crowd that will start filtering in before too long. The quiet corner will be more appropriate for the tough conversation ahead.

Wyatt strolls through the door moments after I have seated myself and barrels his way over without so much as a glance to locate me. He knows me better than I give him credit for.

A waitress is at our table the moment he sits down, flashing flirty eyes and a bit too much cleavage his way. Wyatt doesn't spare her a single glance. He turns all his attention to me after giving her his drink order. "Look, man, if you're about to drop a cancer bomb on me or some shit, I will kick your scrawny ass."

He might not be joking, but I have to laugh, anyway. "I'm six-three, asshole. I might not be the Jolly Green Giant, but I'm far from scrawny. And no, I don't have cancer."

He nods, satisfied that I'm not dying. "Well, good. So, why do you look like your dog died or something? Hank and Harriet alright?"

I run my hand over the back of my neck, carefully considering my words. I want this to come out right, but I don't know that such a thing exists. "I'm in love with Maddie." So much for carefully. The words tumble out of me and land on the table like a grenade.

Wyatt eyes me like I'm speaking Mandarin.

The silence forces me to keep talking. Fucking shrinks and their mind games.

Much to my annoyance, it works. I talk and talk, spilling my guts over everything that has happened and everything I have been feeling these last few months. They flow like a raging river, crashing into my quiet, stoic friend. I pick at the napkin below my drink as I talk until it is shredded into tiny, indistinguishable pieces.

His face gives away nothing, but I can't say I'm surprised. He has always been slow to process things. He looks at the facts first, considers them carefully, then allows his emotion to come into play and considers everything all over again. I can only wish I had that level of control.

Finally, after ages of deafening silence, Wyatt scratches his head, rubs his left eyebrow, and downs the drink he had yet to touch.

I'm man enough to admit that I'm scared shitless. Wyatt is my best friend. He's been by my side my entire life through the worst moments and every one of the best. The idea of him being disgusted with me was never something I considered. It sits heavy, crushing me under its weight.

The way I feel about Maddie isn't going anywhere. This conversation is inevitable, though that doesn't make it any easier.

"That's a pretty big bomb to drop there, man. I probably should be more surprised. Probably should knock your damn teeth in." He stops and returns to rubbing his jaw and scrubbing at his face. "What's Maddie's part in all of this? Does she feel the same?"

"Far as I can tell, yeah, she feels the same."

His hand goes up, flagging the waitress for another drink while I sit and pick at the label on my beer. After a single rum and Coke, I made the switch, deciding that drinking on a school night was asking for a world of hurt tomorrow. With the way my week has gone, I don't trust myself not to go too far, so it's best to quit while I'm ahead.

"All that is beside the point. Have you slept with her?"

"No, I swear."

"Good. Don't."

I nod in agreement, fully aware that would be a bad idea.

Wyatt studies me, his eyes moving over me like he's searching for my intentions. "Look, I'm not saying I con-done this, but you're a good man, despite what you think about yourself. And Maddie is an adult in ways that have nothing to do with her age. She's smart, and she can make her own decisions. She also has a long road ahead of her, but she's tough as nails and is far more capable of love than she realizes. She deserves to know what true love looks and feels like and fuck, I can't believe I'm saying this, but maybe you are the right man for that." He scratches at his eyebrow again and takes another drink.

"Now, I also can't stand the idea of you losing your job and getting a label slapped on that you don't deserve. So, with that in mind, keep taking things slow and get to know each other. If things get more serious after that, the three of us can sit down and talk and figure out a plan that won't ruin both your futures. Alright?"

Wyatt downs the last of the drink that had appeared while he spoke. If it was anybody else, two straight shots of whiskey would have them on their way to feeling pretty good. For somebody Wyatt's size, I would guess that amount of alcohol is more like drinking a beer.

Boy, I sure as hell was expecting to walk out of here with a shiner. Can't say I could have predicted things going this way.

"It's still early. Don't get too comfortable. Maddie is a damn good person. Harrison, don't fuck this up."

"I won't," I say with as much sincerity as possible.

Wyatt laughs to himself suddenly.

"What's your deal?" I question.

"You know, now that I'm sitting here thinking about it, in another life, I might have tried to set the two of you up. As fucked up as it seems to say, I can't picture a better match."

That almost sounds like a compliment. Almost.

"Uh, thanks. I think. But do you really believe that? With everything you know about me."

Wyatt scowls and drums his fingers against the table top. "The hell is that supposed to mean?"

I tip my head back and sigh. "Come on, man. I'm nowhere near good enough for her. What if I turn out to be just like Hudson? What if, one of these days my anger gets the better of me? What if I can't keep a lid on it and end up loosing control? What if I hurt her?" Just saying the words is like a knife to the gut.

A large hand slamming against the table sends me jerking backward. All eyes in the room fall to Wyatt who is seething before me. "Knock that shit off, you hear me? Dammit, Harrison, what's it going to take for you to see that you are not your fucking brother! You might as well be yin and yang. Polar fucking opposites. Stop letting the weight of his decisions crush you."

"Maybe."

Wyatt hits me with another pissed off stare. "No, not fucking maybe. It's the truth and I swear I will beat it into you if I have to." Moisture grows in his eyes. "You know Fallon wouldn't want that."

I'd like to think that is true. I nod my head but remain silent, trying to accept his words as truth and consider what believing that might mean. Harleigh, Maddie, and now Wyatt have all said variations of the same thing. Logically, I know they are right but getting my heart to believe that is going to take a little time.

All things considered though, a small sense of relief washes over me. I suppose I owe my sister a thank you for pushing me toward this. Wyatt's got an enormous heart, and I have to admit it, the guy is pretty damn wise. Not that I would ever say that to his face.

With the heavy conversation behind us, we switch gears and launch into easier topics like sports, classes, and normal things like that. It feels like it always has, and that alone is enough to extinguish a small corner of the blazing fire of guilt that's been burning me alive.

I may not have all the answers, and I still don't know what comes next, but at least I have gotten some of the shit off my chest and can breathe a bit easier for the time being.

Chapter Twenty-Nine

"Holy hell, it's cold out there!"

Harleigh bursts through the door of the diner, bringing a tundra of frozen air along with her. She's not joking about the cold, Jesus! I bet it's dropped at least fifteen degrees since I arrived early this afternoon. Losing the heat from the afternoon sun must have brought the temperature plummeting with it.

Fuck, I hate the cold. Why do I live here again?

With all the confidence in the world, she plops herself down directly next to me in the fading black booth and pulls a tan beanie from her head that makes her hair stick up all over the place with static. She still manages to look flawless with hat head whereas if that were me, I'd look like I escaped from a mental ward.

"What are you up to this beautiful evening?" Her perky attitude reminds me of Kenna, and like with Kenna, I can't find it in me to be annoyed by it. I should introduce these two.

"Funny you should ask. I'm currently plotting your brother's murder." With my pen, I stab at the paper in front of me to drive the point home.

"Sounds fun! What did he do this time?" Harleigh grins, then pops out of the booth and helps herself to a menu from the counter. Damn, I suck as a waitress.

She slips gracefully back into the booth and opens the menu, pouring over its simple contents like don't both already know exactly what she's going to order. Too many more of these late night visits and Pauly is going to start hating me.

"His job." I roll my eyes, more irked with myself than Harrison. "He gave us these journals at the beginning of the year, and we're supposed to write in them daily. The idea is to get into a routine of writing and developing the habit. Simple right? He doesn't even read the damn things unless we tell him to."

"So, what's the problem then?"

I smack my head down on the table in front of me. She's right. It is not a big deal at all. There shouldn't be a problem, especially since we have been doing this same thing every day for months.

"Do you want some coffee or something?" I shove her on the arm to get her to let me out of the booth and then slide across the slippery vinyl.

"Hell yes."

I make my way over to the counter and gather two cups. "I suppose the problem is that I know what I want to write, but I don't know that I want to write it." I carefully make my way back over to the booth with both full cups in my hands and gently set them on the table, then go back for the cream and sugar. I drink mine black, but I know Harleigh likes to load hers down with an ungodly amount of sugar.

"I think that makes sense. But, remind me where the murdering my brother part comes in?" She's smiling, so at least I don't have to worry that she's offended.

I slide back into the booth on the opposite side. "It doesn't. It's not his fault; I'm sorry, I'm in a pissy mood, and he's an easy punching bag since he isn't here."

She reaches her hand across the table and folds it over mine. It's such a strangely intimate gesture that I don't know how to react. I have to will my stiffening muscles to relax.

"You don't have to apologize to me. We're friends, Maddie. That means pissy, happy, sad, excited, or whatever the hell you want to feel, I got you. I'm not the kind of person you have to pretend to be happy for. Trust me, I can be a big-time hothead when I get fired up. I just learned not to go there very often."

I have a hard time believing that Miss Perky Pants gets all that mad, but I won't argue. At least, not now when she is trying to be kind.

"Now, tell me what the deal is with this journal thing. Why don't you want to write whatever is on your mind? Especially if my brother won't read it." She pulls her hand back and returns to ripping the little paper packets of sugar open, dumping one after another into her mug.

I groan again, tip my head back, and then force myself to be honest. "That's the thing. I want him to read it. But if this wasn't obvious, I don't like to make myself vulnerable with people, and the thing I want to write is pretty raw."

"Hmmm," Harleigh taps her chin thoughtfully. "Does this have anything to do with the kiss?" An infuriating combination of joy and mischief fills her perfect face. Meanwhile, I almost drop my boiling hot cup of coffee down my shirt.

"The what?" Even though I know we're alone, I look around to ensure nobody heard her.

Harleigh waves a hand in the air, brushing it off like nothing. "Did Harrison not mention how close we are? Besides, I can read that guy like a book. I knew something was up the moment he came home the other night. It took some master-level sister pestering to get it out of him. To be fair, I already knew something was up with you guys, so I think he conceded because of that."

She takes a sip of her coffee and groans. I can't imagine how good it can be with that much crap covering the actual taste of the coffee, but whatever. To each their own.

It's hard to say whether I'm relieved that she knows, mortified, or scared shitless. Something about that simple fact makes it all feel more real. In what way, I have no idea. It might not make sense to anyone else, but it does to me and I'm trying to learn that that's enough. A small part of me also feels giddy at the idea of Harrison telling his sister about me, about...us?

"Fine then. Yes, it has everything to do with that. I don't know what he told you, but I suppose, at least for me, whatever is there with us feels real. I want it to be real and healthy and normal, and from what I've heard, that means sharing things about yourself with the other person, and that's hard as hell for me to do."

Across from me, Harleigh locks me in an intense stare, forcing me to look her in the eyes. "He's serious about this too, Maddie. He's only ever been in one serious relationship, if you can call it that, and believe me, that girl was a bitch. She was never right for him, not like you. I think you get him in ways that nobody else does. He doesn't share that side with me. Our brother is a pretty taboo subject for the whole family but I know he still has a lot to work through there. He blames himself and it's made him think he's unlovable." Harleigh takes another sip of coffee, then smiles at me over the cup.

"He's different with you. I think you make him feel hopeful. Now look, I can't claim to know jack shit about how to have a healthy relationship, but I can tell you that I think being honest and open is a damn good way to start, even when it's hard. You are worth knowing, Maddie, and if anybody can handle seeing the parts of you that you hide from the world, it's Harrison. Let him in. Or at least try. I think you two have a real chance at something pretty amazing."

A hot splash of coffee lands against the side of my hand, burning the shit out of my skin and making me aware that my hands are trembling. I have to put the cup down before I maim myself permanently.

I wasn't expecting our conversation to go this way, and I'm lost on what to say. I feel a single tear escape the corner of my eye and burn its way down my cheek, hotter than the coffee. Her words mean more to me than she can know. At the same time, they scare me just as much.

Every instinct I have is trying to run like hell in the opposite direction of whatever is happening with Harrison. Yet, through that fear, I have the urge to write down every one of the thoughts charging at me so I can come back and look at them again with a clear head. I have a feeling Wyatt would agree that they are all lies.

"I'm not saying it's not messy. You guys have a lot in your path, but if you ask me, which I know you aren't, but I'm gonna say it anyway, it's worth taking a chance on."

Harleigh says her piece and then lets the comfortable silence take over as she enjoys her sugar with a side of coffee. This gives me a moment to process my thoughts. I'm tempted to text Harrison, but I don't know what I would say. We haven't talked since the other night since there was no school yesterday or today, and I don't know how to open that door back up. I haven't been brave enough to try.

"So, what are you up to tonight?" I feel awkward and need to move the conversation away from myself. I hope Harleigh will go along with it.

She doesn't respond at first, and the silence forces me to find something else for my brain to latch onto. Unfortunately, that something happens to be the blank notebook taunting me from its spot on the table. I slam it closed, but it doesn't feel like enough, so I pick it up and fling it across the room. It doesn't go nearly as far as I would have liked, but lands with a soft thud, which is about as much satisfaction as I suppose I am going to get.

I'll regret it later when the pages are all dirty and wrinkled, but for now, fuck it.

"Cheering you up, apparently!"

"Ha, good luck with that."

The notebook continues to torment me from a few feet away. The idea of folded-up corners and creases in the otherwise crisp, fresh pages makes my skin crawl. It takes about ten seconds before I cave and slide back out of our booth to snatch it from its place on the floor.

I'm bending down to grab it when another gust of frigid air bursts in with the obnoxious chime of the door. My heart rate picks up from just the simple sound, hoping Harrison will be there when I turn around. Instead, I find Bea heading over to Harleigh to say hi. She's alone, and Pauly is here, so I'm confused. She must read the look on my face when she turns toward me. "Inventory, remember?"

Uh no. I have no idea what she's talking about. "Of course. Was I supposed to have gotten started on that?"

She reads right through me. "Did I forget to mention it? Crap, I'm sorry, Maddie! I have way too much on my mind these days."

"No big deal. What do you need me to do?"

"Nothing. I'm closing down early. Caden is with his grandparents, so I have the night to myself, and damn if I'm not going to enjoy it. I'm going to crank the radio, dance around and knock this out in a night. What I need from you is to get the hell out of my way, and I mean that in the nicest way. Enjoy your Friday night, babe. You're eighteen. Act like it for once!"

Like I know how. Harleigh grins and claps her hands, jumping up out of the booth. "You're so coming home with me!"

Her excitement is enough to make me smile. "We hardly know each other!" I slap my hand to my chest. "At least buy me dinner first." I wiggle my eyebrows, and she laughs out loud.

"Done!"

"Wait, what? I was kidding."

"You might be, but I'm not. We're going back to my place, ordering pizza, and having a good old-fashioned girls' night. I insist!"

As surprising as it is, the idea sounds kind of fun. It's been far too long since I've had a night off to enjoy and do something normal. I would feel bad about not spending it with Kenna, but she has to go to some formal charity dinner with her parents tonight in the city, so she's not even an option right now.

I'm about to agree when I remember where Harleigh lives. Or rather, who she lives with. "I'm pretty sure that's a bad idea."

I would offer up my apartment as an alternative if I didn't hate that place, and something feels wrong about inviting somebody there with its bare walls, basic, second-hand furniture, and not a single picture, decoration, or touch of personality whatsoever. It's depressing and not at all the right vibe for a girls' night.

Hadleigh's face falls, and Bea winces. "I'm sorry, I shouldn't have assumed. I'm sure you have plenty of other things you would rather do with a night off."

Ah, shit. That came out all wrong. I would love to get to know her better and make a new friend—Lord knows I could use one or two of those—but going into Harrison's home without him being the one to extend the invite seems like a huge boundary issue. I'm not so sure we are to the point in our, whatever we are calling it, for him to be okay with me peeking in his shower. Because let's be real, I absolutely would.

I've never understood going through somebody's medicine cabinet, if people have those anymore. If I want to know something about a person, how many bottles of shampoo they have, whether they brush their teeth in the shower, and how much hair is clogging up their drain will tell me a lot more than the fact that they get the occasional headache.

"No, it's not that at all. I would love to! I just don't want to make your brother uncomfortable."

Out of the corner of my eye, I see Bea shoot me a goofy look, raising her eyebrows dramatically and winking.

"Oh please, if that's the only reason you're saying no, I'm considering the matter settled. You're coming with me, and we are having ourselves a sleepover. I haven't done that in ages! It will be so much fun, I promise. And if not, we'll call it a night, and you can go home—no big deal. I swear I won't hold you against your will. Please give it a chance. Harry won't mind; I can almost guarantee it."

How am I supposed to say no when she's just short of begging me on her hands and knees? It has nothing to do with the thought of seeing Harrison again, P.K.—post kiss—or of being in his home.

That smells like him.

Where he sleeps.

And showers.

God, I'm like a creeper.

Libido aside, the thought of being face-to-face with Harrison again does scare me. We haven't talked like we said we would, and most of that is on me. I want to have my head on straight and know what I want before we get to that little chat, and I have yet to make that happen. The thoughts in my head were a mess before this all happened, so now I'm more confused. My heart knows it wants, but I don't trust that traitorous bitch. She's overly soft and gullible and easily won over.

A little pathetic if you ask me.

On the other hand, my brain might be as bad for the opposite reasons. It's cynical and jaded and angry and hurt and wants to say fuck the world, so that nobody ever comes close enough to hurt me again. That voice says Harrison can't be trusted. It says I'm not good enough. It says I'm broken and messed up and have a lifetime and a half's worth of issues to work through that nobody deserves to have to put up with my insufferable ass.

I truly thought I would be fifty before this became a problem. Not once did I think I would be anywhere close to the possibility of a relationship for a long, long time and by then, I figured I would sort of have my stuff figured out.

Underneath it all, when I weed through all the lies and the voices feeding me things that have no basis in reality, I find a glowing beacon of light. It's just enough that if I let it, it might shatter through the darkness. That light is what tells me that the level of connection, friendship, attraction, and unbridled trust that Harrison and I seem to share only comes once in a lifetime, if a person is lucky.

"Alright, if you say so, I guess I'm in!"

Chapter Thirty

I'T'S BEEN A LONG day of meetings and I'm exhausted. The last thing I want to do is stop for groceries on my way home. With bad weather predicted for the weekend and a pantry and fridge whittled down to condiments and stale cereal, I don't have much choice. Lucky for me, everybody else has the same idea, so the grocery store is packed, which delays me getting home that much more.

To add to the fun, the roads are covered in thick, sloppy, wet snow that pulls my tires wherever it pleases as I try to navigate home. Cars slide into the ditch all around me, forcing me to take it slow. My standard twenty-minute drive home takes over an hour. This all comes at the end of an already long two days that have been filled with meetings from seven in the morning until six at night.

I can't even find it in me to be happy that it's Friday.

With the students being off the last two days for these mandatory teacher training sessions, I haven't seen or heard from Maddie since our big kiss. The distance put me on edge long before tonight's sprinkle on the top of the cake. At this point, I want to hunker down in my office with a good book or maybe a movie marathon and drown my anger and frustrations in a butter-soaked bag of popcorn.

When I finally make it home, I load my arms with grocery bags and shove my way through the door, praying none of them rip open and scatter through the house. I got all the ingredients for hot chocolate, soup, fresh bread from the bakery, and, of course, popcorn.

I've about reached the kitchen when I see a sharp, pointed edge from my popcorn box piercing through the thin plastic grocery bag. In slow motion, I make my final steps to the kitchen and drop everything on the counter just in time to avoid casualties. *Phew*.

"Lee, you up? I was thinking of a *Lord of the Rings* marathon. Or maybe *The Hobbit* would be better?" I holler through the quiet house. It's early enough that I don't have to worry about her being in bed yet.

By the time I have all the groceries put away, I still haven't gotten a response, which isn't that unusual. She likes to walk around with her Air Pods in, music cranked loud enough to burst an eardrum. With that in mind, I move across the house toward the four-season porch at the back where she likes to hang out, hoping to plead my way into some company for the evening.

Of everything I might expect to find, Madalynn Klein curled up on the couch with brightly polka-dotted fuzzy socks covering her feet would have been the last on the list. She's got her typical black leggings and a heather-gray sweatshirt with *Be cool. Be Kind* written in the top corner. Her hair is up off her neck in her signature bun.

The sight is absolute perfection. I barely have time to take it all in before I realize I don't ever want her to leave. I could come home to the sight of her every day and never grow tired of it.

Maddie is chewing her fingernails, intensely concentrating on the two thousand tiny puzzle pieces scattered on a mat before her, searching for the exact one she needs.

Harleigh and I are puzzle junkies. It's something we inherited from our parents. Every Sunday night for as long as we can remember, we would sit at the dining room table after supper and work away at one for hours before it was time for bed. Ma would hum along to whatever classic country song was floating through the room, and Dad would sit back and watch. Occasionally, he would throw in his two cents or taunt us with a particular piece we were hung up on. He was the best at puzzles out of all of us and yet rarely participated.

Hudson rarely participated.

When frustrated, I'd hover my fingers over the table, moving slowly to the left or right as he guided me. Yet, never once did he give up the actual location. Instead, he would cough anytime I got close. The closer I got, the bigger the coughing fit.

I stand in the archway to the living room for at least ten minutes, watching Maddie in this relaxed state. It's not until Harleigh gets mad, pounds her hands on the ground, and declares a snack break that I'm discovered.

"Harry, you're home!"

Maddie, still engrossed in the puzzle and not as quick to give up as my sister, practically flies off the couch when she realizes I'm standing here like a weirdo watching her.

"I hope you don't mind that I invited Maddie over. Bea closed down shop for the night, and I happened to be there at the time, and well, here we are!" Harleigh, with her back to Maddie, shoots me a heavy look that lets me know that I better not kick out her new pal. Not that I would.

"I don't mind one bit. How are you, Maddie?" I wince at the overly formal tone that accidentally comes out, gaining another dirty look from my nosey sister.

"Uh, cold. And annoyed with this damn puzzle. How do you two have the patience for these things?"

"It's so calming!" Harleigh chimes in, which makes me chuckle. Maddie throws a confused glance at us, unaware of the inside joke she just missed.

"Harleigh likes to throw tantrums like a toddler when she gets stuck. Her doing a puzzle can turn quickly into the equivalent of a teenage boy playing video games. Lots of yelling and cursing. A table has been known to be flipped." I wink at Maddie, who smiles back at me.

"That is so unfair! I flipped a table one time, and that was completely justified! It was an all-white puzzle; what kind of sadism is that!?" Harleigh stomps a foot, helping to prove my point about the tantrum, and looks to Maddie for some backup.

Maddie, in turn, glances back and forth between us. Her eyes sparkle with amusement, almost hiding the despair tainting her happiness. It makes me realize that having a sibling to share memories and tease is something I have taken for granted.

That won't happen again.

And Maddie will never have to miss out on any of it from here on out, if I have any say.

"Maddie?" Harleigh urges when she hasn't responded.

Maddie throws her hands up at chest level from her corner of the couch, pleading the fifth. Smart girl.

Everything about this evening feels surreal. I have to believe that some overarching entity keeps pushing Maddie and me together. The coincidences are too many and too significant, which doesn't begin to account for the all-consuming draw I have to be near her.

It's taking everything in me to stop myself from dropping to one knee and begging Maddie never to leave my side.

But I can't do that.

For her sake and for mine. It's taking a lot for me to open up to the idea of being with Maddie. No matter how badly I want to, I still have this lingering resignation that I'm not good for her. Every time the thought comes up, I feel like the very blood that runs through my veins is burning me from the inside out. Poison will do that to do you.

Even without my own reservations, I know I still need to bide my time and allow us both the chance to come to terms with whatever is happening with us. We each have so much of our own healing to do and while part of me is inclined to believe we need to figure it out before going down whatever road we are on, the other part questions why we can't do it together. In our own ways, we each have a lot of self-forgiveness to work through, so maybe by leaning on one another, that mountain won't feel quite so daunting.

Chapter Thirty-One

Harrison strides over to where I'm sitting on his couch and settles down directly next to me, as close as he can be. Just shy of sitting on me. The heat from his body radiates in waves, warming me all over. I want to snuggle into him, maybe lay back and watch his nerdy movies.

Every hair on my body stands at attention like they are all simultaneously reaching for him, soaking in the proximity, basking in his touch. I also can't ignore that he feels comfortable enough to be this close to me in front of Harleigh.

Or in general.

It's far too close for acquaintances and definitely too close for a teacher and student. Maybe that should seem obvious since we are well past that point, but it stands out when I spend every minute questioning if this is real.

His signature vanilla bourbon scent invades my senses, making me warmer from the inside out. Harrison feels like home. Being here, in his space, feels like home. I never want to leave, and I'm fully aware of how crazy that sounds.

I'm allowed to sniff the man I'm headed into a relationship with, or maybe already there, right? Eh, no. Still weird.

I need a minute to myself since I'm not thinking straight. Besides, this night was supposed to be about hanging out with Harleigh, yet I've gotten completely wrapped up in Harrison instead. "Bathroom?" I get up quickly while they both point to my left.

"Straight down that hall, all the way to the end."

I will my legs to move at a normal pace instead of sprinting out of the room like they want to. I'm following Harrison's directions down the hall but stop short of the bathroom when two partially opened doors to the left grab my attention. The first is his bedroom. That feels too private to look at, so I avert my gaze, which causes my eyes to land on the second door. No amount of self-control can keep me out of there. I can't help but push my way into his office.

If I never wanted to leave before, they are going to have to drag me out of here wailing like a banshee now.

I've never wasted time wistfully planning my dream home before, but if I had, this would feel like it had been plucked straight from my brain. The only thing missing is that little bookshelf ladder that wheels along the room so you can reach anything you need, like in *Beauty and the Beast*. What book lover hasn't dreamed about that library?

I seriously consider crawling under the desk and hiding out until they forget I'm here, emerging only when the house is quiet and still to curl up in that cozy leather armchair and write or read until my eyes bleed. I could do that night after night, and nobody would be the wiser.

Every detail comes together perfectly, from the way the light stain of the desk makes the space feel brighter against the contrasting dark green walls, to the artwork that is simple and subtle enough not to distract from the books, which are the real trophies of the room. It's perfect in every way imaginable, down to the smell that is so distinctly Harrison.

The bookshelf begs me to come closer, and that's a request I cannot resist. There are rows upon rows of classic novels ranging from Austen to Homer to Steinbeck, followed by a single row of poetry, no thank you, and then a range of nonfiction, which includes everything from psychology and self-help books to cookbooks and everything in between. I have been in bookstores that would kill for the collection Harrison has.

He has contemporary fiction, science fiction, war novels, detective novels, true crime, thrillers, horror, and even some children's books.

My fingers float carefully over the spines, flowing between the firm weight of the hardbacks, over the soft creases and ridges of the older paperbacks. I wonder about the pristine covers with their uncracked spines.

Were they gifts or maybe books tucked away for a special occasion?

I can't help but reach for one that catches my eye, pulling the deep red spine out and away from its place on the shelf to scan over the first page.

Would Harrison let me borrow one? Or all of them? I could stay in this room for days reading, but it would never be enough. The desire to hole up here forever is only partly due to the books and a good majority to do with the owner.

I think somebody might have to pry me away from here.

Chapter Thirty-Two

As Maddie leaves the room, I turn to my sister and throw my hands up. I hate this strange limbo phase we are in right now where I don't know where Maddie and I stand.

"I don't want to push her, but this is killing me. Am I supposed to go after her or give her space? How do I ensure I don't cross a line if I have no idea where the line is?" I rub the back of my neck before sliding my hand into my hair, pulling on the ends.

"Chill out over there, brother. I think your wheels are spinning in entirely the wrong direction." Harleigh has returned to her puzzle and doesn't spare me a glance as she speaks.

"What's that supposed to mean?"

"Maddie's into you. I would hope you're not too blind to see that. But that doesn't mean it isn't as hard, if not harder, for her. Give her a chance to figure her shit out before you go assuming things." She grins as she finds the piece she's been searching for, snapping it into place with ease as I sit feet from her on the edge of sanity.

"What if she doesn't, though? Figure it out, that is. I can't stand the thought of pressuring her."

"You're thinking about this like such a man. In your mind, A plus B equals C. It's a hell of a lot more complicated for us women. There are hundreds of different variables at play constantly. We can't rely on logic alone like you do.

"Look, Maddie strikes me as somebody who loves hard and fast, but given her history, I get the feeling it will take a little bit for her to accept that. She's scared to open up, scared to fall on her ass and get hurt again. Hell, I wouldn't be surprised if she's the one scared of hurting you. I might be completely wrong. I don't know her that well yet, but that's the vibe I'm getting."

Her attention remains on her puzzle, a waterfall landscape, as she drops her wisdom on me, leaving me once again gaping at my baby sister, trying to figure out when she grew up and turned into such an insightful woman. She still has yet to let me in on why she moved in with me so abruptly, but moments like this make me really thankful that she did.

As much as I would love to track Maddie down and make her talk to me, I won't hijack her night with Harleigh. Maddie deserves the opportunity to have a normal night to relax and hang out with a friend. I'm glad to see that her and my sister are getting along so well. Harleigh is a good person and Maddie needs more of those in her corner.

So, I force myself to walk away and head for my office, intending to spend the evening reading. I need a break from anything work related, at least for a night. With finals coming up, it seems like all I have been doing lately is grading assignments that are weeks overdue as kids scramble to fix their grade before it's too late.

As I round the corner to the hallway, I find a soft light spilling out from a door cracked open to my left. At the end of the hall, the door to the bathroom remains wide open revealing an empty room.

I should have known my office would pull her in. The books that line the shelves often feel like they have a life of their own, calling to me and luring me in whenever I haven't spent enough time living in the world that I love so much. It's no surprise that they have the same effect on her.

For the second time tonight, I find myself standing out of sight, watching the woman I'm in love with, with a smile on my face. She's perched on the ottoman, sucked into a novel she seems to have plucked off my shelf.

By the way, she's sitting, I can tell she didn't plan on reading more than a page or two. I've been there my-self plenty of times to understand. The thought makes me imagine spending hours browsing the shelves in a bookstore or enjoying a cup of coffee and talking about a novel we read together. I can picture the day we take our kids on a rainy afternoon, chasing them around the store, sharing our childhood favorites with them as we read in the little plush chairs they keep in the kid's section. It's a thought that should scare me. The fact that it doesn't should scare me even more.

I'm gonna need to build a bigger library.

But I need to get on the same page with our imaginary kid's mama first.

Maddie belongs here, even if she hasn't seen it yet. In this short time, the way she acts here or at the diner is a stark comparison to the person she is at school. There, she's rigid and tense, walking around like she's running from something, avoiding eye contact and shuffling from place to place.

Here, she's relaxed and comfortable. There is a twinkle in those pale green eyes that I love so much.

She's lighter.

Free.

It's far from the same person, and I hope that will work in my favor.

"I see you found my sanctuary." I enter the room with a gentle smile, hoping she takes it as reassurance that I'm not upset to find her here.

I must not be as effective as I hoped. Maddie scrambles to her feet, dropping her book with wide, panicked eyes.

"Fuck, I'm so so sorry. I didn't mean to snoop. I saw the open door, and I couldn't help myself. It's so perfect!"

I close the remaining few feet separating us and pull her into my arms. I can't resist not touching her any longer. Within seconds, the tension in her body puddles at my feet, her muscles give in and the weight of her body sags against me. Her head lands against my chest, so I take the opportunity to kiss the top of her head and hug her to me.

"Spend as much time in here as you want, babe. It's my favorite room in the whole house, in case that wasn't obvious."

"It's incredible, I can see why. You might have to pry me out of here."

Not a chance.

"I would love to have something like this in my own home one day. It's silly, but I was that little girl who wanted a huge library like Belle. It was the only Disney movie I ever liked. I never cared about the frilly dresses or the dancing or even the love story. That library, though, called to my soul, even as a kid."

I make out the faintest smile and blush on her cheeks from where she's still leaning against my chest.

"I'm sure we can make that happen." I should let the words die on my lips. My heart is stronger than my head and wins the tug-of-war. I immediately worry about her reaction and kick myself for ruining this moment.

But she surprises me, as always. Instead of tensing up as I expect, she nuzzles deeper into me and breathes a content sigh. One more puzzle piece is sliding into place with that simple little action.

CHAPTER THIRTY-THREE

I HATE THINKING OF Andrew and Harrison in the same sentence, but it's hard not to compare them in times like this. Part of that is probably because Andrew is the only "relationship" I've ever had. I don't have much else to go by.

The way Harrison looks at me is a stark contrast to Andrew. Sure, I could see the attraction in Andrew's eyes. He had charm and would smile and laugh; things that felt perfectly normal at the time. But when he thought I wasn't paying attention, that look would turn into something you might see on Animal Planet—a starving animal about to rip apart a piece of meat.

I was a prize. Some victory he had won.

At the time, it made me feel desirable and confident. I would walk a little taller, push my shoulders back, and do whatever I needed to ensure his attention remained on me.

Looking back now, it makes me feel cheap, dirty, and used.

My skin crawls with the memory. It's those kinds of moments that make me hate myself. How could I not see what was right there? Knowing I pushed him to it, how can I claim not to have deserved what happened?

I didn't say no.

I should have said no.

I shake the thoughts from my head and pull my focus back to Harrison.

I can't change the past, but I can appreciate what's standing right before me.

Harrison looks at me the way people look at Christmas lights or their homes after being away for a long vacation. He looks at me with this peaceful content mixed with a tiny bit of awe. It's like he wants to dive into my soul and learn every part of me, which is utterly unnerving.

I don't want him to see the ugly parts of me.

Like he always seems to, Harrison senses the shift in my thoughts. I need to work on telling my face to shut the hell up. Whatever he sees has him pulling me in closer again, kissing the top of my head and holding me. He feels like he's trying to keep all those broken pieces together.

It gives me hope, a foreign but not unwelcome feeling. I haven't figured out how, when we are together, everything makes sense. It feels right, like we are on the same page, headed in the same direction. But then, as soon as we part ways, the doomsday part of my brain kicks back in and reminds me of why it can't or won't work.

Harrison deserves somebody normal—somebody far better than me. I'm only going to drag him down into my depravity. My darkness will stomp out his light, and we will both end up miserable. He will grow to resent me and then where would that leave us?

I should suffer on my own.

Every time I convince myself that I need to walk away now, before my heart gets too deep, moments like this happen, and the sun breaks through the clouds and tells me that it's my depression and trauma talking.

I'm doing my best to build a better future for myself. I want to be happy, and maybe I can be if I keep putting in the work to make that happen.

I can be worthy of a man like Harrison.

Right?

But is it fair to ask him to wait around while I'm still deep in the trenches? I don't know how to be a good friend, let alone a girlfriend.

"Let me in, Maddie. Please?" Harrison pulls away, but only to reach down and cup my face. He brushes a stray hair away from my eyes. His fingers trail down my cheek, tracking a tear on its path downward.

I choke on the words, holding back a sob. "I can't." I force myself to walk away, pulling the door closed behind me.

I find Harleigh right where I left her, with more than a quarter of our puzzle completed. She's tossing individual popcorn kernels in her mouth, studying the scene unfolding before her.

When I sit down next to her, she takes in my puffy eyes, snotty nose, and tear-streaked face. Instead of saying a word, she matches her brother's canny ability to know exactly what I need and passes me the popcorn bowl. She points out the missing piece she's trying to find and lets me plunge into the simple yet tedious task.

In another life, I would love to have a sister like Harleigh.

My attention span must not be as refined as hers because I quickly lose interest and get pulled back to my thoughts. The longer I think, the harder each kernel lands in my mouth until one hits me in the back of the throat, sending me into a coughing fit.

When I can breathe normally again, scratched tonsils aside, my anger has peaked. I want to scream, to beg to understand why there isn't a single soul on the planet that can understand what I'm going through. I try hard to stay away from the pity party line of thinking, but for fuck's sake!?

As awful as it feels to think, at least when you go through a tragedy like a fire or losing a loved one, there are other people with whom you can commiserate and share stories. They understand how it feels and can relate. There is common ground that can help make a person feel better and validated.

I've tried joining these online support groups and shit, but they make me feel worse. I can't come right out and say the horrible things that live inside my head.

I don't belong there because I'm not a victim.

Harleigh and I spend hours sitting there alternating between the puzzle, which slowly starts to come together, no thanks to me, and chatting about mundane things. I show her videos of people detailing their cars online, which she agrees are satisfying as hell. Rugs too.

It's past midnight, at which point she can't stop yawning. "I'm so sorry, but I have to get to bed. I can't keep my eyes open any longer."

I'm feeling much better by now and have her to thank, so I'm not sure why she's apologizing. "I don't think sleep is in the cards for me quite yet. I think I'm going to go ahead and head home. This has been fun, though. Thanks for inviting me over."

Harleigh raises an eyebrow as she pulls herself off the floor and starts folding blankets, picking up trash, and tidying up our mess. I jump in to join her, grabbing our empty soda cans and the discarded popcorn bowl.

"Yeah, that's not happening. It's snowing cats and dogs out there. That's a real saying, right? Anyway, there is no way in hell my brother or I are letting you go home in a blizzard. Especially not when you don't have a car. You would freeze to death!"

Shit, I had forgotten about the snow. God, I hate winter!

"You're stuck with us until tomorrow. Sorry!" She shrugs with a cute little smile that says she's anything but. "Make yourself comfortable! There's plenty of soda and water in the fridge; Harrison has a million books you can read and his laptop is in his office, too. He won't care if you're in there. I would stay up if I could, but trust me, I'm total bitch if I don't enough sleep. But I'm serious about helping yourself. Snacks are in the pantry, blankets and pillows in that cabinet over there."

Harleigh walks off before I can open my mouth to argue. I both love and hate how well she seems to know me already. Am I that easy to read?

I strongly consider leaving despite her protests. It can't be more than a mile to my apartment, and sure, it's probably cold, but dying in a snowstorm seems like it's got to be less painful and weird than staying here, wandering around my teacher's house all night.

As much as I like the sound of that, I'm not suicidal.

At least not anymore.

I can't stand being cold, and if I made it that far, the walk home would be beyond miserable.

Looks like I'm stuck here.

I might as well make the time pass quickly. It doesn't take much convincing to head back toward Harrison's office. That room is like my wet dream come to life. I don't hate the idea of being bent over that desk or the ottoman, and... nope. Not going there. That line of thinking is so not helpful to my situation, especially with temptation next door. Like literally. Right. Next. Door.

Does he sleep naked? Or in a pair of tight black boxers? Both ideas are equally appealing. It wouldn't be hard to pop on over and find out.

Get it together, Maddie!

I flick the lamp on so there is enough light to read by and settle into the chair with my feet propped up on the ottoman. There's a blanket draped over the back of the chair that I pull off and snuggle into. Harrison's signature scent envelopes me, lulling me into a state that's about as relaxed as I can hope to get. It's heavenly.

I pull my journal, with its newly soiled pages, from the bag that I grabbed on my way in here. I'm still pissed at myself for throwing it earlier.

Despite the crinkles, the pages beg to be filled with some form of beautiful and poetic prose. Sorry to let you down, little paper. In this story, nothing is beautiful.

The words rip through the page, painting a harsh picture of my life even before Andrew came along.

No part of my story has even been a happy tale.

Fat, ugly tears pour from me for the second time today, but I push through them as the little blue lines on the page blur with each drop that lands on the delicate paper.

As painful as it is to relive, the more ink that spills out, the lighter the burden of the memories gets. Pulling each moment out of my head and sticking them to the page removes their power over me. The pain lingers, but it's more like a healing scab than a freshly throbbing wound.

I write with the idea that nobody but me will ever read it, holding nothing back. I write like I hold the power over these words instead of them holding it over me.

The story I weave doesn't begin to describe my darkest moments. Instead, it's more like the tipping point where everything went from bad to worse.

It takes me over an hour to finish.

When I do, my body sags like I just completed a marathon. All the adrenaline and energy I poured out leaves me spent, but satisfied. It's enough to have my eyelids drooping, trying to pull me under into a dreamless sleep. I can't find it in me to fight against it, so I give in and allow the darkness to suck me under.

Chapter Thirty-Four

I GIVE MADDIE THE space she needs and let her spend her night as she intended. As hard as it is for me to stay away, I'm adamant about respecting her boundaries.

That being said, it's far more challenging than I thought. In order to distract myself, I hole up in my bedroom with my latest book and lose myself in tales of water horses and dead fathers for hours.

I polish the novel off around two in the morning. It's not the first or last time I have gotten so wrapped up in the pages of a novel that I lose track of time. I can't count the number of times I have wanted to go out and tell Maddie about it, though, and that's made it hard to focus. I hope I can talk to her about it tomorrow and maybe let her borrow the book to read for herself.

But since it's not the middle of the night, or perhaps early morning, depending on how you look at it, I figure it's safe to come out. The house went quiet hours ago. Harleigh turns into the Wicked Witch of the Midwest if she doesn't get enough sleep.

Thankfully, she's at least aware of it and didn't stay up too late.

I need to use the bathroom and tame my rumbling stomach, so I head out of my room and down the hall. As I pass my office, I glance over and find that the lamp was left on. After a few steps into the room, I realize the reason why.

Maddie is curled up in my favorite chair, my grandmother's crocheted blanket draped over her body, fast asleep.

If it weren't the stalker move, I would snap a picture to stare at it when she's not around.

I creep into the room and notice the blue notebook I handed out at the start of the semester resting over her stomach and her pen on the floor below. I'm happy to see her using it, even if she's never let me read hers.

My fingers itch to reach for it, to read anything from her for the slightest clue how to break through those walls she's built so well around herself, but I could never break her trust like that.

I'll be here ready to listen if and when she ever decides to open up to me.

I do reach for it though, but only to close the cover and set it down next to her bag and pen.

The movement is enough to wake her.

Sleepy, pale green eyes blink at me, and a slow, lazy smile spreads over those perfect pink lips. I like knowing she's happy to see me.

"Hi," she whispers, stretching her body like a cat in the sun.

The blanket falls away with her movement, revealing her stomach's bare, creamy pale skin where her shirt has hiked up in her sleep. I have to clench my fists to keep from reaching out and running my fingers over the perfect porcelain expanse of her abdomen.

My lips tingle with the desire to run them over every inch of her perfectly flawless body, drinking in the sweet taste that makes up Maddie. I have no doubt I would be instantly addicted.

The quiet of the world around us, blanketed in heavy snow that seems to have shut down any signs of life, leaves us in our little bubble outside of reality.

She feels it, too.

It's enough to give me the courage to reach out and lift her, settling myself into the chair, warm from her body heat, legs stretched out on the ottoman, and Maddie perched on my lap. I sit her sideways with her thick ass settled on the outside of my thigh and her back resting against the armrest of the chair.

She gives me a surprised but content smile. It's brief, but I catch it and latch on.

Maddie nuzzles into my neck, curling her body into me, still sleepy and chasing that peaceful half-asleep state she doesn't get to enjoy often enough. I gladly pull her body tight to mine and rub my hands gently down her back. Her hand rests against my chest, rising and falling subtly with my heartbeat, the cadence appearing to comfort her.

"Ready to talk?" I have to ask. The question that's been fighting to get out for days.

Her head turns upward to meet my eyes. Striking green eyes study my face, but I don't know what she's looking for—she might not know either.

"Maybe you should read first?" She drags her eyes away from mine and scans the surrounding area, looking for something.

It takes a moment for me to make the connection and reach down to grab her journal for her. "I promise I didn't read it," I say as I hand it to her.

"I know, I trust you. But I'm giving it to you now so you can." She flips through the pages until she lands on the most recent ones. "Specifically, these."

I'm about to take it from her, eager to understand any part of herself she is willing to share with me, but I stop and hand it back. "Read it to me?" I ask. "Or tell me what it says."

Her confidence falters. "Do I have to?"

"Of course not."

Her fingers drum against the pages.

Eventually, she gives a small nod, clears her throat and begins to read. Her words start out so softly that I have to lean in to hear them.

There's a vacant disconnect as she reads like she's saying words instead of telling a story. As she continues, the filter starts to fall away, and instead of reading, she starts to speak from memory alone. The notebook, clutched in her hands, drops to her lap and then to the floor.

She bares her soul to me, if only a tiny part. I take it and cherish the words she gives me, no matter how much they feel like daggers slicing at my heart.

Chapter Thirty-Five

"I'VE BEEN A CLICHE since the day I was born. The girl whose mom got knocked up in a drunken one-night stand with a guy never to be seen or heard from again. I don't know my father's name, and I don't think my mom does either.

"I remember being little and wondering if she ever tried to find him. Did he know I existed? By the time I was six, I finally realized that no, of course, she didn't. Trying to find my father would mean that she knew I existed, and aside from having given birth to me, I'm confident she tried to forget about me as often as she could.

"Which is how I ended up living with my grandmother."

The words come out robotic. I can't look Harrison in the eye, but the steady beat of his heart against my cheek is enough to keep me going.

"I know there are grandparents who bake cookies and cut the crusts off sandwiches, buy their grandkids toys and spoil them endlessly. I've heard enough classmates brag about it when we returned from winter break to know that it was a real thing outside of a story on TV. But, it was never my experience.

I can't complain too much since the woman did take me in and let me live with her. She could have left me in my mother's empty apartment, wondering when I would eat again or how long we could make it before losing power.

So, I knew it could have been far worse, and I was grateful to have an alternative. At the same time, though, I never got those warm fuzzy feelings from her. She made it clear I was a burden from the day I walked through her door.

"For context, my grandmother got pregnant at a pretty old age, at least old for childbearing. At the same time, she was far too young to become a widow just a few years after my mom was born. I don't know where it came from, but I always used to imagine that she was a wonderful, caring mother until she lost her husband and checked out on life. She drowned in grief for the love of her life, which left her this shell of a person who didn't care much about anything or anyone anymore, including my mother.

"The result was my mother being left to raise herself, and so it was never her fault that she couldn't love me. Nobody had ever taught her how. Life dealt them both a shitty hand, and somehow, I got to pay the price for it all."

Harrison listens to every word without reacting. He gives me a safe space to talk and share without judgment. This is more than I could ask for, and he encourages me to continue telling him my story.

"I was eleven when my grandmother died—the day started as usual. I got myself up that morning, threw in a load of laundry, washed the dishes, and walked three miles to school. I spent the forty-five-minute walk grumbling about having gym that day.

"Six miles of walking a day felt like more than enough exercise. What would playing dodgeball with a bunch of assholes do to help my physical fitness? Not to mention, whoever had the horrible idea to let a bunch of brutal, judgmental teenage girls all change together in a big open room with literally zero privacy is a complete asshat."

Harrison's fingers dance over my back, mindlessly tracing patterns on my skin as I talk. His other hand is firmly gripping my thigh. He seems to understand that the physical contact keeps me grounded in reality and prevents the panic attacks from sneaking up on me. I could love him for that.

"I was one of the fat kids because I wasn't a size zero. I developed far quicker than my peers at that age, so where they were still in training bras, I was searching the bins at the thrift shops for something with a bit more support. I guess when you are eleven, having an ass and boobs the size of a grown woman somehow translates to eating two boxes of donuts for breakfast every day. So yeah, the locker room was a pretty shitty place for me back then." I roll my eyes at the painful memory and push myself to keep talking.

"Anyway, the walk home that day took a bad day and made it worse. It started down-pouring around lunchtime and hadn't let up by the time school ended for the day. I waited half an hour, hoping it would let up before conceding to my fate and booking it the three miles back home. By the time I made it, I was sopping wet and beyond pissed.

"I blame the terrible day for not noticing something was off, but I had tunnel vision. I wanted to get out of my wet clothes and soak in a hot bath, which is exactly what I did, followed by burrowing into my bed with a book for hours.

"I think it was probably around nine that night before I remembered the laundry I put in that morning. I hated having to rewash it, especially when I needed a clean shirt to wear the next day, so I bolted up and raced down the stairs into the basement with the stupid idea that it might not be too late to get it in the dryer if I hurried."

God, I was dumb.

Retelling this story brings back every sensation from the day. My bones feel the deep cold from the rain and that smell. I will never, ever forget that smell.

"It hit me as soon as I reached the top of the stairs. At first, I thought maybe water had gotten in from all the rain. It had happened before. Or maybe the laundry was that bad from sitting there all day, wet like that."

I almost gag remembering it all these years later.

"Turns out, laundry doesn't produce that kind of smell. Death does."

Harrison sucks in a sharp breath, the first reaction I have gotten from him this entire time.

"I still can't tell you how long she'd been down there before I found her. The coroner told me it was probably the night before, but they couldn't say for sure without doing an autopsy, which I definitely couldn't afford. At seventy-eight, there was no reason to suspect anything but natural causes, so they basically told me there wasn't much point in it anyway.

"Since we hadn't seen or heard from my mom in about five years, I had to make all the decisions. CPS and the cops tried to track her down for weeks, but she was a ghost. Come to think of it, I don't even know if she's still alive."

I can feel the tears coming at this point. At the time, those few days felt like the worst of my life. It's funny how, looking back, they didn't make the list of the top ten worst days anymore.

"With no other family to speak of, I was shipped off to the foster system. The first few months were a nightmare. I remember thinking how badly I wanted to return to being left alone. At least with my grandmother, I got to do what I wanted. She didn't bother me as long as I ensured bills were paid, groceries were delivered, and chores were done.

"It took her dying for me to realize I never loved her. I never loved a single person my entire life. But to be fair, nobody had ever bothered to love me either."

Harrison grinds his teeth. His grip on my leg tightens, but he stays quiet.

"My freedom ended pretty quickly after that. I cycled through a few homes, mainly being used as a built-in babysitter during those first months. I was pretty lucky, though. My caseworker, Jackie, was still one of the few in the system that cared. She quickly caught on to it and pulled me out of those places.

"I think it was about six months after my grandma's death that I was placed with the Garrisons, and for the first time in eleven, almost twelve years, I felt this hope like I had finally found a family. The moment I stepped inside their house with its literal white picket fence and a dining room table used for something other than folding laundry and storing bills, I wondered if I had finally caught a break."

I take a breath, remember that moment and that feeling, and compare it to being here. I thought stepping into the Garrisons felt like home, but now, I don't know if that's true. I felt normal, sure, but also like it was staged. It was like they were painting a picture of how they wanted to appear instead of living it. But at eleven, something like that isn't easy to see. It could also just be hindsight blurring my perception.

"I guess when you take a tragic, neglected, and naive young girl who has absolutely no self-esteem and give her the tiniest bit of attention and a chance at hope, you can fool her into believing anything you say so long as it's wrapped up in a pretty box with a charming smile, warm hug, and a compliment."

The self-loathing in my voice is hard to hide, but it's no secret to Harrison that I'm not exactly my own biggest fan. I'm working on it, though. I want to forgive that little girl who didn't know any better.

I haven't ever told this story to anybody, not even Andrew. When he asked, I told him my grandmother died and left it at that. The parts about finding her decaying body and the bullying I faced, I kept to myself until now. Writing it down felt good, but sharing it with somebody who might care feels freeing on a level that heals parts of my soul.

Saying it out loud makes me realize how fucked up it all was. I survived that. I was a kid and had gone through some seriously messed up stuff and still survived. I'm fucking strong.

That little voice threatens to shut down my moment of empowerment by reminding me how pathetic it probably sounds to somebody else. I mentally punch that fucker in the face. It can shut up because I'm done believing those lies.

It strikes me that Harrison's silence makes me feel heard and accepted. He absorbs my words, processes them, and allows me the space to do the same without being tainted by somebody else's perspective. He wants me to feel proud of myself, not know that he's proud of me. At least, I think that's what is happening.

He pulls my body back against him, rests his chin on the top of my head, buries his nose in my wild hair and breathes in the smell of my shampoo.

I think I might be in love with Harrison James.

Chapter Thirty-Six

NOTHING BETWEEN MADDIE AND me happens the way I expect.

One moment, I'm holding her, trying to will my thoughts into her mind since I know that my words won't come out right. There is anger simmering below the surface that I'm fighting to keep at bay. Thankfully, my amazement over her strength and resilience outweighs my rage.

Since my words fail, I do the only thing that feels right. I kiss her.

I pour the weight of my feelings into her. I try to tell her I love her without saying it directly. I tell her how strong and brave and fucking amazing she is.

The last time we kissed, I held back. This time, I give her everything.

I could do this every night and never grow tired of it. Through my kisses, I beg her to keep letting me in. I want to know the story behind every scar, every freckle, every laugh and smile. I want to know what makes her cry and what makes her laugh. I want to suffer through her pain alongside her, stand strong next to her when she feels broken and help her find all the missing parts of herself that she lost along the way.

Maddie may not know who she is right now, but I sure as hell do, and I love her exactly as she is.

My hands cup her face. I can't keep them there for long. I need to feel her. With a desire that matches my own, she moves her body to straddle my thighs.

I move over every inch of her body, roaming around and exploring. I remember how her back arched when my fingers trailed over her spine the other night and repeat the action. She whimpers and arches into me, exactly the way I was hoping.

My fingers inch down and grasp her ass, pulling her closer to me until every inch of her front is plastered to mine. Her breasts smash against my chest. Her hips grind into me as we kiss. I know she can feel me. Every hard inch presses against her center, separated by two thin pieces of fabric that conceal very little.

Maddie moans into my mouth, and I capture it. I store that sound at the forefront of my mind, so it's accessible anytime I want, though I hope I won't need it since the real thing is right here.

Maddie's fingers grip my shirt as she writhes against me. I imagine she feels like this moment will slip away if she lets go. I need her to see that I won't let that happen.

Her skin is burning with a bright-red heat. The way she responds to every touch is like I'm stroking raw nerves. Every time my hands move, she shudders against me, her eyes rolled back in her head.

My teeth sink into the plump flesh on her bottom lip, enough to sting but not enough to hurt. I gauge her reaction, which isn't hard with the way she sinks deeper, another moan filling the silent air around us.

Every moan, every squeak, every whimper that falls from her gorgeous lips sends a jolt straight to my dick. If I didn't know better, I would say she's making them on purpose as every twinge nudges against her sex. I can feel the wet heat radiating through the flimsy fabric.

"Are you sure you want this?" My voice is raspy and low, almost like a growl.

"Fuck yes. Please, Harrison. I've wanted this since the moment I laid eyes on you." Maddie throws her head back as I push up harder into her, burying my face in her neck and nipping at her sensitive flesh.

"Is that so?"

The confirmation is all I need. To Maddie's surprise, I rise quickly from the chair with her legs still wrapped firmly around me. She tightens her grip on me with both her legs and arms around my neck and squeals, clinging to me like a damn little spider monkey.

Each step I take while carrying her has her body bouncing against my cock. Fuck, I need to get her naked. I can't wait to taste every perfect inch of my girl. I'm going to show her what it means to make love. I need her screaming my name.

We make it to my bedroom, where I kick the door closed behind me and toss Maddie onto my bed. Then I take a moment to look at her.

"Light?" she asks. If she thinks we are doing this in the dark, she's fucking crazy.

"Not a chance babe," I respond and continue roaming my eyes over every inch of her.

Her hair is wilder than normal; her chest rises and falls in deep, heavy pants. Her cheeks and lips are stained red from my facial hair scratching against her delicate skin. I like it, though. It's like my own personal mark on her, telling the world to fuck off.

She squirms under my gaze at first, crossing her arms over her stomach, twisting and turning her head like she's worried about how she looks flat on her back.

"God you are beautiful," I whisper.

Maddie finally seems to relax when she understands that I'm not going to stop staring at her until I am good and ready. Instead, she takes the chance to turn her own appraising eye on me. I can feel her unzipping my pants with her eyes. Practically see the drool forming in the corners of her mouth as she stares blatantly at my dick, still straining to be free from my sweatpants.

"Shirt. Off. Now." My tone is firm and commanding. I'm taking a risk speaking to her like this. I have no idea how she will react, but I suppose I'm about to find out.

Maddie pauses, a flash of fear filling her eyes at the thought of me seeing her naked. But then she moves her hands slowly down, grasping the hem of her hoodie and peels it over her head, revealing a bright-red, skin-tight tank top.

Her breasts are close to spilling out of the top, begging me to pay them attention. So that's exactly what I do.

I'm across the room and on the bed in seconds, pushing Maddie to her back, straddling her legs, but careful not to rest all my weight on her. I don't need to crush her the first time we sleep together.

Slowly, I trail my fingers up her sides, making her shiver and arch up into me.

"Please, Harrison," she whines.

"Please, what, baby?"

She grunts, twists, pushes herself up, anything to gain contact. I like seeing her wiggle beneath me. I fucking love seeing her beg. I want there to be no doubt after this all ends that she wanted it.

"Words, Maddie."

"Jesus, touch me! Please touch me already. I need you!"

As you wish.

Not able to hold off any longer, I dive in, burying my face between her full, heavy breasts. My hand continues to trail over her body with the softest of touches. It drives her crazy, and damn, does that do something to my head.

I feel like she's an instrument that only I can play.

With my other hand, I find the fabric at the center of her breasts and yank down, moving it out of my way right along with the cups of her bra. Maddie helps me out by slipping her arms free of the material, allowing it to pool around her waist, leaving her bare chest right there for me to appreciate in all its glory.

My God, my girl is perfect. My fingers itch to explore every bare inch of her.

I'm not blind, I've seen the way Maddie tugs at her clothes, or winces at her reflection. I make it my goal to worship every part other body, especially the ones she seems to hate so much.

Slowly, I work my way down over her stomach, gliding my fingers over the small white marks embedded in her flesh. She flinches and tries to pull me away, but I refuse to budge. I take my time, kissing every inch of her stomach, the soft flesh of her thighs, even down to her feet. I remember her making a comment about them being "too big for a woman," whatever the hell that means.

When I drag my finger over the arch, she squeals and tries again to pull away. Like I will let that happen. I don't care how long it takes to make her believe it, I vow to make sure that Maddie learns to love every inch of herself the same way I do.

Her nipples pucker, making me drool. I need a taste.

While I take my time sucking on each one, pulling at her with my teeth and then soothing the bite with gentle laps of my tongue, Maddie scratches and claws at my back, she goes from cursing to begging to moaning round and round in circles as I work her body.

Chapter Thirty-Seven

Holy shit.

I didn't know my body could feel the things Harrison brings to life with ease. My brain disconnected from my body somewhere after that first initial kiss. He once again quiets the ugly, cruel voices in my head. He's like my new drug.

I want to live in a world where nothing outside the two of us exists.

Every nerve, fiber, and organ in my body sings. I drink in the sensations, focusing on nothing other than how he makes me feel.

The pads of his fingers are rough and calloused. They scrape against my flesh, leaving small red marks occasionally. They embed themselves into the swell of each side of my ass. I feel his bite marks littering my neck and along my collarbones. They aren't deep or angry, so I know they will be gone by morning, but I like knowing they are there for now. I feel claimed, owned, possessed.

I want to have the same effect on him. I match his marks with my own. My fingernails dig into his back, pulling him against me, desperate to get more.

Our bodies were designed for each other. It's clear now that neither of us was ever meant to be touched by another. We fit together too perfectly in a way that can't be replicated. The contours of my body flow directly along the ridges of his. We are two pieces of a puzzle that only belong together.

I cup his face, savoring the sharp sensation of his prickled hair against the palm of my hand. My teeth nip and pull at his bottom lip. His mouth captures mine, taking ownership of our kiss. He makes it clear he is in charge here, and I'm all too happy to comply.

I gasp. He groans. I arch. He ruts. I kiss. He bites. It's the perfect dance.

Despite my urgency, Harrison takes his time. He treats this moment like it's the first of many more. Like he has all the time in the world to love me. Like he wants to memorize every detail of my body. He doesn't once shy away from a single part of me. Even the places that are too soft or squishy, too dimpled or pale. He savors me. Worships me. Makes me feel like maybe those parts aren't as ugly or gross as I've always believed.

Every stroke and gentle caress of his fingers, even in the feverish passion flowing between us, makes me feel cherished. I lost count of the compliments he's showered me in at this point.

Enough of that, and I might start believing him.

I swear we spend at least an hour like this. Kissing, touching, and exploring one another. Apart from the heavy attention he pays to my breasts and nipples, nothing beyond kissing has happened. He's still fully clothed, and technically, so am I, if you don't count my shirt bunched up around my hips.

I'm high on the smell of vanilla bourbon, consumed by it all around me in the best possible way. The salty taste of his sweat combines with the sweetness of butterscotch and lingers on my tongue. I need more.

"Harrison." I practically purr his name like a needy bitch, but since that's exactly what I am, I don't give a damn.

"Yes, baby?" Asshole. He knows exactly what I want but enjoys fucking with me.

"Fuck me, Harrison. Please, fuck me already."

"You sure that's what you want?" He rocks his hips against me, grinding the tip of his dick as close as he can to my clit...holy shit. I could cum like this.

I nod vigorously.

Harrison leans in until his lip brush over my ear. His breath is hot against my skin, sending a chill down my body. "Take off your pants."

I scramble to comply, hooking my fingers in the waistband of my leggings and thong and shoving them down my legs along with my tank top and bra.

Harrison leans back on his heels and drinks me in. His eyes turn to molten lava, burning a trail over my already overheated flesh everywhere he looks.

"Jesus, Maddie. I don't think I will ever get enough of you."

I can't take it. I need him.

Now.

I'm over this taking it slow thing that he seems to be enjoying so much, so I attempt to take over, leaning up far enough to grasp his pants and tug them down. His sweatpants slide easily down his hips, shocking me with his lack of anything underneath.

I let out a soft cry that causes him to hum with satisfaction.

Every bare inch is right there before me, and it's all mine. Hell, the throbbing and deep purple head is because of me. Talk about a heady thought.

If anybody had asked me on the first day, walking into his class, that we would be here, I would have laughed in their face. No way in hell would an Adonis like Harrison James want anything to do with a nutcase like me, and yet, here we are with little room to argue that he does want me.

My fingers wrap around the wide girth as I stare at Harrison. His nostrils flare, and I can feel the way he struggles not to buck against my touch. The muscles in his thighs are rigid from the effort it takes to remain still.

"Tell me what you like," I ask.

"Fuck Maddie, are you trying to kill me?" His voice is thick with lust, sending waves of desire through me. I'm surprised I can't feel the wetness leaking down my thighs at this point. I don't think I've ever been so turned on. "You. I like you, so no matter what you do, I promise I'll love it."

I sit up, spurred on by his words, and gently shove his shoulders, sending him backward. Now, he's lying on the bed with me on top.

I wrap my hand around his cock.

It jumps with the contact until I tense my fingers, getting a firm but not painful grip and start gliding my hand up and down, running my thumb over the tip, gathering some of his pre-cum to act as lube.

My thumb swirls around his head, making Harrison hiss. His hands move up. They tangle in my hair, the grasp giving a small bite that's strangely erotic.

I'm panting, simmering with need, my legs shake with anticipation. I need him inside me. I can't wait any longer.

"You ready?"

There he goes again, reading my mind.

"Please."

Harrison moves us again, positioning me on my back with him propped up on his elbows over me. His skin is hot against mine, creating this maddening construct between that and the cold air swirling around us.

In one swift, graceful move, he positions himself at my entrance and then looks me in the eye, asking for permission. I give a slight nod, and it's all he needs to push slowly inside me, sinking in and joining his body to mine.

I don't recognize the noises that spill from me as he moves, thrusting deep inside me. I'm panting, withering, gripping the sheets, pulling him closer.

My legs wrap around his hips, matching his movements thrust for thrust.

Holy Mother of God.

I fall apart in minutes. Screaming, chanting Harrison's name like a prayer.

He follows right behind me, roaring as he empties himself inside me. I can feel the heat of him merging with my body. I want to keep him there forever. I want him to be a part of me always.

My body relaxes, spent from the late hour, physical exertion, and emotional weight of this entire night. I feel myself drifting almost immediately, vaguely aware of Harrison leaving the room and coming back moments later, the warm sensation as he takes a washcloth and cleans me up, then pulls the covers over my limp body.

The bed dips, and then his solid arm wraps around me, tugging my body into his until we are molded together.

In his arms, I have never felt more relaxed in as long as I can remember. Sleep pulls me under where I dream of happy endings.

Chapter Thirty-Eight

Holding onto Maddie feels like holding onto air. I'm fighting like hell to keep a firm grasp on her, terrified she will slip through my fingers at any given moment.

She feels like a dream. If I close my eyes and focus too hard, everything gets blurry and fades away.

Dark wavy hair covers my pillow, and pale, flawless skin presses gently into my mattress. I'm hit with the sweet, cool scent of watermelon shampoo with every inhale.

I can't help but run my fingers over the softness of her belly, the curve of her ass, the top of her nose nuzzled into my neck.

I pray for the sun to stay low, hidden beneath the horizon, thinking that if I can get it to hold off long enough, we might have a chance at carving this night into stone.

I pray over and over throughout the night, while Maddie snores softly beside me for her to wake up without any regrets. I beg her to open her eyes and smile, knowing this is where she belongs.

We may not have been in love at first sight, but looking back now, I can see that her soul called out to me on that very first day. I couldn't hear the message yet, but I do now. I'm here and not going anywhere.

I used to think my parents were crazy for diving into marriage so early in their relationship, but now I get it. In years of dating, I've never once thought about marriage. I've longed for it, sure, but I have never been in a relationship that ever made it to the point of consideration. Yet, with Maddie, we aren't even in a relationship, and I'm ready to marry this girl.

As I run through everything in my head, I trace little circles around a cluster of freckles that paint her shoulder. The brush of my fingers on her bare skin makes her stir but only to burrow deeper into my neck, her arm draped over my chest and leg swung over mine. She sighs peacefully as she gets comfortable and drifts back into a sound sleep.

I know she struggles with nightmares, so I'm happy to see her resting undisturbed, from what I can tell. I would happily let her sleep in my bed every night and lay here to chase the monsters away if it meant she was healthy and getting needed sleep.

Eventually, sleep also claims me as the sun creeps through the curtains. I fall asleep holding onto the woman I love with nothing but faith that we will figure out how to navigate the challenges before us.

Hours later, I wake covered in sweat.

I'm burning up from my little heater. The sun is shining in full force through the window, blinding me. It takes a few moments for my corneas to chill out from the assault, but once they do; I become aware of Maddie, who is propped up on her elbows, watching me.

My little stalker.

"Hi." I flash her a smile, happy to see her still in bed with me. I half expected to wake up and find her gone.

She returns my smile with a radiant one of her own. "Hi."

Needing some form of contact, I pull her to me despite my discomfort over the heat permeating the room and plant a kiss on the tip of her rounded nose.

"How'd you sleep?" I ask.

"Amazing. Thanks for that."

"Not sure I did much, but you're welcome."

She looks like she wants to say something more, opens her mouth to do so, but then stops and closes it again, keeping her thoughts to herself. I want to push her to find out what it was, but I decide not to, for fear of scaring her away.

"You didn't tell me you sleep hot." I glance down at my sweat-covered chest, and her eyes follow. It's brief, but I catch the blaze of fire in her when she looks down at my body. I fucking love that.

"Care for a shower?" I ask.

Maddie doesn't hesitate to hop out of bed, letting the sheets drop to the floor. I'm surprised at the confidence she displays, but I am not complaining in the slightest at the opportunity to drink in her naked form in the light of day.

She's so damn perfect.

"Lead the way!"

I follow her instructions and peel myself from the bed, slipping on a pair of shorts and throwing a clean t-shirt in her direction. I have no idea what time it is, but I'm guessing late morning. I don't think either of us feels like giving Harleigh a show this morning.

Right before opening the door to the bedroom, I reach over and smack Maddie's bare ass, making her squeal. I don't think I will ever get enough of the freedom to touch her whenever and however I want.

Looking up and down the hallway, I'm pleased to find it void of any signs of life. My sister is either still holed up in her room downstairs, or maybe the plows have already been by and she went out this morning. I'm hoping for the latter.

I grab Maddie's hand and pull her toward the bathroom, giving the water a minute to warm up. While it does, I use the time to give her a proper good morning by lifting her onto the countertop and capturing her lips with mine.

She gasps, most likely from the cold marble that presses into her bare ass, but quickly loses herself to me. Her hands snake up my chest and wrap around the back of my neck. My fingers find their way under her shirt, pulling it back over her head and tossing it somewhere behind us.

I didn't intend for this to turn heated, but I can't seem to control my urges around her. I feel like a teenage boy again when Maddie is around.

She ends up being the one to pull away, smirking at me before shoving me backward, hopping off the counter and strutting to the shower, where she pulls the door open and steps behind the glass.

I happily follow.

We stand under the spray, her back to my front, my arms wrapped around her middle, head resting on her shoulder as the water cascades over us. It feels incredible for so many reasons.

"Oh my God, I knew it!" Maddie suddenly pulls away, snatching my body wash from the shelf and holding it over her head like a trophy.

"What on earth are you talking about?"

"This! Vanilla Bourbon. I knew it!"

I have to laugh. I love seeing her so carefree and happy about it, as much as I love that she's been smelling me, and I've been doing the same.

"Well, aren't you astute?" I lean in and kiss her again, my hands finding their way through the tangle of her wild curls to the root and grasping a fistful. I use the handful to move her like my own personal puppet, pulling her head back and giving me access to her throat. My lips trail over her skin, placing little kisses all around her neck, drinking in the soft little sighs that each kiss earns me.

"Watermelon," I say as I pull away from her.

"Huh?" Her eyes are half-hooded, still drunk with lust, while she blinks up at me.

"You always smell like watermelon."

"Oh, um, right. Yeah, that must be my shampoo. I've never paid attention. I buy the cheapest bottle."

Her words strike a chord. I have to physically bite my tongue to keep from saying anything.

If I've learned anything about Maddie, it's that she's fiercely independent and sometimes prideful. If I say anything about her financial situation, I get the feeling her mood would turn south pretty fast. So, I keep my mouth shut and reach for a bottle of girly shit my sister keeps in here to wash her hair with.

I take my time massaging the gel into her hair, running my fingers over her scalp and working the soap into her hair. By the time we finish, the water runs cold, sending us scrambling to get out before we freeze.

Maddie's giggle fills the bathroom by the time we finish. That sound is the final seal in my resolve to do whatever it takes to ensure Maddie and I have a future, even if it means throwing my career down the drain.

The job offer in Georgia has been playing around in the back of my mind since it was presented to me. I haven't given an answer yet and won't until Maddie and I have the chance to discuss it. I won't upend her life if it's not something she's entirely on board with. At this point, it could go either way.

Chapter Thirty-Nine

I WANTED TO RUN.

Boy did I want to run.

Waking up in Harrison's bed, his body molded to mine after everything that had happened over the last twenty-four hours, sent me into a panic. I got so far that I was slipping my shoes on, one hand on the doorknob while he slept peacefully ignorant feet away.

I stopped, though.

I don't know what it was other than looking back at him and feeling like if I opened that door and left, it would be the end of something that never had a chance to start. It felt like I was about to walk away from the only chance at a happy ending I would ever get.

So I didn't. I made the choice to be brave and bold, to be strong, to take control of my life, and to stop letting Andrew run the show.

I can't heal from him and the things he put me through if I don't stop letting the fear he inflicted in me have control over my life. So, I silently slipped my clothes off and climbed back into bed. The moment my body hit the mattress, Harrison's arm was around me, pulling me back close to him. I happily went along, plastering myself to his side with a smile, and fell back asleep.

Bea texted me late last night to give me a heads-up that she was shutting down the diner due to the weather. This gave me a day off to spend the weekend with him.

It was the happiest I have felt in probably forever. After our shower, Harrison made breakfast, which consisted of throwing frozen waffles in the toaster and chopping up fruit. Fine by me. I'm more of a coffee-for-breakfast person, anyway.

Harleigh emerged from her room sometime in the afternoon with a ridiculous, shit-eating grin on her face. She immediately wrapped an arm over both our shoulders and told us how happy she was. So, it's safe to say she knew what happened last night, minus the details. She's been calling me "sis" ever since. I roll my eyes each time, pretending not to love it.

I finally had to pry myself away late yesterday afternoon. I had a night shift at the diner, and I needed to do some dreaded laundry, polish off a few final projects due before winter break started in a few days, and, as much as I didn't want to, think through some things.

Harrison and I had gone from zero to sixty pretty damn fast, and my head needed a second to catch up to it all. I could tell Harrison had his concerns about letting me leave. I'm pretty sure he was worried I would change my mind, but waking up alone this morning reminded me of what was waiting for me a few blocks down the road.

I wasn't about to let that slip through my fingers.

Somehow, in such a short period, life had flipped on its axis in my favor for the first time since before I was born. Happiness was right there for me to reach out and grab. Sure, there were some details, pretty major ones at that, to work through. Those details weighed down a little heavier at the thought of sitting at a desk across from Harrison today and not kissing, touching, or undressing him with my eyes.

It's pretty hard to look a guy in the eye and pretend they mean nothing after a weekend of screaming their name. But I guess I would have to figure out how to do precisely that.

Despite a small amount of anxiety about today, I'm in a great mood as I drive to school. I've got the radio blasting, singing out my favorite songs, and enjoying how the snow clings to the branches of the trees, casting a perfect white blanket over everything in sight.

My phone pings from the passenger seat as I'm driving, and I can't help but take a glance. Along with three missed called and as many voicemails from an unknown number, is a text from Harrison. I ignore the missed calls and swipe open the text. I know I shouldn't be texting while driving but I can't seem to help myself from at least looking.

Harrison: Waking up without you this morning sucked. Stay with me tonight?

I pry my eyes away from the phone with a ridiculous smile still plastered on my face. Thankfully, nobody can see me on this deserted stretch of road, or my sanity might be called into question.

Something catches my attention from the corner of my eye.

A little white car is driving right alongside mine. I'm already going five over the speed limit, so the temptation to flip this person off is strong. *Pass me already, asshole.* I can't help but crane my neck to see if the person is as big of a jackass as I assume. The face doesn't register at first. My brain blocks it out as some kind of survival instinct.

I roll my eyes and turn my head back toward the road. The car is still driving right next to mine. Why isn't it passing me?

This time, when I look over, the dark-brown eyes staring back at me finally register. The blood drains from my face. My hands start to shake. I'm clammy and cold.

Andrew.

How could I not have seen this coming?

Oh, right, because the man is supposed to be in jail!

I have spent the last year and a half looking over my shoulder at every turn, jumping at every loud noise, and panicking at the slightest touch from other people. Yet, I can't say I ever honestly expected to come face-to-face with him again. Even knowing I would have to face him in court when that day finally came hasn't set in.

I dare to glance back over and see him frantically motioning with his hand.

He wants me to pull over.

I might, too; he would never hurt me, right?

But what would I say?

The look on his face is desperate, a little deranged.

It shouldn't surprise me, but it does.

The restraining order in my backpack screams at me. I was told to always have it with me, but now I can see how pointless that is. What is that damn little piece of paper ever going to do for me? It certainly wasn't enough to stop him from coming near me.

Why the FUCK is he out of jail?

Shit, my phone.

Where the hell did it go?

I have to pry a hand off the steering wheel, but don't dare take my eyes off the road. I use one hand to swat around at the seat next to me, hoping to connect with the silicone case.

Part of me thinks Andrew wouldn't do anything stupid, and another part wouldn't be surprised if he started veering his car over to force me off the road.

It's one of those things that I can't tell anymore.

What ends would he go to?

Finally!

My hand grasps my phone, and I glance down long enough to unlock it and find Harrison's name.

I bring it to my ear as the sound of it ringing blasts through the silence.

Please answer, please, please, please!

My eyes dart back and forth between the road and the raging lunatic beside me. He is still waving, pleading with me. I can see his lips move, but can't look long enough to figure out what he could be saying.

The only thing I can be sure of is the rage threatening to shred the mask he has kept so firmly in place since the moment I met him. He's trying to contain it, and a year ago, I don't think I would have picked up on it, but now, I can see the cracks. I can see small glimpses of what lies beneath. It scares the shit out of me.

I speed up, hoping I can lose him.

His speed increases right along with mine.

Where the hell is everyone? Why is there not a single car on this road?

I need somebody to come along and make him pull out of the wrong lane. I try slowing down, only for him to copy.

I should turn.

No, all the side roads lead to the middle of nowhere. That would be a stupid move.

"Morning, beautiful." Harrison's voice has never sounded so perfect.

"Help! I need help! What do I do, please? I'm so fucking scared." I keep my eyes trained forward. Looking over at Andrew only freaks me out more. I need to be calm. I need to think. Breathe.

"What do you mean? Maddie, are you okay? What's going on? Talk to me, baby."

I take another breath, slow my shaking voice and explain to him what's happening.

"You are doing great, okay. I know it's hard, but I need you to stay calm. Whatever you do, do not pull that car over. Promise me? Don't pull over. But I need you to hang up and call 911. Can you do that for me?"

"No," I sob. "Don't hang up! I need you. Please!"

"I know. But it's going to be okay. You are going to be okay, Maddie. Where are you? I need you to drive straight to me, okay? Straight to the south entrance by the teacher lot. Do you know where that is? Go straight there. Break as many fucking traffic laws as you need to but be safe. I will be right here and see you soon, but baby, you need to call the police. I need you to be strong and be brave. Hang up now and call them. You can call me right back."

It about kills me, but I do as he says. I get the number dialed and am talking to the operator when I notice the car beside me disappear.

I whip my eyes to the rearview mirror and see Andrew's car jerking to almost a stop, then he disappears. The tires screech as he whips his car around, flying off in the opposite direction.

I breathe a small sigh of relief, but the confusion doesn't let me relax too much. Andrew is among the most determined, competitive people I have ever met.

He doesn't give up.

Ever.

Who fucking cares?

He left, that's what matters.

Focus on driving. Get to Harrison. He will keep you safe.

I keep driving, slowing down my speed only slightly.

The sheriff I speak to starts asking questions. So many damn questions, and I start to panic again because I don't know the answers.

"What color was his car?"

"Um, white." I think.

"What make?"

I try picturing the little emblem on the front, but it's blurry. "I don't know."

"Model?"

"I don't know."

"License plate number?"

I don't know that either.

"What direction was he headed?"

"Dammit, I don't know!"

The opposite of whatever fucking direction I'm going. That was five minutes ago now; he could have turned eighty times by now.

"I don't know, okay!"

Tears pour down my face, and my body shakes with my uncontrollable sobbing.

The sheriff tries to direct me to their office, but I refuse. I tell them where I'm going, but I don't know if the man can understand me by now. I'm crying so hard my voice comes out in hiccups.

I fucked up.

I should have paid closer attention to the car, the details, where he went when he drove off. But I didn't, and I think I will hate myself forever for that. I don't need them reminding me of my incompetence.

I keep driving, and within five minutes, I'm peeling into the south parking lot, throwing the car in park right outside the sidewalk, my eyes landing on Harrison.

He stands outside the building despite the cold, pacing back and forth. His hands drag through his hair, pulling on the ends, making it stick up in all directions.

As I run toward him, I hear him swear and kick the side of the building, drawing the attention of several teachers walking past him.

Then he turns. His eyes land on mine.

They close and his body deflates, like he exhaled the breath he's been holding.

I keep running until I land with a thump against his chest. He falls to the ground with me in his arms, pulling me tightly against him, whispering in my ear, promising me that I'm safe. The words are as much for him as they are for me.

I suddenly feel his body stiffen, and he looks up, frantically checking the road behind me.

"He left. I don't know where," I whisper, though it takes up all my energy.

We sit on that sidewalk outside the school while people pass us, staring down and whispering.

I sob in his arms, and he holds me, stroking my hair, whispering in my ear that I'm safe, over and over and over.

I have no idea how long we sit here for. I'm numb everywhere, both from the cold and from my body shutting down.

Eventually, a car door slams nearby. Harrison lets me know it's a sheriff coming toward us. The man ushers the last remaining people inside, urging them toward the building and to their classes.

Harrison doesn't budge, and neither do I.

Chapter Forty

'VE ONLY EVER FELT fear like this once before. It's not a moment I ever wanted to relive and yet, when Maddie's frantic voice came through the phone, my entire body went cold. That sheer panic will haunt me for a long time to come.

My rage, sitting beneath the fear, is familiar—amplified. I haven't felt this angry in years, but I force myself to keep a lid on it and focus on my girl.

Waiting on those cracked cement stairs, not knowing what was happening and whether Maddie was safe, made up the longest ten minutes of my life.

I'm proud of myself for managing to call Wyatt. He didn't answer, and I got stuck with his voicemail. I can't imagine that whatever words left my mouth made a damn lick of sense, so I have to hope I gave enough for him to find me.

By the time Maddie's car comes flying into the lot, I'm on the verge of losing my mind.

I don't think about who might see us as we sit on the freezing pavement, dusted in a layer of snow. I still can't bring myself to move when I see a man in a brown uniform and a ridiculous hat. I walked away from Fallon ten years ago and the regret of that has consumed me every day since. As stupid and irresponsible and reckless as it might be, I won't do that again with Maddie. Nothing is worth leaving her alone right now, not even my career.

My ass is numb and sopping wet from the snow melting beneath our bodies. I can't imagine what this guy must see in us as he approaches. If he's a halfway decent cop, he's figured out that I'm a teacher or at least work here and that Maddie is not, but once again, I don't give a damn. They can haul me out of here in cuffs so long as she is safe.

If he does think twice about it, he doesn't say anything. Once he clears the crowd, I reluctantly pull myself and Maddie off the ground to face him. Her eyes are still filled with terror, and it takes everything I have to step aside when the guy asks to talk to her alone.

"Let's go inside at least," I suggest. "There is a meeting room inside the door you can use. Maddie, I can come with you or wait outside. It's your call."

Wyatt chooses that moment to come bursting from the heavy metal doors. For a man his size, he sure runs fast.

"Maddie, what the hell is going on? Harrison? Somebody tell me what the hell happened!" he demands, slightly breathless.

"Let's go inside and talk now, please. Sir, can you show us that room? I would strongly prefer to speak with her alone. But I can have a female officer down here in a few minutes to sit in if that would make you more comfortable," the man says to both Maddie and me. His tone is calm, and his actions are considerate. I trust him as much as I can at a time like this, but this is Maddie's choice. If she wants me to stay, he's going to have to drag me out of there by my ankles.

I nod to the man and lead the way inside, placing my hand on the small of Maddie's back as we walk.

Let them see.

She is the only thing I care about right now. Her body trembles in my arms. I can assume it's from the morning's adrenaline rushing through her veins.

Our walk inside the building is silent, and not in a comfortable way. My nerves are on edge. I want to take Maddie home and hold her.

We reach the room where I hold the door open for them to go in and flick on the lights when Vice Principal Gill comes barreling down the hallway as fast as his stumpy little legs can carry him.

I really hate this guy.

He sweats profusely—he carries a little rag around that he wipes across his face every five minutes. The smell of sweat can announce his presence before he rounds a corner. It's disgusting.

His balloon-inflated face looks ready to explode as he stomps toward us. It takes everything in me not to march up to him and shut whatever words are about to come out of his sloppy mouth before he can form them. I don't imagine anything he will say is going to be pleasant.

Before I act, Wyatt steps in and intervenes. He holds out his hand to stop me before I take a step in the man's direction. "I'll handle this."

He meets Gill in a few strides, stopping him in his tracks and forcing the plump little man to crane his neck to look Wyatt in the eye. Since Wyatt knows him far better than I do and has a better rapport, I gladly let him handle this one, at least for now.

While I wait, I continue pacing the hall. Back and forth, back and forth. I feel entirely helpless, and I hate it. The waiting also gives me time to stew, and my anger quickly builds.

After about fifteen minutes—though it feels like an eternity—Wyatt returns to the hall. Gill stomps off in the opposite direction, but I can't read either one of them.

"I need details. What the fuck happened this morning?" Wyatt demands when he reaches me.

I fill him in on what little I know. I fill him in on the weekend, which might be a mistake, but he's my best friend, and I won't hide this from him. I don't want to hide it from anybody. I want to climb up onto the roof of this building and proclaim to the world that I'm in love with Madalynn Klein.

He listens intently, taking in every word I say with a straight face and calm demeanor. I could never maintain myself. I don't consider myself a hothead; it takes a lot to get me fired up, but when I care about something, I'm passionate, and that passion can lead to intense anger. This time it's warranted, so I don't feel bad about it.

I hadn't planned on sleeping with Maddie. At least not yet, so I wouldn't blame my friend for ripping me a new asshole over that one, but he doesn't. I think he knows how much I care for her, and while he might be pissed, he gives me the benefit of the doubt.

Once he understands the situation, we use the opportunity to discuss the next steps. After today, I don't want to let Maddie out of sight. Especially if we don't know what is happening with this fucking Andrew clown or where he could be.

"Did they catch up with him? Arrest him again? I heard this morning that he had been released over the weekend. I didn't want to worry Maddie until I could sit down and talk to her in person. Jesus, I should have done something!" He's worried, too, and since he knows far more about the situation than I do, that makes me feel worse.

We both fall silent and wait.

Maddie and the sheriff finally emerge from the room. He gives Wyatt and I each a curt, somber nod, then shows himself out. Maddie lunges herself back into my arms.

No matter what happens, I'm not going anywhere.

CHAPTER FORTY-ONE

HOW IS IT ONLY eight a.m.?

I want to crawl back into bed and sleep, pretending this day never happened. I've had my share of hard days, but I think this one takes the cake. My emotions are all over the place, and adrenaline still surges through my veins. I have never felt fear like that in my life.

Harrison hasn't left my side, no matter how bad that can come back to bite him in the ass later. He picks up where I can't and refuses to let me fall.

What now?

Do I go to class now and continue my day as if this morning didn't happen? Going home sure as hell isn't an option. The thought of Andrew there waiting for me scares the shit out of me.

I'm not sure how I'm ever going to feel safe again. I don't know how he knew where I lived. I chose that apartment long after contact had been cut off, and I can't imagine him getting my address from anyone with half a brain. I don't understand—one more mystery to add to the list.

Either way, where does this all leave me?

I don't get the chance to consider it for long.

Officer Ingles had disappeared from the building when I look over and catch him turning back around. He walks straight toward us again. Did he think of more questions?

I can't imagine there is anything else I can tell him. I could hardly answer the questions he already asked me, so what else could there possibly be? Or maybe he is now registering Harrison and me, so he's coming back to deal with that issue.

Fuck, no. Please don't do that. Turn around and go on your way. Please.

He approaches me slowly, and I brace for the worst.

"Miss, I don't know how to tell you this…" Nothing could have prepared me for his next words. "We found Andrew Garrison. Best we can tell, he pulled off the road into that old parking lot on the side of Highway 4. Madalynn, you're safe now. He can't hurt you anymore."

They got him! But how can he stand here and tell me I'm safe? I was supposed to be safe before. He was in jail and look what happened!

How am I supposed to believe it won't happen again? Black dots start to dance in my vision. My ears pick up a high-pitched ringing.

I don't understand what's happened.

Except, somewhere in my brain, I do. I don't want to accept it. His words start clicking together.

No.

That's not...

He couldn't have.

Holy fuck.

"I don't think I...I don't understand. What are you saying?" I need to hear them say it.

Harrison inhales a sharp breath behind me and pulls me tight to his chest. His hold feels like it's holding up all my weight. I can't tell. I can't feel my legs. I think he knows I am seconds from crumbling.

The ringing gets louder. I pick up on fragmented words. "Self-inflicted. Instant. Murder. Suicide. Kept driving. Saved your life..."

No. No. No. That can't be possible. This can't be happening. I don't—

The darkness pulls me down, and it all goes blissfully quiet.

I don't know how long I've been down. It feels like hours, and it feels like seconds. I start to come to, feeling something hard propping up my head. One small inhale, and I know who it is. Harrison. My head is resting on his thigh as he sits in the middle of the hallway, acting as my human pillow.

When I muster the strength to open my eyes, Wyatt and Officer I Forgot His Name are crouched down over me.

Harrison is the first to notice my consciousness. His finger runs down my cheek with more care than I have ever felt. "Guys, give her some space."

It's probably the last thing I should be thinking about at a time like this, and yet, Harrison is the loudest thought among thousands running through my head right now. He's been a rock through this entire clusterfuck of a day. I didn't think when I called him. I was in a completely panicked, fight-or-flight state, and yet, he was my first call. That has to mean something. He is the only person I want by my side right now. Not to say I don't appreciate Wyatt and love him in my own way, but it's different.

What we have is worth fighting for. That is clearer at this moment than it ever has been. Harrison is worth every risk. He hasn't walked away yet, and while it might still be pretty early in the day, he doesn't appear to be leaving my side anytime soon. That gives me hope amid the new worst day of my life.

Wyatt clears his throat, gathering our attention. "We might want to think about moving this to a private space. Classes will be released soon, and I don't think we need to add...well, you know." He gives Harrison a look over my head.

A silent conversation plays out between the two, but that's fine. I trust them both, so whatever they are saying, they don't think I need to hear. Again, that's fine by me. I wouldn't mind not having another person talk to me the rest of the day.

Whatever it is might have something to do with getting sheriff guy out of here. Interestingly, he can tell there is something between Harrison and me—it's not like we have been subtle today—and yet, he hasn't once commented or looked at us with concern of disgust or anger. I can't say I understand that, but I'm not going to look a gift horse in the eye or whatever the fuck that weird saying is.

He seems to get the hint. He kindly reminds me that I have his card and tells me to call him if I have any more questions or need anything.

Wyatt holds out a hand, helping me to my feet. *Wait, how is Harrison here with me and not teaching his class? Fuck, was he fired already? Holy shit, did I ruin his life? Fuck!*

By the time we cross the threshold of Wyatt's office, I'm spiraling again. Fast. The thoughts my brain had been filtering out start slamming into me all at once—so many terrifying questions. The image of Andrew's brain splattered against the window of his car has me dry-heaving.

I haven't caught my breath when the words from minutes ago start to come through whatever filter I had up. Murder? Lucky to be alive? Holy fuck. They think he was going to kill me. Could he? Would he?

Yes.

That isn't even a question anymore. How I went from assuming he would never hurt me to being so sure that had today's events gone differently, they would be scraping my body from that car too—I turn and empty the minimal contents of my stomach in the trash can at my feet.

How many times had he threatened to kill himself if I left him? I should have seen this coming. I should have warned somebody. I should have fucking known! How did I not know?

I never thought he was serious, though. I thought he was being dramatic. I was very, very wrong.

Maybe if I had pulled the damn car over, he would still be alive? I hadn't wanted ever to see him again, but that didn't mean I wanted his death on my conscience. Had I never walked through the door of that house and came into his life, he might still be here. How am I supposed to deal with the weight of that?

And yet, a horrible part of me is relieved. No more looking over my shoulder, worrying about facing him in court and reliving every moment of those years I would rather forget about. No more sleepless nights waiting for that knock on my door or the text to ping through on my phone.

Wyatt is the first to break the silence. "Maddie, I can't begin to understand how you must be feeling right now ..."

"No!" I scream. I have officially lost my ever-loving mind. Nothing makes sense. My thoughts spin in circles, chasing each other around and around.

"You don't get it! Nobody fucking gets it! You all keep painting me as this pathetic victim. Why can't you stop for one goddamn moment and consider that I'm as sick and twisted as him? I loved him! Do you understand that? I fucking loved that man! Jesus, at least I thought I did. I thought we were together. A relationship. We were partners, equals." My emotions crash inside me, clashing against one another, building up so much energy I can't contain it. My arm swings out, sending the lamp on Wyatt's desk flying across the room. The cord jolts it back before it can smash into the wall, and the object clatters to the floor instead.

"Sure, there were bad times, but what relationship doesn't have that? Now that it's all over, I still don't know what to think. I hate him, so why is there this disgusting part of me that still loves him? How can I be sad he is gone? And also happy at the same time?

"I keep hearing that word...rape. He abused me. I'm a victim or survivor or whatever name people want to use, but it doesn't feel right. That doesn't fit because I'm as guilty.

"You have no idea how many times a day I sit and wonder if he loved me. I wonder if it was a lie like everybody tells me, or if it was genuine. Maybe he never meant to hurt me. Maybe he loved me. People love people they shouldn't all the damn time! I want to know if any of it was real. Am I only now questioning that because I have other voices telling me what to think?"

A humorless laugh spills from my lips. I sound deranged. "I will never know now, though, will I? Because he is dead, and it's all my fault. I came into his life and ruined it. I might as well have pulled the trigger myself." My lungs burn, and tears blur my vision.

I might throw up again.

"But I also feel so fucking angry! How dare he? How dare he get to take the fucking cowardly, easy way out and leave me here to deal with this alone? Why do I have to pay the price of what he did? It's not fucking fair!" I cry. Tears pour down my face, splashing against the toes of my sneakers.

Every unspoken word that I have bottled up for months, hell, for years, spills from me without any thought. I can't believe I'm saying this out loud, but I can't help it. I can't think enough to stop the word vomit that keeps spilling out. I don't know if I believe what I'm saying.

Something heavy flies across the room and shatters. It jerks my awareness back to the present and forces me to focus on the two men still in the room.

"Dammit, Maddie! Is that what you have been holding back this entire time? Why didn't you tell me sooner?" Wyatt yells.

Wait, what?

He should be throwing me out the door, calling that sheriff back here to arrest me. At the least, I should be met with a face full of disgust at what I admitted.

"Maddie, don't you realize that when they took your phone, every single text, email, note, and photo became evidence? It was poured over by several people and then filed into a report given to me, among others. You never considered that we didn't already know all of that?"

"I...um. No."

Wyatt takes a loud, deep breath. I see him gathering his thoughts, deciding how to proceed or what to say to me. He leans forward, hands on his desk, bent at the waist, and meets my eyes.

"Let me ask you this: How did things start with him?"

Oh, hell no. There is absolutely no way in fuck that is happening!

"Safe space, Maddie. No judgment. Nothing you say leaves this room. It's important, okay? I need you to do this. Be strong," Wyatt says.

"I...I don't remember exactly." I have to stop and think, sorting through so many memories. "I guess the first time I can remember something feeling...odd, I suppose, was this conversation about favorite movies. I think I had been living with him for a month or two. Maybe less."

"Tell me what the conversation was. What did he say, what did you say, who started it?"

I inhale and close my eyes, forcing my brain back into that moment. I can picture where I was sitting and the scene on the TV before me. I remember the feeling in my stomach.

"We were talking, chatting and trying to get to know one another. I thought he was trying to make me feel more at home. It was weird for me. Nobody had ever cared enough to ask me what I liked or didn't like. Um, then he asked my favorite kind of movie. I remember thinking how odd it was to phrase it like that. He didn't ask what my favorite movie was. But what kind of movie." I rub my hands over my face, dreading the next part. Is he going to make me keep going?

The nod I get answers my unasked question. "I don't know what my answer was. It wasn't important—maybe romance or drama. I don't know. But then I asked for his answer."

I don't want to continue, but Wyatt urges me to continue. "Porn. That was the answer. I think it was 'tits and ass' specifically. Zero hesitation. He said it like he would have said action or horror."

I can't look Wyatt in the eyes. It's too embarrassing and so uncomfortable. In my attempt to look anywhere but, I notice the veins in his arms bulging, his fists are balled tight, and then he slams one down against the desk, rattling the entire thing.

"How old?" he grits out through clenched teeth.

"Huh?"

"How. Old. Were. You."

It takes every ounce of strength to mutter, "Twelve." The room grows eerily silent. I hold my breath, waiting to see what happens next. But I get it. I get why he made me go there.

I've often thought about how I never stopped it at the beginning. At the time, the churning in my gut told me it wasn't normal for him to say that to me. So why didn't I tell anybody?

I hate the answer as much as I hate myself for not doing anything. I was desperate to be loved. I wanted a family. I wanted to be happy and normal. Up until that moment, and even directly after, Andrew gave me attention. I was his primary focus, especially once his wife started traveling more. He took me to do things. He called me pretty. He made me feel good about myself for the first time.

"He apologized as soon as he said that. He told me he was sorry. I thought it was a slip. Like he forgot who he was talking to or didn't know how to talk to a pre-teen girl. It was a simple mistake."

Wyatt's hand curls tighter around the edge of the desk.

"Next. What's the next thing you remember happening? Or the next time a conversation or action stood out as strange?"

I have to think about it again. I can't say if this was the next thing to happen and if it was if it was hours, days, or weeks later. That entire time is such a blur.

"It was about a dream. Um, he told me he hadn't slept well because he had a weird dream. At first, he told me it was about him helping me wash my hair. I found that weird, but I told him it was fine. I fed him his own excuse about seeing me as a daughter. It's normal to help your kids do stuff like that." I stop there, afraid to continue.

Of course, looking back now, I realize it was a disgusting thing to say to a kid. But I didn't see myself as a kid at the time. I was constantly being told how mature I was for my age. Adults and teachers would comment on it all the time. It was easier to talk to people in their thirties than it was to my peers.

I suppose that was one thing I liked about Andrew, too. He treated me like an adult instead of dismissing me as a kid.

"Then what?"

I huff, wanting to be done talking about it. Acid burns in my stomach, creeping its way up my throat until my mouth is filled with disgusting bile. "He started pushing a little further. Suddenly, he apologized because I was in the shower, not the bath. I think I said so what, or something like that. That's when he finally added the part about him washing my hair in the shower with me. I guess that was probably the biggest turning point."

"Explain. Turning point for what?"

I raise my eyebrows at him, starting to get annoyed now. He knows what. Why is he making me do this?

"I don't know, Wyatt! What do you want me to say? That was the day I opened the door and painted a huge fucking target on my back? The moment when I put a flashing sign that told him how easy I would be to manipulate? How desperate I was to be loved that I would let him do or say anything he wanted? Jesus! I was stupid and gullible and so fucking desperate for love and affection and acceptance.

"Andrew let me be whoever the hell I wanted! I could say anything, do anything, and push as many limits as possible, and it was all okay. He let me and told me I was normal. Told me we were right, and the world was wrong. He never judged a single thought or word I said, even when I would purposely say the most ridiculous or crazy things to test him.

"He told me how common relationships like ours were. He said people didn't talk about it because they couldn't. He challenged my mind and made me wonder why eighteen was this magical number that permitted people to love, die, and do as they wanted. He challenged society and morals and values. He made me think, and I liked it! I didn't see that he was only pretending to open my eyes; he was only opening them to his warped reality. It was all a lie. I get it, okay!

"I was the center of his universe and reveled in it. It felt so damn good, so no matter how uncomfortable I was, no matter how sick I felt, I never walked away. I stayed because I liked feeling like I mattered!"

It all spills out like lava, leaving me an empty shell. I can't hold my body up anymore. I fall to the floor in a puddle of flesh and bone. It's hard to tell if I'm crying anymore. My face is numb. My limbs are mush. I just finished a boxing match and came out the sore loser.

"I know you don't want to hear this, but I have to say it because you *need* to hear it. What you just described is the very definition of grooming. Even the most typical teen who grew up in a stable and loving home goes through this massive shift at that age where your entire identity is called into question. That leaves you vulnerable. It's when you start experimenting with who you are and the person you want to be. It's a prime age for hormones, crazy emotions, and peer pressure is at an all-time high. It's the perfect storm for a predator like Andrew. They know that, feed on it, and use it to get inside your head.

"Maddie, you've always been smart, and he knew that. He knew that he had to sandwich those bad moments in a hell of a lot of good ones. The more he showered you with compliments, praise, and attention, the smaller the other stuff would be.

"You were taken advantage of because you are a good person with a kind heart. Even if you swear more than anybody I have ever known and have that tough shell around you, you want to believe the best in people. It's a good thing, and you did nothing wrong. It's people like that who are wrong, sweetheart."

Everything he says makes sense. At the time, I felt so grown up, and now, looking back, it's painfully evident that twelve is still very much a child.

It's so obvious if I think about it in terms of anyone else. So why is it so hard for me to apply that to myself? Why can't I give myself the same love I could give Kenna, Harleigh, or almost anyone else?

"It will take time, but you will move past this. It's hard to see now, but there will be a day when you don't think about it. Then it will be a week, and eventually, you will get to a point where you only think about this time in your life at certain moments, and I hope you can start to see how hard you have fought along the way. I want you to look back and be proud of yourself for all you have survived and accomplished.

"I can tell you from experience that hardship changes people, and often, it's not for the better. For many, the pain is too much. You are an incredibly strong woman who will get through this. Fight like hell to reclaim your life. I have no doubt you are on the path to doing that. Don't give up, Maddie."

Wyatt's words draw tears from my eyes. I want to believe him so badly, and maybe there is a piece of me that does. It's buried under a massive amount of rubble. I think Wyatt is telling me it's time to start digging.

It's only now, though, that I remember Harrison. He's still in the room, so he heard everything I said.

Every. Single. Word.

Chapter Forty-Two

I HAVE TO LEAVE the room and I hate myself for that. It's the last thing I want to do to Maddie. I wish I were strong enough, but I can't be in here a second longer. I'm going to fucking explode. I know she needs me. I know I need to say something to reassure her. I know I should be showering her with calming words or love or holding steady right here for her.

I can't do it.

Every part of me is shaking; my body physically vibrating with the rage I'm trying like hell to shove down long enough to get out of this room. I need to make it outside. I can't be in the stuffy building for one more second, or I'm going to burn the goddamn place down.

On second thought, I change paths and storm into the weight room. There is a punching bag in there that can take the blows of my anger.

I beat the shit out of it.

Her words play repeatedly in my head with every punch, and I take all of it out on the heavy swaying bag before me.

My knuckles bleed. I may have broken a finger, but I don't fucking care.

With every swing, I imagine myself beating into Andrew. I want to beat him until he stops breathing.

Just like I almost did with Hudson.

I've lived with the regret of that night for ten years. And here I am making the same mistake with Maddie. But maybe it's not too late. I can still go back in that room and be there for her the way I wish I had been there for Fallon, even when she had long since stopped breathing.

I have to do better.

I don't know how to do it yet, but I'm dead set on learning whatever it takes to make sure she gets through this. That starts with apologizing for walking out and promising never to do it again. I need to be sure she understands that my actions had nothing to do with her and everything to do with making sure she didn't witness that explosion. I need her to know it won't happen again.

I will never walk away from her again.

When I push that heavy metal door back open, Wyatt gives me the deadliest look I have ever received. I fucked up by walking off, but I'm here to fix it.

"I'm sorry about that. I needed to clear my head for a minute, but I swear it's not because of you, baby." I kneel before Maddie, taking her hands into mine, pleading with her with my eyes to understand. "I promise to ensure that my anger never interferes with being there for you, okay? I know it's not an excuse, but I was just so fucking livid at the idea of somebody hurting you like that. Imagine how you would feel if it were our daughter. I know you're not my child, but, fuck, this isn't coming out right.

"I love you, Maddie. That's what I'm trying to say. I love you."

Well, that was bad timing. I had no intention of dropping the L word on her today of all days. I've wanted to say it, but I've held off.

I was waiting.

For good damn reason.

I didn't want the first time I told her to be under circumstances like this. Or in a school office. With my hulking best friend hovering over us. Talk about romantic.

I'm bracing myself to get punched, slapped, screamed at—all the above.

Instead, Maddie flies from the chair, dropping to her knees with me, and flings herself into my arms. She buries her head in my neck and inhales.

She sniffs me.

Weirdo.

I fucking love it.

I will do everything I can to help Maddie learn to love herself. Then, I hope that she will be able to love me, too.

Chapter Forty-Three

I'VE SURVIVED SEVEN DAYS.

One week since the worst day of my life.

It still doesn't feel real most of the time. I haven't begun to wrap my head around everything that has happened. What I have done, though, is cry.

A lot.

I'm so sick of crying.

My pillowcase is hardened with snot, and it's fucking disgusting. I let myself have time to wallow, grieve, and be angry. The shattered glass still littering the floor by my bed is evidence of that. But I also promised myself that today was the day I get up and reclaim my life.

Today is the day I start fighting for myself.

Harrison has kindly given me my space. No matter how many times I have wanted to call, text, or beg him to come lie with me, I have refrained. I needed this time to worry about myself. It was my way of finally practicing some self-care.

I try not to worry about how much mental and emotional work I will have to do. It will take time, and as much as I want to empty the garbage bag on the floor and start digging through it all at once, I know it doesn't work that way.

I can't tackle a lifetime's worth of pain overnight. If there is one thing I have learned, it's that trauma has a way of creeping into the moments you aren't expecting it. For that reason, I think it will be years before I uncover all those triggers and deal with all that pain I have shoved down for so long.

I'm ready, though, as much as I can be.

My goals for today are getting out of bed, cleaning up that damn glass, washing my bedding, and maybe a shower.

I sniff myself.

Yup, definitely a shower.

I know I left a shitshow in my wake. My phone chimes with unread messages, emails, calls, and voicemails every five minutes, and I ignore every single one. One of the voicemails let me know that the police have some additional questions. Yay.

Another four are from Wyatt, asking me to provide proof of life. He also says he has some stuff to talk to me about, but mostly wants to make sure I'm okay. Kenna knows better than to call me, so I have forty-nine unread texts from her. I'm scared to look and face her wrath. For somebody so happy, she sure can be scary.

And then there is Harrison.

Part of the reason I've avoided him is that I don't want to face the damage I've done when it comes to him. I dread the moment he tells me he no longer has a job because of me. He won't say the "because of you" part, but I'll hear it, anyway. I never intended to ruin his career or his life, for that matter, and I'm struggling with the feeling that that is exactly what I have done. If I had stayed away from him...

Nope, stop. Don't go there, Maddie. We are done with that shit.

I finally muster up the strength to stand and damn. Muscles I didn't know I had scream. Everything aches from not moving for days. As I step into the shower, the hot water instantly starts to work its magic, relaxing my body and washing at least some of my pain down the drain. It also washes away the funk that has started coming from me. Gross.

I stand under the spray for at least half an hour, letting the healing power of the water do its thing on my aching body. By the time I turn the knob to the off position and step out, the mirror is coated in the thick fog that fills the bathroom.

As I'm wrapping a towel around my body and cinching it tight at my chest, I start hearing a pounding on the door that makes me jump and almost slip on the wet floor.

Thankfully, I avoid cracking my skull open and can creep slowly to the door and look out the peephole. My long, sopping hair leaves a trail of water behind me, since I didn't get to throw it up in a towel yet. I try to keep the panic at bay, but can't deny the relief I feel when I find Harrison staring at me through the door.

I unlock the doorknob and the deadbolt slowly. He might not be scary compared to the alternative, but I can't say I love the idea of facing him right now. I had been avoiding this for a reason. The idea of disappointing the man I love churns my stomach with guilt.

I step out of the doorframe, motioning for him to enter, since I can't find the courage to speak. What am I supposed to say in a situation like this? *Sorry, I got you fired. Sorry, I ruined your life?*

I don't need to worry about what to say because Harrison barrels through the door, cups my face, and slams his lips to mine.

It's the most alive I have felt in days. My body lights up from his touch. It reminds me I'm still here and have something to live for, something to fight for, something to keep me pushing through these awful days because if these tiny moments with Harrison are any indication, there is so much potential for happiness for the two of us. His kiss fills me with hope, so I cling to it like a little baby spider monkey.

I kiss him back, matching his fever, and we get lost in the moment. We float above all of our problems, the world, and life. Every voice telling me it won't work, it's wrong, or I'm too broken for him is silenced.

By the time we part, I'm breathless, my cheeks and lips swollen and raw from the slight scratching of his beard. It's a sensation I have quickly grown to love.

"Um, I should probably go throw some clothes on."

Harrison growls. "If you must."

I scurry off, narrowly avoiding my water trail and falling on my ass again. I snatch the first clothes I find in a pile near the dresser, stepping into the bathroom to change. My hair has dried into a frizzy mess by now. That's what happens when it goes without product or a hairbrush.

I gather the tangled mess and wrap a hair tie around it, securing it to the top of my head as usual. I skip any form of makeup and go right to getting dressed. I grab an old, faded pair of plaid pajama shorts and a t-shirt. Looking down, the shirt makes me laugh.

It's my butter shirt—literally a yellow t-shirt with a giant stick of butter across the front. I saw it one day and knew I had to have it. It was absolutely ridiculous, which I love.

As I exit the bathroom, Harrison sees my shirt and chuckles. I'm filled with a silly sense of pride and happiness that he noticed.

"I would offer you something to drink, but I only have tap water. Pretty sure I can't do that because I have no clean glasses either..." I fidget, pick at the skin around my nail beds, cross and uncross my legs, bounce on the balls of my feet. I'm awkward. That won't likely be changing anytime soon.

Harrison motions to the couch. "Can we sit?"

"Shit, yeah, sorry." I glance around, embarrassed that he is seeing my place like this. "Sorry for the mess. It's been, well, you know. I usually keep it clean."

"Babe, it's fine. I don't care about that. I'm so fucking happy to see you. I've been worried sick. We all have." He strokes my cheek lovingly.

"We?" I question.

"Yes, we. Wyatt, Kenna, me."

Right. "So, how bad?"

Harrison gets a nervous look on his face, which makes me sweat. "We should probably talk about that. I am sorry for barging over here like this. I know you were ignoring us all for a reason, and I swear I wanted to honor that need for time and distance, but after a week of not hearing from you, I was starting to get scared, Maddie. I can't lose you."

"Shit, I hadn't considered that. I'm so sorry, but please know I would never do...that. I'm not going anywhere. The thought never crossed my mind, and I wouldn't do that to you. I didn't mean to scare everyone. I am sorry about that. My head was in an ugly place, and I knew I needed to spend some time alone, facing my feelings and whatnot. I also didn't have it in me to face you yet," I admit.

"Why me? I mean, I have to assume I got you fired, right?"

Harrison chuckles, and it throws me completely off. Can't say I was expecting that sort of reaction.

"I will be the first to admit things are complicated, but Wyatt and I have come up with a plan, and in the last few days, we have been busy putting together the pieces to make it all come together. If you are interested, that is. That's what we need to talk about."

In the hundred different ways this conversation has played out in my head the last several days, none of them were remotely close to this one. It's leaving me feeling a bit lost and confused.

"Alright, so what's the master plan you speak of?"

Before he answers, Harrison reaches over and pulls me closer to him, settling my legs across his lap. His fingers drag along my legs, and I cringe, remembering I haven't shaved in over a week. He doesn't seem to mind, but, ew.

"Alright, so, have you ever considered online classes? Wyatt thinks it would be a good fit for you and was already planning to propose the idea since he has been working with the administration team at the school to get a program in place for online learning. If you are interested, he is already prepared for you to help pilot the program with him, work out the kinks, and report on what works and what doesn't. It's been approved already so all you have to do is say yes. But only if it's what you want to do."

"Yes. Done, yes. I hate that school so damn much. That sounds perfect! But what about you? Does that mean you get to keep your job?"

"Sort of. They can't prove that anything is going on between us. I'm sure you will get questions about it, so I guess that could change, but Wyatt was able to downplay what everybody saw last week. I don't love that because I hate denying us. Either way, I was advised that it might be in my best interest to find a different position somewhere else, but we are at the end of the term anyway, so I will finish the last few days and then, well, that's the other big thing we need to talk about." Harrison rubs his hand along the back of his neck and then looks nervously back at me.

"You know my parents moved to Georgia, and Harleigh, and I have been toying with the idea of moving there since before I met you. My dad called a while back and had this job opportunity for me, and well, I did a virtual interview. The job is mine if I accept. But I won't do it or make the move without you. I know that is a huge step, and it's asking a lot. I don't want us to rush this, and I don't want you to feel pressured, so please take all the time you need and think about it, okay? We make this decision together."

Holy shit.

Seriously, holy shit.

I can't believe the things I'm hearing right now. He wants me to move to freaking Georgia with him? Is he that serious about this?

"I know this is a ridiculous question, especially right now, but does that mean we are dating? Boyfriend and girlfriend sound like we're ten, but I don't know what to call it."

Harrison doesn't respond immediately, but he pulls me closer once again, bringing me so that I'm sitting on his lap, straddling his thighs, facing him. He cups my face and gives me a light kiss.

"I don't know how to say this without freaking you out, Maddie, but you are the only person I want to spend my life with. I know it's early, which is crazy, but I believe in soul mates. When you know, you know, and baby, you are it for me. I can't promise things will always be perfect. Every relationship faces hurdles and challenges, and they all require hard work. But I want to do that work together, every day, for the rest of our lives. I want the good, the bad and every mundane moment between you."

"Yes." It's the only word I can manage to say.

"Yes?" he questions.

"Yes to all of it. Yes to Georgia, yes to living with you, yes."

I just said that. And I meant it, too.

"Wait! Oh my God, I need to ask you this first."

Harrison instantly gets concerned. "Okay, what is it?"

"What's wrong with you? I mean that completely seriously, too. Do you chew with your mouth open, snore loud, serial killer, meth addict? What's the catch here?" I am only partly joking.

He laughs at me but does consider my question. I respect that. "I hate dogs."

I bolt off his lap, standing up before him. "You're joking. Tell me you are joking?"

"Dead serious. See this scar here?" He points to the small mark under his left eye that I have wondered about several times before. "I was playing in the park when I was little, and this dog ran up and attacked me out of nowhere. Been scared of them ever since."

"Oh, come on. I'm sure it didn't attack you for no reason! Dogs are the best; they are so sweet. Who doesn't like dogs?"

"Well, there may have been a hot dog involved that I refused to give up, but still. It was my hot dog, and he tried to eat my face over it! As a four-year-old, that's some scary shit. I had nightmares for weeks. I had to sleep in my parents' bed and refused to return to that park for the entire summer. Haven't eaten a hot dog since then either."

He's lucky he has a semi-valid reason for being a dog-hater. I do have to laugh, though. We are totally getting a puppy.

"So, is that it? Any other horrifying confessions you want to lay on me?"

He smiles again and rubs the back of his neck. "No more crazy confessions, but Maddie, I'm far from perfect. I'm a man and I am working on letting go of my brother's sins but I still have plenty of my own. I have a handle on it, but I still have all this anger inside of me that sometimes doesn't come out in the best ways. I've broken a lot of dishes, punched a lot of walls, that sort of thing."

He sighs again. "Aside from that, I can't cook to save my life. I never remember to put the toilet seat down. Ask Harleigh; that one drives her crazy. I'm overly tidy, which sounds like a good thing, but not when it means I can't fall asleep until the dishes are done or I can't relax until things are cleaned up. It annoys me at times, so I know it annoys others. I have my faults, trust me. I'm sure you do as well.

"So no, Maddie, I'm far from perfect. But I think every one of us has room for growth. I want to do better and be better for and with you. That is what love is in my eyes. Two people who bring out the best in each other and push and challenge one another to strive for more." Tears blur my vision, streaming down my fast as he continues to talk.

"If there is one thing I have learned through my parents, it's that love takes work. A lot of it. It requires constant communication, even when that's hard. It means being open and honest, respecting one another and being committed to making it work. There will be fights or disagreements, and we might face moments when we want to throw in the towel. The difference between couples that work and those that don't is that the ones that last are the ones who decide on day one that divorce is off the table. No matter the problem, they have the commitment to one another to figure it out together, no matter how tough times get. That's what I want with you, Maddie. That's our future."

I can't find the right words to respond to that. I never imagined anything so perfect being said to me, of all people.

I also happen to agree wholeheartedly.

It might be hard for somebody like me to imagine that love like that exists because I have never once witnessed it, but there is a hopeless romantic buried within me that latches on to that idea and insists that it can exist if I want it to. Besides, I have seen a good handful of couples well into their eighties and nineties come into the diner, share a cup of coffee and pie, sit on the same side of the booth, and hold hands. There is no faking a love like that.

"Am I allowed to admit that the idea scares me? I want that more than anything, and I think it's possible, but it almost sounds too perfect. My head is still so messed up, Harrison. I haven't begun to process everything from these last few years, and that won't happen quickly. I can't promise I won't get all looney tunes at times. More so here in the beginning. It doesn't feel fair to trap you into all that crazy." My voice trembles as the words tumble from me.

"Oh babe, you are not trapping me. I'm walking into this with eyes wide open. I want to be here for you and help you heal however I can. I want to show you you are worthy of love, even on the worst days. You are worth fighting for, and I want to prove that. Love is beautiful and selfless and giving. I plan to show you that daily until you understand what it means to be loved, valued, and appreciated. You are worthy of a lifetime of love and happiness, and while I might not always hit the nail on the head, I want to spend the rest of my life trying."

"Well, shit. When you talk like that, I don't think you leave me much of a choice but to marry you," I joke.

His face lights up, making me worry that he wasn't getting the joking part. That thought must be written all over my face, because Harrison laughs. "Chill, I know you were kidding. For now. But even saying those words as a joke makes me ridiculously happy. But getting back on track with the whole point of this conversation. How do you feel about our plan?"

I like the idea. I have wondered about online classes more than once before, but I didn't think it was an option for me. I despise that school, and I had no issues never stepping foot in that building again. And as far as moving, I like that idea, too. A fresh start feels like exactly what I need, and let's be real. I would follow Harrison anywhere.

"Let's do this. I'm in."

"Wait, seriously?" he questions.

"Seriously. I'm ready to start moving forward with my life. I want the happy ending, Harrison, and I want it with you."

Trigger Warnings

The Ugly Parts of Me includes content that might not be suitable for some readers that includes:

Sexually Explicit Scenes
PTSD
Profanity
(Remembered) Emotional Abuse
(Off Page) Rape/Grooming
(Remembered) Child Abuse and Neglect
Death
Death of a Parent
Discussion of Mental Health
(Off Page) Suicide
(Off Page) Murder
Open Door Explicit sex

Reader Discretion is advised.
All characters in this book are of legal age.